Homefront

Homefront

DORIS GWALTNEY

Simon & Schuster Books for Young Readers
New York · London · Toronto · Sydney

SIMON & SCHUSTER BOOKS FOR YOUNG READERS
An imprint of Simon & Schuster Children's Publishing Division
1230 Avenue of the Americas, New York, New York 10020
This book is a work of fiction. Any references to historical events, real people, or real locales are used fictitiously. Other names, characters, places, and incidents are products of the author's imagination, and any resemblance to actual events or locales or persons, living or dead, is entirely coincidental.
Copyright © 2006 by Doris Gwaltney
All rights reserved, including the right of reproduction in whole or in part in any form.
SIMON & SCHUSTER BOOKS FOR YOUNG READERS is a trademark of Simon & Schuster, Inc.
For information about special discounts for bulk purchases, please contact Simon & Schuster Special Sales at 1-866-506-1949 or business@simonandschuster.com.
The Simon & Schuster Speakers Bureau can bring authors to your live event. For more information or to book an event, contact the Simon & Schuster Speakers Bureau at 1-866-248-3049 or visit our website at www.simonspeakers.com.
Also available in a hardcover edition.
Book design by Jessica Handelman
The text for this book is set in Weiss.
Manufactured in the United States of America
First paperback edition January 2010
10 9 8 7 6 5 4 3 2 1
CIP data for the hardcover edition is available from the Library of Congress.
ISBN 978-0-689-86842-9 (hc)
ISBN 978-1-4169-9572-2 (pbk)
ISBN 978-1-4169-9573-9 (eBook)

For Will, Mary, and Ben,
with love

Acknowledgments

Particular thanks to Bill O'Neill at the War Memorial Museum in Newport News, Virginia, who pointed me to so many pertinent facts concerning World War II; to the librarians at the Smithfield Branch of the Rawls Memorial Library for help with reading microfilm of the *Smithfield Times* for the years 1941–1945; and to John and Anne Edwards, the present owners of the *Smithfield Times*.

Part One

Elizabeth's Bedroom

You can love a person and not really enjoy their company. I know, because that's the way I feel about Grandma Motley. For the past five years, ever since Paige and Polly were born, I have been sleeping in Grandma's bedroom. I have one dresser drawer for my fold-up clothes and my quilted satin handkerchief box, and about five inches in the closet to hang my dresses. I even have to keep my Sunday shoes in a box under the bed, with my hat sliding around on top of that.

The only other thing Grandma allows me to keep in the room is a bookcase my brother Johnny built for me, and she fusses every day about how she can't get to the window anymore. Of course, she's the one who said to put it there in the first place.

And Grandma never lets us forget that this is really her house either. "Until I die," she says, "I will see to certain things around this farm. There's a way things ought to be."

One day I heard Daddy say to Mama, "Emily Ruth, you have got to be the best person that ever lived to put up with my mama. She's always had her way, and I guess she'll always get it." So I know I'm not the only person who feels that way about Grandma. I mean, if she's awake, she's talking, and if she's asleep, she's snoring.

But I won't be listening to her snores much longer. I'm counting the days, four to be exact. And then my sister Elizabeth will be off to the State Teachers College at Farmville and I'll get her bedroom. Then I won't be the only girl in the seventh grade who still shares a bedroom with her grandmother.

And of course, anybody in the world would want a room like Elizabeth's. A couple of years ago she made blue flowered curtains for the windows. And matching pillows for the bed. And a white organdy skirt for the dressing table. And since the room is on the front of the house, you can sit at the window and see the road. Of course you need to hold your head just right to see through the branches of the maple trees and down the long row of cedars that lead to the gate. Sometimes, if Elizabeth is out on a date with Tommy Gray, and if Grandma isn't looking, I open the window and step out onto the porch roof. By the time I take three steps, it starts to slant. I have to grab a tree limb to keep from falling. But it's great. I feel free as a bird. Polly and Paige can't find me. Grandma Motley can't find me. None of the eight people who live in our house can find me. It's wonderful to feel sneaky like that.

One night when I was out there, Tommy and Elizabeth came home early from a date. I could see the headlights of the car as it got closer and closer. I was afraid to move. So when Elizabeth started to open the car door and the light came on, I saw how they kissed each other good night. I hung on to a big limb with one hand, and I leaned down as far as I could go. Then I could see their lips opening up and moving toward each other. Just like a movie. Maybe like Carole Lombard and Clark Gable. I opened my lips and I was thinking about how in four years when I was sixteen and could have dates, I would be kissing somebody too.

But then Tommy opened his eyes and looked up through the windshield and saw me.

"Is that you, Margaret Ann?" he hollered.

I didn't answer. I jumped back inside the window and hid until Elizabeth came upstairs. And then I begged her not to tell Mama and Daddy.

"Please, Elizabeth, please. I promise I won't do it again."

Then actually I could see relief in Elizabeth's eyes, and it came to me that she might not want everybody to know about her and Tommy kissing either.

"This can be our little secret, Margaret Ann. How about that?"

Elizabeth started laughing, and I got to laughing too. We

had to stick our heads in the closet so we wouldn't wake Grandma. I knew Mama was still awake. She never goes to sleep until Elizabeth and Johnny both are home from their dates. But Mama never fusses. So we were home free.

During these last days Elizabeth is with us, I eat my snack the minute I get home from school, then dash upstairs to her bedroom. Grandma keeps insisting that I'm bothering Elizabeth and Mama, but they never say so. On the other hand, they don't seem to answer my questions either. And I want to know everything. Is that a new sweater? Where did she get it? Is this a new dress? Did she make it that very day?

Elizabeth sews prettier and faster than anybody we know. She is going to major in home economics, and she says she wants to be a teacher. But you'd have to be pretty dumb to believe that. I'm sure as anything she'll teach a couple of years and then marry Tommy Gray and live the rest of her life about four miles down the road on the Gray farm. She'll make blue flowered curtains for every window in Tommy's house.

The day before Elizabeth is leaving, I come home from school to find Grandma Motley's old steamer trunk sitting in the middle of Elizabeth's bedroom. I get kind of a funny feeling, and I don't go inside the room right away. Somehow, for the first time, I actually realize what this means. It isn't just that I'll have a new bedroom, it's that Elizabeth won't be here. Almost every day of my life I've seen my sister. Who will tell me my socks don't match? Who will lend me a hairbrush when I can't find mine?

I feel a tear in each eye, just ready to roll. So I stand there, not making a sound, and it's like the socks and silk hose and petticoats and sweaters and shirtwaists are floating through the air. Straight out of the bureau drawers and into the deep drawers of that big steamer trunk. I can't see Mama's hands or Elizabeth's hands. Only the pretty things Elizabeth has sewn. I guess it's the tears that make it look like that.

I hold my breath, trying to be quiet so nobody will know I have a tear in each eye, and I admit it, it comes to me to wonder if the curtains and pillows and dressing table skirt will come floating across too. I never asked Elizabeth if she's taking them with her, and I really want them. I guess that kind of dries up my tears, because when Grandma pops around the corner, out of the back hallway, I am dry as a bone.

"Margaret Ann, I told you not to bother your mama and Elizabeth. They have less than twenty-four hours to get everything packed and ready to go. They do not need you."

"They might. I haven't even had chance to ask them."

"Then don't bother to speak a word. I have a job for you myself."

"What is it? Grandma, I really don't have time . . ."

"You do indeed have time if I ask you. Now, go downstairs and find some game to play with Paige and Polly. Sallie is trying to iron and cannot take a step without them under her feet."

"I don't like to play games," I say. "Paige and Polly are old enough to play something on their own."

"And you are old enough to be some help in this house. Your mama has all she can do around here."

I start to ask Grandma why she doesn't help Mama if there is so much to do.

Anyway, I'd had about enough of Paige and Polly. That's what caused me to move in with Grandma in the first place. When they were born, I was given the choice of sharing my bedroom with them while they were crying half the night and spitting up all this terrible milky stuff or listening to Grandma snore.

"Grandma, listen, this is my last afternoon with my sister. I really want to see if I can help her."

"You can help by doing what I ask you. Now, go downstairs and get the twins from under Sallie's feet."

"Grandma . . ."

"Margaret Ann Motley, you are being disrespectful. I won't hear another word. Go downstairs to the kitchen this minute and get those children. Take them outdoors and play with them."

"Play what?"

Grandma's face is really red, like it gets when she's mad, and I don't wait to hear the answer. I run past her, along the back hall to where it meets the stairs and down into the kitchen. But I don't play a game with the twins. I take them down to the dog pens where Daddy keeps his foxhounds. It doesn't take long for the three of us to be happy together. If there is anything better than a dog for comfort, I don't know what it is.

Tommy Gray is invited to supper that night, so we eat in the dining room. But we don't use Grandma's best set of china. Grandma's best china only appears when the preacher comes. We have baked chicken, though, just like on Sundays.

I sit in my usual place beside Daddy, with the twins right next to me. Their eyes bug out whenever Tommy Gray is around, and he's sitting right across the table. They love him to distraction.

Johnny is on the other side of the twins, and Mama is at the end of the table. At the very last minute she stirred the gravy one final time and ran upstairs to put on her blue silk dress with the lace on the collar. She and Elizabeth are almost exactly the same size. They both have tiny waists you can get your hands around if you extend your thumbs and cheat a little bit. My heart's wish is that someday I will look like them, but I know it will never happen. On the other hand, a few weeks ago I measured my waist with Elizabeth's measuring tape, and it was only two inches larger than hers and Mama's. And when we measured my top—my breasts, I mean—they were the same as Elizabeth's.

I sneak a look at Grandma across the table. She doesn't allow talk about breasts or anything like that. I don't even like to think about it in her presence because Johnny and Elizabeth both have told me Grandma is a mind reader. I believe it.

I look back at Mama and I feel like I can read her mind a little bit too. Her eyes are sad, even though she's smiling. I guess I'm doing the same thing, because I'm not exactly sure how I feel about the whole situation. I look across the table at Elizabeth. She looks really happy. So why shouldn't I be? I mean, I really do want that bedroom.

One thing the rest of us don't have to worry about is making conversation. You can't get a word in edgewise between Grandma Motley and Tommy Gray. If it hadn't been for Tommy, I would've thought that women talked and men listened. Daddy and Johnny are men of few words. But Tommy loves to talk and he loves to tease everybody, especially me. He starts out with the twins, but I know it will be my turn soon.

"What are you two little lookalike girls going to do without your big sister?" he asks.

There they are with a chance to break into the conversation, and all they can do is snicker behind their fingers. Tommy doesn't give them a second chance.

"How about you, Grandma Motley?" he says.

"I expect I can manage. After all, it was my idea for the child to go to college in the first place. And I'm the one paying for it. Now, I never had the chance to go to college, but I have spent as much time as possible on reading the Bible and the *Progressive Farmer*. Because a farm wife is just as important as her husband."

Tommy keeps opening his mouth at the end of every sentence Grandma speaks, but she talks on and on as Sallie brings in the chicken for Daddy to carve, and Mama and I go to the kitchen to get the bowls of vegetables. Somehow Tommy finds the opportunity to break in, because when we get back, he is talking.

"What do you think about the peanuts over at the Darden place, Mr. Motley?"

"Been too busy to look," Daddy says, and keeps on carving and passing plates.

"Our corn sure looks good in the home-place fields. Won't be long before we can start picking. I don't suppose you want to lend Johnny to us for a few days, do you?" Tommy laughs, so you know he's making a joke. But Daddy answers him like it's a serious request.

"Can't do without that boy," Daddy says.

Johnny smiles and stuffs his mouth with a big bite of chicken.

"Keep it in mind, Johnny. If you ever need a job, let me know," Tommy says.

While we're all laughing at Tommy's joke, Grandma starts in on her usual speech about how things used to be at harvest time. To hear her tell it, everything, even the weather, was better when my granddaddy was farming this place.

"It's all these machines," she keeps saying. "You can have your machines if you want them, but I say it destroys the quality of the crops. The human hand can cut and pick so there is no waste. Now, you take cotton, for instance. We continue to pick cotton by hand and there's no loss. There's nothing left in the fields when the hands get finished. But once somebody invents a picker . . ."

"Now, that's an idea, Mrs. Motley," Tommy says. "The man that designs a cotton picker is going to be rich. He won't need to touch a boll of cotton again in his lifetime. What you think about it, Mr. Motley?"

"I have no doubt it will come one day. But I think Mama's right about the waste."

"How about you, Johnny? What do you think?"

I look down the table at Johnny. I know he thinks whatever Daddy thinks. Daddy is a good farmer, and he has taught Johnny about every phase of farming.

"I don't see any need to change," Johnny says.

"How about you, Margaret Ann? I heard today Mr. Holland was getting a fancy new tractor. Anything to that rumor? I mean, you ought to know what's going on over at the Holland place."

"Maybe," I say. I can feel myself blushing. I don't half care, except that I don't know the answer to the question. It's no secret about Bobby Holland and me, but the thing is, he should have told me something as important as that. The Holland farm is right next to ours, just up the road a little, and Bobby usually tells me everything that's going on there.

Before we started school, Bobby and I used to play together nearly every day. When we were in the third grade, I got to be friends with Joyce Darden, and we started talking about girl stuff and what we were going to do when we got older. Joyce said she didn't want Bobby hanging around with us all the time. So I told him, "Leave me alone, Bobby Holland." And he did.

Last year, when we were in the sixth grade, suddenly all the girls in our class, even the town girls, wanted him to be their boyfriend. I realized that I did too. I knew what he liked to talk about. Dogs, and hunting, and farming. That was what I knew about too, so we got back together.

"Seems like you don't want to tell us what's going on over at the Holland place, Margaret Ann."

"The child doesn't know," Grandma Motley says. "When

I was twelve years old, I had my mind on more important things than the boys on the next farm."

"Is that so, Mrs. Motley? Well, I guess you're right. It doesn't pay to think too much about boys. Right, Elizabeth?"

Tommy leans forward so he can see around Grandma.

"I guess not," Elizabeth says.

Just then Sallie comes in for the plates, and I help her take them to the kitchen where there is a huge chocolate cake in the middle of the table.

"When did you make this, Sallie?" I ask.

"While you were at school. Then I hid it so no little fingers would be picking the frosting off."

"I wouldn't do that."

"And I wasn't talking about you. But if you remember, you have two little sisters who would nibble the world if it was set before them."

"It sure looks like it's enough for everybody and then some."

"If we can keep the boys and the twins from eating it all, I thought Elizabeth could take what's left with her tomorrow. I've got the perfect box to put it in."

Sallie carries the cake and I take the dessert plates to the dining room. We put everything in front of Elizabeth, like it's her birthday.

"You have to serve it, Elizabeth," Mama says.

All the time Elizabeth is slicing the cake and passing the plates, Tommy rattles on about stuff like how many people are being hired at the shipyard in Newport News to build battleships for the war in Europe. I close my ears. I don't want to hear about it. I know Daddy doesn't either. Daddy fought in World War I—the Great War, he calls it. The only thing I've ever heard him say about it is: "If you've been there, you can't talk about it." Sure enough, he's looking down at his piece of cake and poking it with his fork.

"I think these people are just crazy," Grandma says. "Particularly that Hitler. A gun is for providing food for family needs. Anything else and I call it clear evil."

"I agree with you, Mrs. Motley. A gun is for hunting. But sometimes you have to use it for something else."

"Just wait till you try it, boy," Daddy says. "You'll never want to hear about it again."

Everybody gets quiet. So quiet we can hear Grandma yawning behind her hand. Grandma's yawns are a signal, and everybody knows it. The meal is over.

"I don't think you gentlemen are going to settle a thing here tonight," she says. "I bet Margaret Ann hasn't done her homework. And I know Sallie wants to get these dishes washed so she can go home."

"And I want Tommy and Johnny to bring my trunk downstairs so we won't have to do it tomorrow," says Elizabeth.

Grandma stands up and places her napkin an exact inch from the side of her plate.

"Where you going, Grandma?" Tommy asks.

I hold my breath. I keep expecting Tommy to go one step too far one day. But Grandma smiles, not a real smile, but the kind she does when she is too fed up to speak. She nods to everybody at the table, one by one. And then she walks out of the dining room and closes the door behind her.

"I'm sorry, Tommy," Mama says. "She doesn't mean anything."

"Sure she does," Tommy says. "But I understand. I have a grandma too, you know."

"You're kind not to take offense," Mama tells him.

"Not after a meal as fine as this," Tommy says. "I sure thank you for having me."

"You're welcome anytime, and you know that," says Mama.

"Yes, ma'am, I do." Tommy half bows toward Mama and then Daddy, and then Elizabeth. "Okay, let's go get that trunk. That suits you, eh, Margaret Ann? I hear you're ready to move in as soon as we get Elizabeth down the stairs."

"Well," I say, "if you put it that way, then yes. I mean, if she has to go off to college, then yes, I want her room."

"Good for you, Margaret Ann," Tommy says. "Here's a girl that knows her own mind and doesn't mind speaking it."

We all get up from the table, and I slip out of the dining

room before anybody can ask me to clear the dishes. Johnny is right behind me.

"Come on, Margaret Ann," he says. "Let's go upstairs and clear Elizabeth out of your bedroom."

When we are halfway up the steps, I look back over my shoulder. Tommy and Elizabeth are standing on the bottom step just kissing away.

"Come on," I say. "We don't have time for stuff like that."

"Maybe you don't," Tommy says, and goes right back to kissing.

The next morning Mama says I can stay home from school to be with Elizabeth. Tommy Gray had planned to take her to Suffolk to the train station, but his truck broke down and so did one of the Grays' tractors. Tommy is the only one of the Grays who knows how to repair motors, so Daddy has to drive our truck instead of the car. That means there is room for only three in the cab, and Grandma Motley says she has to go. She says Elizabeth has always been her favorite, and it's a grandmother's place to be on the platform to say good-bye to her favorite granddaughter.

As soon as the truck drives out of the yard, Mama goes to her bedroom and I know she's in there crying. It isn't that Elizabeth is her favorite. Mama loves all five of us the same. But Elizabeth is the first to leave home and that's sad to me too. I snuffle for a few minutes, but then I want to get my stuff moved into Elizabeth's room before Grandma Motley gets back from Suffolk. I don't ask any questions. I just start moving.

Paige and Polly are standing at Mama's bedroom door when I get back upstairs.

"Mama, Mama," they say. First one and then the other.

"Leave Mama alone," I tell them. "She's resting."

"But Polly and I are sad about Elizabeth. We need to talk."

"Talk to me, then," I say, though I could have bit my tongue off. If there is one thing I don't need, it's the twins. But I've issued the invitation, and so they follow me down the hall to Grandma's bedroom.

"Aren't you sad, Margaret Ann?" one of them says. I can never tell the difference between the two of them. "Don't you miss Elizabeth?"

"In a way. But after all, Elizabeth wanted to go to college. It was her decision."

"Are you sure of that?"

I hesitate. After all, last night at supper Grandma told us it was her idea, but I didn't think she actually forced Elizabeth to go.

"Look," I say. "I'm sure Elizabeth wanted to go to college. Now, you two go outside and play while I get moved into my new bedroom."

"We can help. Please. Please let us."

"Promise to be careful?"

"Oh, yes."

"Okay, then, you can take this box of books and I'll bring the bookcase."

Off we go down the hall, straining every muscle. We make four trips to get everything, and suddenly I realize we've made everything messy. It isn't pretty anymore.

"Okay, girls. Thank you. You can go play now. I've got to clean up."

"We don't want to go. We want to play in Elizabeth's room."

"It's not Elizabeth's room. It's mine."

"But she's coming back, isn't she?" one of them asks. "What are you going to do when she comes home for Christmas?"

Oh my gosh. I never thought of that. What a dim bulb I am.

"What are you going to do, Margaret Ann?"

"Yes, what are you going to do?"

I look from one of them to the other. They even sound alike.

"Look, Paige," I say, and she takes a step forward to listen to me. Aha! I know which is which. But I don't know the answer to their question. Elizabeth had always been peculiar about her bedroom. She didn't want us in there, night or day. But now it will be different. Maybe.

"You can sleep with us when Elizabeth comes home,"

Polly says. "Our bed is big enough for three people."

"Ah . . . that's okay. I'll just sleep with Elizabeth. But I'll tell you what. If you go to your room and be quiet until I get settled, I'll play a game of Uncle Wiggley with you."

The twins are so happy about playing Uncle Wiggley, it almost makes me ashamed that I never want to play with them. And that it is so easy to trick my way out of it. Then I wonder what I am going to do when they get old enough to realize I don't know them apart. Maybe by that time they won't wear matching dresses and have their hair cut just alike.

Actually, if I wasn't twice as tall as the twins, people might not have been able to tell the three of us apart. Until a couple of years ago, Mama had cut our hair just alike. Kind of square around our heads with bangs halfway down our foreheads. Now I insist on growing my hair long like Elizabeth's, and I roll it up on rags every night so it curls. But we all three have brown eyes and a nose just like Daddy's. Kinda short and pudgy.

Elizabeth's nose is like Mama's, thin and delicate, and everybody says the two of them are beautiful. My brother, Johnny, looks like Mama too, except for being a boy. The girls at church all tell me how handsome he is. They ask me all these strange questions, such as what he likes to eat and what kind of shaving cream he uses. Crazy stuff. I usually tell Johnny what they say, but it doesn't matter to him.

• • •

As soon as the twins leave, I start to work. I hang my dresses in the closet, and actually they don't take up much more than the five inches Grandma had allotted me. I put my shoebox on the shelf, and then I put my Sunday hat into a hatbox Elizabeth left behind.

I have four dresser drawers all to myself, so I use one for underwear and one for socks and my one pair of hose. Then I put scarves and my handkerchief box in another drawer. That leaves one drawer perfectly empty. I decide I'll have to think about what to put there later.

After I arrange every book in its place in the bookshelf, I have to face the fact that there is nothing else to do.

"Girls," I call. "Come see my new room."

They come running down the hall and jump through the door together.

"Is it pretty?" I ask.

They stand silently, staring around the room and then at each other.

"Do you like it?"

"It's okay," one of them says.

"What do you mean, 'okay'? It's beautiful."

"But not like Elizabeth had it."

I look around me.

"Maybe not, but it's like me. It's like I want it."

"It's okay, then, if you want it to look like you."

I stare at the girls, from one to the other, trying to think of an answer. There isn't one. "Well, I like it," is all I can think to say.

"So do we."

"Now let's play like you promised."

"After you have insulted me and my bedroom? You expect me to play with you?"

"Oh, but we love it. That's what we meant. It's more like a real place now that we can go to."

"We always felt like Elizabeth would get mad if we came inside her room. But we'll visit you, Margaret Ann."

You've never seen such smiles as they had on their faces. Later on I'll lay down the rules about visiting my bedroom.

"Okay," I say. "Let's get this game started."

We play Uncle Wiggley for what seems like hours, but finally Daddy drives in with the truck. Shortly after that we hear Grandma's voice.

"Margaret Ann. Margaret Ann."

She continues to call all the way up the back stairs. She must have stopped off at her bedroom, though, because everything gets quiet. Then Mama's bedroom door opens and I can hear Grandma talking to her.

"Yes, Elizabeth got off. There were no problems. And I see Margaret Ann has wasted no time moving into Elizabeth's bedroom."

Mama says something I can't quite hear and then Grandma says, "You better watch that girl." How she thinks anyone can watch me more than she already does is beyond anything I can imagine.

The very second we hear the tractor driving in from the field, I jump to my feet.

"Let's go see Johnny," I say.

"But we haven't finished our game." I don't know if it's Paige or Polly.

"Look, you wouldn't want to disappoint Johnny, would you?" I ask.

"No. Oh, no."

"We would never disappoint Johnny."

All of us girls love Johnny to distraction. Maybe it's because there is only one of him and four of us. We leave the game on the floor and run for the back stairs. When we get to the tractor shed, Johnny is climbing down from the tractor, beating the dust off his pants with his hat. He hugs Paige and Polly.

"How's my pretty girls?" he asks, and then he looks at me. "Elizabeth get off all right?"

"Grandma said there was no problem, so I guess that means she's okay."

Johnny looks down at his wristwatch.

"She ought to be there. Wasn't it five o'clock she was getting to Farmville?"

"I think so."

"Well, it's six-thirty now. I guess she's all settled in her dormitory."

"Maybe she's eating her supper," one of the twins says.

"I'm ready to eat mine too," Johnny says. "What's Sallie cooking tonight?"

"I have no idea. I've been moving my stuff to my new bedroom."

"You didn't waste any time, did you?"

"Would you?" I ask.

Johnny laughs and hugs me so tight I nearly leave the ground.

"No, Margaret Ann, I wouldn't have waited another night. Reckon you can sleep, though, with no snoring?"

"I'll let you know in the morning."

That night when I go to bed, I don't even want to sleep. Elizabeth's pillows are so comfortable. And the sheets are smooth. I turn my chin from side to side on the top hemline and feel the stitches where she embroidered her initials. E.E.M. Emily Elizabeth Motley.

I stretch out my hand and pat the other side of the bed. No Grandma Motley. I roll over into the middle and stretch my legs. Back and forth. Only then the sheets aren't so smooth anymore, so I stop and lie real still.

For the first time in years I can actually hear something

besides snoring. People who live in town think the country is so quiet at night. But there's lots to hear if you know what to listen for. If there's any breeze at all, you hear the trees. Sometimes they whisper, but if a storm is coming up, they sound almost like they're roaring.

And in the summer you can hear birds. Particularly owls. Elizabeth never liked hearing owls. Somebody told her if you tied a knot in the bedsheet they would quiet down. Sometimes it works; sometimes it doesn't. I guess that means owls do what they want to.

I turn my face toward the door and listen. I hear Grandma Motley snoring, but it's a long way off. There is no sound at all coming from Johnny's bedroom, which is right next to Elizabeth's—I mean mine. I turn back the other way, and I don't hear Grandma anymore.

I remember one day a few years back—I must have been eight or nine years old—I asked Grandma about why she snored.

"Women do not snore, Margaret Ann," she said. "It's your daddy who is doing all the snoring. I think it's all the dust they breathe in the fields. I expect Johnny to start snoring any day now. None of us will be able to sleep a wink with two men in the house snoring."

I used to believe that about men snoring. I remember one day I asked Bobby Holland if he snored and he looked at me like I had lost my mind.

"No, I don't snore," he said. "Do you?"

"Of course not."

"Then why do you think I do?"

"Because Grandma says men snore because of all the dust they breathe in the fields."

He got to laughing so hard I just walked off and wouldn't have anything to do with him for a week.

But I still wonder if Bobby Holland snores, even a little bit. Because I know Daddy does. And every now and then I hear Johnny give a snort or two when he drops off to sleep in the living room listening to the radio. Daddy and Johnny work really hard. And so does Bobby Holland. I think all three of them are truly happy working in the field. Which is good, because all three of them will be in the fields now till dark, harvesting.

Some farmers with as many men working for them . . . and as much land as Daddy has . . . don't work at all. My uncle Waverly Saunders doesn't. . . . He dresses up every day like it's Sunday . . . drives to town . . . goes visiting with his wife, my aunt Janice. . . . I close my eyes and drift off.

Back to Grandma's

Elizabeth's bedroom is all I ever hoped for. Beautiful curtains. And pillows. And the white organdy dressing table skirt. I actually use the dressing table as a desk to do my homework on. It is so great not to have to use the dining room table anymore. And it doesn't hurt that I can look at myself in the mirror from time to time while I'm studying. I've asked Mama to buy me some bobby pins, and she says she will. That's what most of the girls at school use to curl their hair. I can keep them in the little candy box Elizabeth left in a dresser drawer. That way the twins will never find them. Then again . . .

Speaking of the twins reminds me of the best thing about this room: the doorknob. I can twist it closed, all the time explaining the rules to Paige and Polly, just like Elizabeth used to do to me.

"You are never to cross this threshold without my

permission. Is that clear? Whether I am at school or at home, you must never enter without my permission. Okay?"

I'm not completely sure the twins will stay out while I'm at school, but I do think they will clean up any messes they make. That's what I used to do when I was little.

So one day I go smiling off to school with something new to tell Joyce Darden. Mama says I can invite her to spend the night on the third Friday in October. And Johnny says he'll take us to Smithfield to the movie, and Bobby Holland can go too. Things are really great.

On Tuesday of the very week in October that Joyce is supposed to spend the night, everybody but Daddy gets a real surprise. For Grandma Motley and me, I think you can call it a shock. I step inside the pantry to find an apple to put in my lunch box, and I hear Daddy telling Grandma that my aunt Mary Lee Liveley is coming to visit. That might sound like a simple thing, but it isn't. In the first place, I'm not sure I had ever really believed there is such a person as Aunt Mary Lee Liveley. Not even when Elizabeth was whispering the whole story to me a year or so ago. Nobody ever speaks her name in front of Grandma. And since you never knew when Grandma is going to pop up, no one ever speaks the name Mary Lee Liveley at all.

So when Daddy tells her, Grandma gets real quiet for a minute, and I do too. I can't imagine what Grandma looks like, sitting quiet at the kitchen table. It happens so seldom.

I'm barely breathing because I don't want Grandma and Daddy to hear me and realize I'm standing no more than ten steps away in the pantry.

"John Motley," Grandma says after the longest time, "I will not have it. She made her decision fifteen years ago and she can stick to it."

"Now, Mama, look here. This war in Europe has changed everything. Surely you wouldn't want her to stay in England."

"She's not in England. Don't think because I'm getting along in years that I've lost my eyesight or my brains, either one. I read the newspaper. I know how they've been sending children out of England for somebody to have to take care of in Canada. I know some of the mothers have come too. Besides which, I have seen those letters you hide in your desk drawer. She and that child of hers came to Canada near about a year ago."

"Not that long . . . ," Daddy tries to say.

Without making a sound, I look around the pantry door. And, just as I thought, there sit Daddy and Grandma staring at each other across the kitchen table. Exactly where I left them.

"Why can't she stay in Canada?" Grandma says, her eyes blazing.

I pull my head back quickly just as Daddy answers.

"Because I wrote her and asked her to come home. It's not

some stranger's place to look after my sister. I want her here."

"Well, I don't. You know how Mary Lee is. She'll only make more work for Emily Ruth."

"Emily Ruth doesn't mind. She's more than glad to have her."

"We don't have room for her. Where would she and the child sleep?"

"Emily Ruth says they can sleep in Elizabeth's room. That used to be Mary Lee's bedroom when she was a girl."

I can't help myself. I whistle through my clenched teeth. What is Daddy saying? And Mama—giving away my bedroom without even asking me one word about it.

"I have spoken, John," Grandma is saying. "There's no more to be said. You can write her and tell her not to come."

"It's too late for that, Mama. She will be here this afternoon on the train. I thought you might like to ride to Suffolk with me to pick them up."

"This afternoon? Indeed. I refuse to go."

"Then maybe you can look after things, and Emily Ruth can ride with me."

"John Motley, I don't think you have been listening to me. I said she isn't to come here."

"And I said she is, Mama."

I can hear Daddy's chair scraping back. He must be getting

up from the table. And Grandma doesn't say one word.
Daddy just keeps right on talking.

"I am going to Suffolk to meet the three o'clock train.
And I will be bringing my sister and your granddaughter
home with me. And they will sleep in the front bedroom
until this war is over and she can go back to England to her
husband."

Still Grandma doesn't say a word. I hear her chair scrape
too, and then I hear her heels click across the linoleum floor.
I wait, holding tight to my apple. Then I hear Daddy walking to the back door. I hear the door open and shut. But neither of them says another word.

When I walk out of the pantry door, Mama is coming down
the back stairs into the kitchen.

"Why didn't you tell me, Mama?" I ask. "About Aunt
Mary Lee and her baby. Grandma doesn't want them to
come, and I don't either. It's not fair to take my bedroom."

"Oh, Margaret Ann, please don't be that way this morning.
I simply did not have time to talk to you about it. Besides,
they have to sleep somewhere. Where else can we put
them?"

"They could have stayed where they were. In Canada.
That's what Grandma says."

When I hear myself saying that, I get a real shock. To
think that I'm agreeing with Grandma. But still, I'm not

going to stand here and listen to Mama after she's given away my bedroom.

"I better go," I say. "I sure don't want to miss the school bus today of all days."

"Of course you don't, sweetheart. Hurry on down to the bus now. And don't worry about your books and things. I'll move them myself," Mama says.

That stops me right in my tracks.

"No, Mama. Let me do it."

"There's no time, Margaret Ann. The room has to be ready today."

"But Mama . . ."

Mama hands me my lunch box and my books and hurries me down the hall to the front door. When I get past the third cedar tree, I see the bus is already at the gate waiting. But I refuse to run. Maybe if I get left, I'll find some way to keep my bedroom. But no, that day Mr. Jones, the bus driver, just sits there and smiles and waits for me.

Joyce Darden, Bobby Holland, and I always sit together on the third seat back on the right-hand side. Joyce gets on first, me second, and then Bobby. Mr. Jones has a rule that whoever gets on first has to go to the back. That makes a lot of people mad, but it works for us.

"Hey," Joyce says, even before I can sit down. "What are you going to wear to the movie Friday night?"

"Oh . . . Friday night," I say. "I don't know. I haven't had a chance to think about it."

Joyce looks at me like I'm crazy, and I can't blame her. We've been planning this night for a long time. So, what am I going to do? How can I tell her I don't have a room to myself anymore? I don't think she'll want to come if we have to sleep with Grandma. And Grandma won't allow it even if she does.

I don't know what to do. I'm not even sure I should be telling anybody about Aunt Mary Lee and the baby. Good gosh, I don't even know how old the baby is—or what its name is. Imagine having a cousin and not knowing its name. There has to be something disgraceful about having an aunt you've never seen and a cousin whose name you don't know.

I sure wish I'd asked Elizabeth more about it when she told me. She was whispering it like she didn't want anybody but me to hear her. I remember that. And we were standing in her bedroom by the window, looking down at Grandma and Daddy and my uncle Waverly Saunders and Aunt Janice. They were sitting there in the shade of the maple trees, on our white wooden lawn chairs, waiting for Mama and Sallie to bring out lemonade and cookies. And Elizabeth said that Daddy had a beautiful sister who had gone off to college and met an Englishman. And fallen in love with him.

"Grandma disapproved of him," Elizabeth had said. "I

think it was because Aunt Mary Lee stopped going to church, and started smoking cigarettes, and saying curse words."

"Really?"

"Well, I heard somebody at church whispering about it. But it might not be true."

"Yeah. It might be something else. Maybe it was just because the man wouldn't do everything Grandma told him to."

I was serious about it, but when Elizabeth laughed, I did too. It always makes me happy to say something Elizabeth laughs at.

So I asked Elizabeth to tell me the rest of the story, but all she would say was that Aunt Mary Lee had run off with this man to England and got married to him. Elizabeth didn't know the man's name, and I don't think she knew they'd had a baby either. Or maybe it hadn't been born when she told me all this. I don't know, but she said she had seen a picture of Aunt Mary Lee once. So I got the idea of looking in Grandma's box of pictures while she was sitting under the maple tree, drinking lemonade.

There were lots of pictures of people I didn't know. Most of them had names on the back, but one or two weren't labeled. I decided that not even Grandma would throw away all her pictures of her own daughter, so I kept looking.

Way at the bottom I found her. It didn't have a name on

the back, but it was a girl who looked a lot like Daddy. She was standing on the front steps of our house, dressed up like she was going to church. She was wearing a corsage, so it must have been Easter.

While I was holding it to the light, trying to figure out if her nose was just like mine, I heard Grandma coming down the hall. I stuck the picture way at the bottom where I'd found it. I closed the box. And I shoved it inside the drawer and closed it tight.

When Grandma opened the door, I was already sitting on the bed reading. Which goes to show I was scared out of my mind. Grandma doesn't allow anybody to sit on a made-up bed.

"Margaret Ann Motley, how many times do I have to tell you never to sit on a made-up bed? Besides which, you ought to be outside playing on a nice day like this. Now, straighten the covers and take yourself right downstairs and out the back door."

"Yes, ma'am."

"And don't let this happen again, do you understand?"

"Yes, ma'am."

I remember that I could hear Grandma fussing every step I took down the stairs. Just as plain. Even in the kitchen I could hear her. I never touched that box of pictures again. Never asked Grandma or Mama or anybody else if it really was Aunt Mary Lee. I guess I tried to forget I'd ever heard the name. But there is no doubt of it, this very afternoon I'm actually going to see her.

"Margaret Ann, is there something wrong?"

Joyce is leaning over the pile of books in her lap, looking me straight in the face, and Bobby Holland is grinning over her shoulder.

"Margaret Ann, you haven't answered a single one of my questions. Don't you feel well?" she asks.

"Oh," I say. "I'm fine."

I know I should come right out and tell her I haven't been listening. But Joyce gets her feelings hurt mighty easy. I decide to do what I always do, bluff my way through.

"I'm fine, Joyce," I say. "I was just thinking over our plans for Friday night. It's going to be great. Sallie says she'll make apple dumplings for supper. And Johnny says he doesn't even have a date. He's just taking you and me and Bobby Holland."

"Oh my gosh, Margaret Ann. It will be like a double date."

Oh Lord, Mama and Daddy will kill me if they think I have an actual date. And Joyce's eyes are shining and she looks so happy. I decide I have to tell her all about the change in plans. I can't let her go on thinking things are going to be so good. When I open my mouth, I am really planning to tell her the whole story. All about Aunt Mary Lee and the baby. And about how I am going to have to move back in with Grandma. What comes out is this.

"That's great, Joyce. That's just great."

All that day at school I keep thinking of how I'm going to tell Joyce about Aunt Mary Lee and the baby. Because I know as well as anything that Grandma will say Joyce can't come and that I have to be the one to tell her. But how can I? I don't know, so I keep on putting it off.

I haven't so much as spoken to Bobby Holland since we got off the bus that morning. He sits way in the back of the classroom because Miss Boswell says she can trust him to behave. I sit about in the middle, so I guess that shows what she thinks about me. Anyway, I worry all day long and I can't remember the answer to a single question Miss Boswell asks us. It's like my body is at school and my mind is at home. I can see Mama and Sallie cooking and cleaning. Mama always bakes a ham when company is coming. And Sallie will have to clean chickens and bake them. And make dressing. And cut turnip greens from the garden and cook them. And since Sallie has so much to do, Mama will probably have to clean the bedroom. And probably the living room. So maybe she won't have time to move my things to Grandma's room after all. Or maybe it's all a terrible mistake. Maybe Daddy will change his mind and not go meet the train and Aunt Mary Lee and the baby will go back to Canada.

. . .

I'm still mulling it over on the bus ride home so I don't hear a word Joyce and Bobby Holland say until Joyce pokes me hard in the ribs.

"Margaret Ann, answer me. I have asked you twice about what we have for homework in history."

"Oh. Well."

My mind is a perfect blank.

"I think it's something about Virginia," Bobby Holland says.

"Of course it's about Virginia," Joyce tells him. "This whole year is about Virginia. But what is our homework for tomorrow?"

Suddenly I remember. I can hear Miss Boswell's very words.

"Miss Boswell wants everybody to find out something interesting about Isle of Wight County. Something like what your ancestors did. You know."

"I don't think my ancestors did anything interesting enough to talk about," Joyce says.

"Me neither," Bobby says. "What about you, Margaret Ann?"

"I don't know of anything. But, I'm thinking about looking in our family Bible."

"Oh, yes," Joyce says. "I'll do that too."

So we talk about family Bibles and what color they are and how big they are and what is written in them. I have no idea what I'm saying. I agree with whatever the others say. And when the bus stops at Joyce's gate, I almost shout hallelujah.

"Bye," she says as she gets up to go.

"See you tomorrow," Bobby Holland and I say together.

When the bus drives off, we wave for as long as we can see each other. Just like we do every day. But it seems like Mr. Jones is driving about three miles an hour and we will never get out of sight of Joyce's house. I wish I could stop the bus, jump off, and run all the way home. I feel like I could get there faster on my own.

Just as I'm thinking about the possibility of moving to the front of the bus, Bobby Holland pinches me on the shoulder and moves closer to me on the seat.

"Look . . . Margaret Ann . . . ," he says. "I mean, look at me."

I blink my eyes and then I look at him. He's smiling like he does when he has something important to tell me. He is so handsome.

"Yeah?" I say.

"All day I've been trying to tell you about Princess. I hope you remember Princess."

"Don't be sarcastic. Of course I remember Princess. Do you think I'm crazy?"

"No, I don't think you're crazy. But you're sure acting strange. Anyway, I just want to tell you Daddy says you can have a puppy when they're born. If you want one. I'm going to get one, and I thought it would be great for us to have puppies out of the same litter."

"Yeah. It would."

Just that minute the brakes squeak and the bus stops at our gate.

"Look, Bobby, I've got to hurry. I mean . . . this afternoon . . . it's just that . . ."

Bobby stands up quickly so I can get past him. I guess I've hurt his feelings. I can tell by the way his shoulders are slumping. But I can't help it. Not today.

"Good-bye, Bobby. Thank you. Really. We'll talk more about it later."

When I step down into the road and walk between the two brick gateposts, I can see our car parked at the front door. So they're home. Aunt Mary Lee and the baby are actually here. Because if Daddy had come back alone, he would've pulled the car up to the garage immediately. Two more steps and I can see the whole picture.

Daddy has his head poked through the front window on the driver's side. And Mama is coming down the front steps with Paige and Polly by the hand, laughing and calling out something, which of course I can't hear. I start to run. And then I stop. It's like I can't make my feet move. All I can do is stand there in the lane and watch.

Daddy takes his head out of the car window, turns around, and sees me.

"Come on, Margaret Ann," he says, real loud, so I can't act like I don't hear him. "Come on and meet your cousin Courtney."

That's the baby, I decide. I surely hope nobody expects me to hold her. Mama used to make me hold Paige and Polly, so I can just imagine her telling Aunt Mary Lee: "Oh, Margaret Ann is so good with babies. She had a lot of practice with the twins."

I hang back, even though Daddy is still motioning me to run. And then a young-looking woman who I figure must be Aunt Mary Lee gets out of the front seat on the other side of the car, throws her arms up in the air, then grabs for Mama. They look like they're dancing or something. Just twirling round and round and laughing. The twins are hanging on to Mama's skirt and stumbling over the tree roots.

While I'm watching all this lurching and screeching, I keep thinking, where is the baby? Have they left it asleep in the back of the car? When they quiet down a little, I look back to Daddy's side of the car. And there stands a girl. She looks like she's exactly my height. With hair the color of real clear honey like you eat on biscuits. Dressed in a dark green suit with a skirt halfway to her ankles. She's laughing too. And my Daddy, who usually won't look a chicken in the face, is hugging her and kissing her on that honey-colored hair.

"Come on, Margaret Ann. Come meet your cousin Courtney."

"My cousin Courtney?" I yell back to him. "Courtney the baby?"

Daddy laughs so loud that Mama hears him and says, "What?" And then they all laugh. Mama. Aunt Mary Lee. Even Paige and Polly. I am so embarrassed. My face feels like it's catching on fire.

So my cousin isn't a baby. She is probably my age. And she's the prettiest girl I have ever seen. Prettier than Elizabeth. Prettier than Mama. How am I going to explain this at school tomorrow? What will Joyce say? And what about Bobby Holland?

When I thought this cousin of mine was a baby, I didn't plan to actually dislike her. Of course I didn't want her here. I knew she would be a nuisance. And most of all she would take my bedroom. But this honey-blond girl—the prettiest girl I've ever seen—is a different matter.

While we're all shaking hands and being introduced, I hear Mama telling Daddy: "What a charming girl Courtney is." Nobody ever says I'm charming. Of course, I'm probably not. But still, for your own mama to say someone else is charming—and have your daddy agree—it's pretty hard to stomach.

The twins are hanging on to every word she says.

Probably because they can't understand her. She talks funny. Like somebody has taken scissors to the English language and clipped it to pieces. Almost every word she says is different from the way we talk. At least nobody asks me to go upstairs and help her get settled. Actually they ignore me completely, so I follow close behind Mama into the kitchen.

Mama always serves lemonade and cookies when company comes in the afternoon, and she always uses the same white china pitcher that has a couple of blue rings around it, underneath the handle. She always waits till the last minute to squeeze the lemons, measure out the sugar, and fill the pitcher with water. She says it tastes better when it's fresh like that.

Usually, I can drink the whole pitcher full. This day I'm not thirsty. I feel like I'm full right up to the back of my throat.

"What's the matter with you, Margaret Ann?" Sallie asks.

"Nothing," I say.

"I don't feel no hug this afternoon, so I thought something must be wrong."

Hugging Sallie is usually the first thing I do when I walk in the kitchen. Next is looking in the warming closet of the stove to see what she's kept warm for me there. So I go to the stove where Sallie is standing and she grabs me and hugs me until I get smiling.

"Now," she says. "Help your mama."

"Okay," I say, "but I want to know what's going on around here."

I take a lemon out of the pan of warm water, roll it around on the drain board of the sink, and hand it to Mama. She does look so tired. I shouldn't add to her worries, but I'm worried too.

"Did the twins move my things?" I ask her.

"Of course not. What makes you think that? Sallie moved your things when we were cleaning Elizabeth's bedroom."

"It's my bedroom."

"Margaret Ann . . ."

"I'm sorry, Mama, but I can't help it. Every time I think about it, I get madder. What am I going to tell Joyce about all this?"

"Oh my. Joyce is supposed to spend the night with you Friday, isn't she?"

"Yes, she is. So where are we supposed to sleep? In the living room? On the front porch?"

"I expect we'll have to postpone the visit."

"Postpone? For how long? How long do you expect them to be here? Aunt Mary Lee and Courtney, I mean."

"Lower your voice, please. They'll hear you."

"I don't care if they hear me."

"Margaret Ann, you are being unreasonable. How do you think Courtney feels? First she was taken to Canada, and now here. Put yourself in her place."

44

"Good gosh, Mama, I think you've got that idea exactly backward. Courtney is putting herself in my place. My bedroom."

"Look here, Margaret Ann, I don't want to hear you talk to your mama like that. Good as she is. You ought to be ashamed."

Oh, no. Not Sallie, too. There must be something going on here that I don't understand. Sallie and Mama are not the kind of people to make something out of nothing. I can hear it in Sallie's voice. It has kind of an edge to it. And Mama looks like she's seen something or heard something to upset her.

"Well," I say. "Okay. I'm sorry, Mama. What can I do?"

"You can help me carry the cookies to the dining room."

"Okay, but tell me why we're having refreshments in the dining room," I whisper.

"Because your grandma says—" Mama is whispering too. Just then Daddy pops through the door.

"Hurry up, ladies."

"Sorry, John," Mama says. "You direct everyone to the dining room and we'll be there in a jiff."

Mama takes the tray of glasses, and I take the lemonade in one hand and the cookie plate in the other. While we're walking down the little hallway and into the dining room, I keep asking Mama about what Grandma said. And where in the world is Grandma? Mama has plenty of time to tell me too, but she won't say another word.

. . .

Daddy insists that Courtney sit beside him, which is my place at the table.

"You sit between the twins, Margaret Ann," Mama tells me. It's a fate worse than death. Particularly since we're using the good glasses, the ones with little stems, and I have to keep the girls from turning them over on the tablecloth.

"I know you two are tired," Mama says to Aunt Mary Lee. "We'll have an early supper so you can get to bed."

I'm just about to say that I don't see why it should make you so tired to ride on a train from Canada to Virginia when Daddy reaches out and pats Courtney on the hand.

"How did you like Canada, sweetheart?" he asks.

"Not very well, thank you," Courtney replies.

"I'm afraid we were both a bit homesick, John," Aunt Mary Lee says.

"But you're home now," Daddy says.

Aunt Mary Lee smiles.

"Thank you, John. It is so good to be here and so good for Courtney to see where I grew up. And best of all, for her to meet her relatives. Speaking of relatives . . . where is she? Is she back there? In the kitchen?"

"I guess you mean Mama, don't you?" Daddy says.

"Of course I mean Mama."

"Mary Lee, I'm sorry. She's . . . well . . . you know Mama."

"What do you mean? Surely she was expecting me.

Surely you didn't invite me here without consulting her."

"Look, Mary Lee, she'll come around. Give her a day or two."

"Mama has had fifteen years to 'come around.' When you invited me here, I was thinking it meant she had."

I look at Mama then, and her face is white as a ghost.

"Margaret Ann," she says, like she's out of breath from running to the mailbox or something. "You can take Courtney upstairs to her room and help her get her things unpacked. Take the twins too."

I don't want to go. I want to see what's going to happen next. I want to know what all this is about. But Mama looks at me like she does. She doesn't say a word, but she might as well have. "For me." Whenever Mama says that, "For me," I can't help myself.

"Come on," I say, and start for the door. I can hear Courtney behind me, walking up the hall to the front steps. The twins are behind her. At the bottom of the stairs, I feel like turning and running out the front door. I would if it weren't for Mama.

"Come on," I say again, and start up the stairs. So, I'm the one who has to take Courtney upstairs to my very own bedroom. It's just like *I'm* giving it to her.

Courtney walks straight over to the bed and takes a seat. The twins plunk down beside her and look up at her like they're adoring a saint or something.

"Do you like this room?" one of them asks. "It's really Elizabeth's. Margaret Ann has been sleeping here while Elizabeth is away at college. But now she's back with Grandma Motley."

Courtney looks up at me then. I'm still standing in the doorway. I have no intention of going inside. I have no intention of telling her how Grandma feels about people sitting on made-up beds either. Let her find out for herself.

"Margaret," she says. "I want to ask you something."

I nod my head, but I don't say a word.

"Where is Grandma Motley?"

Just as she is asking, we hear the sound of the tractor motor. The twins jump up and run to the front windows.

"It's Johnny," they say. "Come see Johnny. Look, he's parking the tractor out front. Under the trees."

Courtney doesn't budge. She doesn't take her eyes off my face for a second.

"Is she here? In this house?"

"I imagine so. I don't know where else she could be."

"Doesn't she want to see us?"

"Well . . . ," I say.

"It's true, then, isn't it? She didn't want Mother and me to come at all."

There are few things in this world that I want more than to tell her that Grandma doesn't want her to come, and I don't want her to come either. But it's almost like I can hear

Mama right through the floorboards. "For me." Still, I don't want to lie. How can I manage to do what Mama does? She doesn't lie exactly, but she does what she calls "putting things in the best light."

"You never know about Grandma, Courtney. By next week she'll probably be saying you're her favorite."

By this time the twins are running back to Courtney. They take her hands and pull her off the bed and over to the window. I use that as the perfect excuse to leave.

What Mama wouldn't tell me is that Grandma says she isn't coming out of her bedroom until Aunt Mary Lee and Courtney leave. I find that out when I run in to put on a clean dress for supper.

"Is that you, Margaret Ann?" Grandma asks, all the while staring straight in my face.

"Yes ma'am." I can think of a lot of cute things to add on, but you really don't say things like that to Grandma Motley.

"You can tell Sallie to bring me a tray. I'll just have a piece or two of hot buttered toast."

"Aren't you hungry, Grandma?"

She shakes her head and won't say another word. Which is an even stranger thing for Grandma to do. By the time I get my clean dress on, I hear Mama calling from the kitchen.

"I'll tell Sallie," I say, and run for the back stairs.

· · ·

After supper Mama says I have to take the twins to the living room while the grown-ups stay at the table, drinking coffee. Courtney offers to help me, and even though I insist she stay with the others, she doesn't catch on to the fact that I don't want her around. So the four of us go in and sit down. The twins ask Courtney a zillion questions while I stare into space. Finally Johnny walks in.

"Don't you want coffee?" I ask him.

"I've had three cups. That's enough for one night. Besides, I want to get to know my new cousin."

"She's nice," one of the twins says. "She can tell us apart too. And even Margaret Ann can't."

"So you know," I whisper.

Johnny completely overlooks me.

"Courtney must be pretty smart, then," he says. "What grade are you in at school?"

"Mother says I would be in the seventh grade here. But that isn't what we call it in England."

The seventh grade. My grade. What will Miss Boswell say? What will Joyce Darden say?

Johnny drags the small rocking chair that always stays by the fireplace over to where Courtney and the twins are sitting on the sofa.

"They tell me you lived in London before you came to Canada," he says.

"During the winter we did," Courtney replies. "Mother

and I usually spent the summer at our house in the country. Father would come down on weekends. But now . . . we don't know for sure if the house in London is left standing."

"What do you mean?" I ask her.

"Don't you know?" she says. "About the bombing?"

"Of course I know about the bombing. I can read. But do you mean your own house might have been destroyed by one of those firebombs and you wouldn't know it?"

"Father flies for the RAF. He seldom gets to London. And Mother thinks he wouldn't tell us even if he knew."

After that, Johnny asks one question after the other about the war. I don't say a word. There's no way I can even if I wanted to. But I don't want to. And I don't want to hear the answers either. I get chills just thinking about it. Firebombs and plane crashes. Horrible things. I decide that being upstairs with Grandma Motley is better than sitting down here in the living room.

"Well," Grandma Motley says as soon as I close the bedroom door behind me.

"Ma'am?"

"Well, what's she like?"

"Do you mean Courtney?"

"Is that her name?"

"Yes, ma'am."

"Well, then, I mean Courtney."

"She's okay. The twins like her. And Johnny likes her. And Daddy is crazy about her."

"What about you?" Grandma asks.

I can't look at Grandma when I say it, and I can't say it real loud, but I tell her.

"I don't like her. I wish she'd go back to Canada."

"Maybe she will."

And then I look at Grandma, because it sounds to me like she's laughing.

"It just might be that Miss Courtney Liveley will be leaving this place sooner than she thinks."

"What do you mean, Grandma?" I ask.

But she won't say. She just sits rocking and smiling. I start to feel even worse than I felt downstairs in the living room. Like something really bad might happen to Courtney. Like maybe one of those firebombs is going to cross the ocean and find her and Aunt Mary Lee . . . and maybe us, too.

The very next day at school, I'm sitting in my desk, looking down at the floor and praying Miss Boswell won't call on me because I completely forgot to look up anything in the family Bible, when suddenly, the classroom door flies open. The first thing I see is Grandma's coat. There is no other coat like it anywhere. It is so old that what was once beautiful black chinchilla has started to look like a baby goat. So they're here, is all I can think. But how on earth did Daddy and Aunt Mary Lee get Grandma to come?

It's like a parade. After Grandma Motley there's Daddy. Dressed in his Sunday suit. On a Wednesday. Then there's Aunt Mary Lee, wearing Mama's best hat. Last of all is Courtney, and she's wearing my blue sweater and skirt that used to be Elizabeth's. I've never even worn it because I've just grown tall enough for it to fit me.

Miss Boswell looks at me first off, but I pretend to drop a book on the floor. I reach down like there's something really down there, and I don't come back up until Joyce punches me and whispers, "What is going on?" I whisper back that I don't know. But I do know I have to get back up before all the blood in my veins rushes to my head.

When I get back up, Daddy is shaking hands with Miss Boswell and introducing Aunt Mary Lee and then Courtney. Grandma Motley she already knows. Everybody knows Grandma Motley.

They talk awhile behind the teacher's desk, and then Miss Boswell calls me to the front of the room.

"Margaret Ann, I expect you'd like to introduce your cousin to the class while I go with your family to talk to the principal. It won't take long, but there are a few things we need to check on."

I stand up. I can feel everybody's eyes shifting from me to Courtney and back again. What are they thinking? I don't want to look at Joyce and I don't want to look at Bobby

Holland, but when I get to the front of the room, it's like my eyes are drawn to both of them. Joyce is frowning. I want to go back to yesterday and start all over. Why didn't I tell her? And why didn't I tell Bobby? He's biting his lips like he doesn't know what to think or what to do.

"Go ahead, Margaret Ann. We won't be a minute," Miss Boswell says.

I watch my daddy and the others out the door, wanting more than anything in the world to leave with them.

"Well," I say. "This is Courtney Liveley. She's from England . . . and she has been in Canada for a while . . . and now she's here. In Virginia. At my house."

"How'd she get there?" Jack Hubbard asks. Jack plays baseball with Bobby Holland, and he lives on a farm a few miles away from us.

"Did she come on a train? Did she fly?" a couple of the boys ask.

"Who is she?" asks Joanne Cox, one of the town girls.

"Can she talk?" asks a boy in the back of the room.

"I can talk," says Courtney.

She smiles, and the room gets just as quiet. And then she starts to talk in that funny clipped way that I can hardly understand. But it seems like everybody else in the classroom can.

"Ask me anything you like. I should be glad to answer."

"Do you mean you live in England? Really?" says Joanne Cox.

"Really. But of course my mother and I had to leave some months ago because of the blitz."

"What's the blitz?" John Cofer, one of the town boys, asks.

"Well, it's actually from a German word *Blitzkreig* that means 'lightning war.' It was first used to describe Adolf Hitler's march through Europe when he was conquering Poland, and Denmark, and Norway. We English shortened it to 'blitz.'"

Courtney sounds like Miss Boswell when she's explaining history to us. But the class is listening even better than they ever listened to Miss Boswell. I glance at Bobby Holland. He's looking very serious, and I know he will remember every word Courtney says.

I walk back to my own seat, not looking at anybody, just seeing my saddle oxfords that used to be Elizabeth's before she outgrew them. I'm sure I look like poor old Johnnie Newby, who is crippled and works for us because Daddy says somebody has to look after him. Or like Sallie's husband, Junie, when he got into the hard cider last Christmas by mistake and got drunk. After I sit down and look around me, I realize I really could be crippled or drunk or anything else. Nobody would notice or care. Because every eye in the room is on my cousin Courtney.

When I get home from school that afternoon, I realize that I'm a fortune-teller. Because Grandma Motley stands right beside the kitchen sink and says right out that Courtney is the smartest and prettiest girl she has ever seen. Which means that she is Grandma's new favorite.

"What happened?" I ask Mama after Grandma has gone back upstairs.

"Well, things just worked themselves out, just like they do if you try to do right. I had taken your Grandma's breakfast tray up to her room when your aunt Mary Lee walked in and asked her forgiveness."

I know Grandma really likes to have people ask for forgiveness, but what I can't believe is that Aunt Mary Lee would do it.

"So what happened next?" I ask.

"So then Courtney came in, and we all cried and made up."

"Grandma didn't cry," I say.

Grandma never cries. Her tear ducts have dried up because she's old. She told me that one day when she came back from the doctor.

"I'll bet nobody cried, Mama. Now, tell me what really happened."

"Well . . . you're right about the crying. That was just a manner of speaking."

"So . . . what happened?"

"Well, as I said, I told your grandma that Aunt Mary Lee said—"

"But she really hadn't said anything, had she, Mama?"

"Well . . . no . . . but I could tell what was in her heart. Just like I could tell what was in your Grandma's heart. So I simply suggested to first one and the other how it was."

"Mama, you told a lie. Maybe two lies."

"No, I didn't. All I did was tell the actual truth that was in their hearts . . . to everybody, and that made them see this was no time to be foolish. Anyway, it worked, didn't it?"

"Oh, Mama" is all I can think to say.

Anyway, now nobody seems to notice I'm on the planet. The only girl at school I can count on not to like Courtney better than me is Joyce. And she's wavering. But she did seem to understand perfectly when I told her the Friday night plans were off.

All the boys are in love with Courtney, and the town girls want her for a friend even though she does live in the country. "She's only there for the time being," Joanne Cox says about fourteen times a day. "Actually she's from London. In England." Even Bobby Holland ups and gives her his seat on the bus before Mr. Jones tells him to. And he actually told me one day that I ought to be nicer to my cousin.

Every night at supper, Daddy asks her to sit by him. And every night after supper Johnny comes to wherever we're doing homework and asks her questions about the war. I mean, Johnny never asks questions of anybody, and here he is talking like a maniac.

Sallie and Mama have learned how to make these scones that Courtney likes to have every afternoon when we get home from school. And Grandma brags about the good grades she makes and how she ought to be in the eighth grade, or maybe even the ninth.

I am so lonely that I'm even beginning to wish the twins would talk to me. But not really. So I write a letter to Elizabeth, thinking she'll understand. But when I get a letter back from her, all she can write about is how much she's looking forward to Christmas and meeting our cousin Courtney. Christmas is a long way off, and even having Elizabeth home isn't going to change things. Because she'll spend most of her time with Tommy Gray.

Still with Grandma

Before Aunt Mary Lee and Courtney arrived, I hadn't given much thought to the news coming out of Europe. But now it's like the war is in the house with us. There's a picture of Uncle Walter Liveley on the living room desk, right beside the one of Granddaddy Motley. Uncle Walter has on his RAF uniform and is standing beside his airplane, like he's getting ready to hop in and fly off to bomb the Germans. Grandma says he's the handsomest man she's ever seen.

About the middle of November, Aunt Mary Lee gets one of his letters, which is forwarded from the place they stayed in Canada. Everybody sits down around the tin heater in the living room to listen to it. And guess who reads it? Courtney, of course. After that a letter comes from him once a week.

And every afternoon when we get home from school, in place of my snack that Sallie used to save for me in the warming closet, we have tea. At least that's what Grandma calls it. She makes us all sit down around the dining room table. And Aunt Mary Lee pours the tea out of this beautiful china pot that Grandma says has been sitting in the china cabinet for three generations. I don't think anyone ever touched it except to dust it or maybe to wash it during the spring and fall cleaning.

Here I am starving and longing for one of Sallie's great big apple turnovers or a big, thick slice of chocolate cake, and all we have are these scones, and little cookies that Courtney calls biscuits. Honestly, it's hardly enough to keep a bird alive. And I don't drink the tea. Mama always gives us hot tea to settle our stomachs. So I tell Mama I'm not sick.

After a few days, I begin to like the scones Sallie makes, so I eat those. And I pile on the fresh butter and the straw-berry preserves. Courtney looks at me real strangely when I do. "You're going to eat all that?" she asks.

At these tea parties, Grandma Motley asks a lot of ques-tions about Courtney's other grandmother. And when Courtney tells us about the food shortages in the part of England where her grandmother is, Grandma wants to pack up some jars of strawberry preserves and peach pickles to send to her. Daddy says the package will cost a fortune to mail and it will probably never get there. But Grandma doesn't listen, not even when Aunt Mary Lee chimes in and says there are regulations that make it impossible to send food like that through the mail. Daddy has to actually drive to Smithfield, go inside the post office, and be told by the postmaster that it can't be done.

"Well," Grandma says, "what can we send? There's got to be something."

So Mama and Aunt Mary Lee pack up a container of A&P coffee and a jar of peanuts, and it costs $5.66 to send it to York, England.

It gets there too, because in a few weeks, Grandma gets a thank you letter from Mrs. Walter Liveley, Sr. Grandma talks about it night and day. She reads it over to me so many times I can repeat it from memory.

"Take notice of this, Margaret Ann," Grandma says. "Notice the language. It sounds to me just like the writing in a book. You could learn from this letter."

I want to tell Grandma that I have learned—every word of it, since I've heard it so many times. But I don't. I just hold it all inside, and I am getting madder and madder.

"What is the matter with you, child?" she asks me one day. "I haven't seen you smile in three weeks."

"There's nothing to smile about."

"Nothing to smile about? With a nice, pretty cousin right here in the house for you to play with? When I was a child I used to look forward to the days when my cousins would visit. I do not understand what is the matter with you."

"I'm just not as changeable as you are, Grandma. When I

make my mind up about something, it stays made up."

Grandma is buttoning the top buttons to her housedress. She stops for a few seconds, with her fingers wiggling around in the air like she can't find the buttons or something. She blinks her eyes, and then she looks down and catches hold of the buttons and finishes the fastening.

"That's ugly talk, Margaret Ann Motley, such as I never expected to hear from one of my grandchildren. I'm going downstairs this minute and tell your daddy word for word what you said."

Daddy gets real mad at me. He asks me what I have to say for myself. I just shake my head because there is nothing I can say.

The days drift on like that. I have the feeling every minute of my life is filled with Courtney's voice. Miss Boswell rushed us through the first few chapters of the history book so we can do an extra study of England.

"Most of us will not have an opportunity to spend time with someone from a foreign country," she says. "I think we should take advantage of every moment we have with Courtney."

I look back to see Joyce Darden nodding her head in agreement. Bobby Holland is too. So I have to sit there and listen while Courtney describes every stone and tree in the whole country of England.

At home it's just the same.

"I like the way you cooked this sweet potato pudding, Sallie," Courtney says, smiling that stupid smile that makes everybody smile right back at her. Folks do everything she wants, even before she says the words. I'd smile too if it would get everybody to do everything I want. All Courtney has to do is sit back and say, "Yes, please," or "Thank you."

And she likes to talk about the war.

"The war is creeping closer every day," Courtney says one day on the school bus.

"You're right, Courtney," Bobby Holland tells her. "If I was old enough, I would join the army right this minute."

"No, Bobby. I know you don't mean it," I say.

"I do, Margaret Ann. You just as well get used to it."

"Thank you, Bobby," Courtney says. She smiles and blinks her eyes at him. "I am glad there is someone who wants to help save my country."

I look out the window for the rest of the ride home. I don't trust myself to speak a word to anybody.

We are past Thanksgiving and into December, and the Sears Roebuck Christmas catalog is getting tattered from all of us turning the pages and thinking about what we want for Christmas presents. Paige and Polly want everything. Me too. The only difference is that I know I won't get every-thing, so I'm narrowing it down. But the first week has gone by, and I still don't know which thing I really want most. I decide I better make a choice before the day is over. After all, it's the seventh of December.

We're late getting home from church because, first of all, Mr. Kales preaches too long and, second, because the Harris girls get saved again like they do every year. They have to come down to the altar rail to pray and have the preacher's hands laid on their heads as a sign of forgiveness. I always wonder what those girls are up to that requires all that forgiveness.

Then Grandma has to talk to several ladies about arrangements for the Missionary Society meeting, so we're even later getting home.

Mama and Sallie are in the kitchen getting the dressing ready for the chicken and making the gravy. I have to help Paige and Polly get changed out of their Sunday dresses. And I have to change mine too. So by the time I get downstairs, Daddy, Johnny, and Aunt Mary Lee are sitting in the living room listening to the football game on the radio. It's the Dodgers and the Giants. Johnny, Bobby Holland, and I love the Dodgers, and we know all about the players and their statistics. It's pretty obvious that Aunt Mary Lee doesn't know a thing about football, because Johnny is explaining every little detail to her.

I sit down on the floor beside Daddy's chair. My stomach is growling so loud he looks down at me and laughs.

"Sounds like you're hungry, Margaret Ann," he says. "I can hardly hear the announcer."

It's just like old times to have Daddy teasing me like that. But then the door opens and in comes Courtney. And just that minute the announcer stops talking. A different man's voice breaks in like he's really excited.

"Ladies and gentlemen, we interrupt this program to bring you an important bulletin from the United Press. Flash. Washington: The White House announced a Japanese attack on Pearl Harbor. Stay tuned for further developments to be broadcast as they are received."

We just sit there, looking at each other, not saying a word. I get this quivery feeling in the pit of my stomach. Finally my daddy speaks.

"There's no doubt in the world about it," he says. "This means war."

I shake my head at him. I don't want to believe it. I don't want to think that all the things Courtney talks about that happened in England can happen here too. But I know they can. I know that almost a hundred years ago, there was fighting right here in Isle of Wight County. Right where we live. Grandma Motley tells us all about the War Between the States, which is what she calls the Civil War. Her mama said the Yankee soldiers broke into the smokehouse that is still standing right in our backyard, and they stole the hams and shoulders and sides of bacon. And then the family was actually hungry. That's what I have always thought about war. That it means being hungry and having soldiers in your backyard.

Mama comes in about then to say that dinner is on the table. Nobody gets up or even says a word.

"What's the matter with you folks?" she asks. "Isn't anybody hungry for baked chicken and dressing?"

"I guess we lost our appetite, Emily Ruth. We just heard on the radio. The Japanese have bombed Pearl Harbor."

I look up at Courtney. She has a funny look on her face. Almost like she's smiling. She looks back at me and says right out loud: "Now your country will have to help us. Like they should have been doing all the time."

"You're right, Courtney," Johnny says.

And then he gets up and starts to walk out of the room.

"Where are you going?" I ask him.

"I'm going for a walk."

"Can I go with you?"

"Not this time, Margaret Ann."

It's four o'clock in the afternoon before we eat the chicken and dressing. Mama wouldn't let Sallie stay to keep it warmed and to serve it.

"You'll miss your church," Mama says. "You go right on home."

So we eat cold chicken and gummy dressing and a lot of

sticky vegetables, but it doesn't seem to matter. We just chew and chew and stare off into space like we can't face looking at each other.

From that very moment, nobody talks about anything but the war. Miss Boswell brings a radio to school that Monday morning so we can hear President Roosevelt's speech. She says we all better listen because it's going to be an important moment in the history of our country. And then Courtney, who is sitting in the front seat of my row, turns around and looks straight at me.

"It will be an important moment in the history of the world," she says.

She doesn't even raise her hand or anything. She just says it right out. And everybody waits to see if she has anything else to say. The room is just as quiet. It's like President Roosevelt is waiting for her too. But then Miss Boswell twists the dial again and we can hear his voice.

"Yesterday, December seventh, 1941—a date which will live in infamy—the United States of America was suddenly and deliberately attacked by naval and air forces of the Empire of Japan."

His words come at me like waves I'd seen in pictures in our geography book when we studied Hawaii. I forget about Courtney. I can see that beach. And the ocean. And the navy ships. And then the sailors that died yesterday. More than twenty-four hundred people in all. Mr. Roosevelt's voice is like a mist that is drifting over me, and showing me things I don't want to see, and taking me where I don't want to go.

"Yesterday the Japanese government also launched an attack against Malaya.

"Last night Japanese forces attacked Hong Kong.

"Last night Japanese forces attacked Guam.

"Last night Japanese forces attacked the Philippine Islands.

"And this morning the Japanese attacked Midway Island."

There are so many places. How can the Japanese do all this? And what are we going to do about it? I look over my shoulder at Joyce, but she isn't even looking in my direction. She's staring at the radio as if the president is really there inside it. She licks her tongue across her lips like she does when she's really concentrating.

"No matter how long it may take to overcome this premeditated invasion, the American people in their righteous might will win through to the absolute victory."

Somebody behind me—I think it's Jack Hubbard—says, "Yeah." When I turn to look at Jack, I look at Bobby Holland instead. And he's looking at me. He isn't smiling, like he usually does. I decide he is seeing those waves too. And the ships. And thinking that American boys like his older brothers and like my brother Johnny died yesterday. I look quickly back at the radio.

"I ask that the Congress declare that since the unprovoked and dastardly attack by Japan on Sunday, December seventh, 1941, a state of war has existed between the United States and the Japanese Empire."

When the president is finished, Miss Boswell turns off the radio.

"Well, class, what do you think of that?" she asks us.

And of course it's Courtney who speaks for us all.

"Your president is perfectly right. You had no choice in what to do. Actually, your country has been at war for months. Now you will have to admit it."

I am so confused. I don't want to agree with Courtney, but what else in the world can we possibly do but fight?

And so we do just what Courtney wanted us to do for a long time. We go to war. First we declare war on the Japanese. Then the Germans and the Italians declare war on us, and we declare war on them. And Courtney seems to know everything that is going to happen even before it does.

A couple of nights later we're sitting at the dining room table doing our homework, when Courtney stops writing and says my name. Margaret. She won't say the whole thing out, like everybody else does.

"Margaret," she says. "I was thinking about how things

are going to be. The draft will start up in earnest now."

Out of the corner of my eye I see her shaking her head like some kind of owl or something. I'm halfway interested in what she's saying, but the way she says it makes me so mad I can't really look at her. I just keep writing.

"From now on you will see more boys from Smithfield and all the farms around being called to the army."

"Maybe so," I mumble.

"In fact, Joanne Cox told me her brother came home from college yesterday. He wants to volunteer for the navy. If he waited, you see, he might be called to the army. That's what he told his father anyway. Joanne says he simply wants to be of service to his country."

"Well, I want to be of service to my country too, but I don't see any need to talk about it every minute of the day. I can't even get my homework done with you talking all the time."

I get up, grab my books, and walk out of the room. But where am I to go? Sallie and Mama are in the kitchen getting the dishes washed and the food put away, all the stuff they do every night. Johnny and Aunt Mary Lee and Daddy are in the living room listening to Edward R. Murrow give the news. And Grandma is up in her bedroom reading the Bible and offering prayer for Uncle Walter.

I try Paige and Polly's room, but they're playing paper dolls. I listen long enough to hear the paper dolls saying good-bye to their boyfriends who are going in the army.

"Good gosh, Polly, what are you playing a game like that for?"

"Cause that's what Courtney taught us to play."

I can't believe it. What is Courtney trying to do around here? I think about going downstairs and telling Courtney to keep away from my little sisters, but I know she'll tell on me. And then I'll be in even more trouble. So I go to Johnny's room. I know Grandma never goes there, so I sit on his bed to read my geography book and do my arithmetic problems.

When I finish all my homework, I take out my library book and start to read. I'm off in the mountains with Heidi when Johnny comes in. Since the light is already on, he flips the switch and turns it off.

"Shucks!" I holler. I feel like I'm sliding down a mountain. When I'm reading, I feel like I'm in a different world. It takes me a minute to get back to real life.

"Margaret Ann?" he asks. "Are you in here?"

"Turn on the light and you'll see me."

"So what are you doing?"

"I'm reading my library book now, but I needed a place to finish my homework. This house is entirely too crowded."

"What's the matter with the dining room table? Courtney's down there drawing a map for geography."

"And that's exactly what's wrong with the dining room

table. Courtney's down there talking her head off. I sure wish she had never come here."

"Margaret Ann, you don't mean that. Anyway, I'm sure she would prefer to be at her home. If she still has a home. If it hasn't been bombed."

Johnny closes the door and walks slowly toward the bed. He stands looking at me with this weird look on his face. He doesn't look mad. I guess he's trying to look patient.

"Margaret Ann, I've been noticing how you treat Courtney. And it's not right. She never says anything, but sometimes I can look at her and see how she feels."

"Look, Johnny, I don't want to hear this. Not even from you. I'm sorry I wrinkled up your bed. I'll just go to Grandma's room and listen to her praying. I've got nowhere else to go."

My arms are so full of books I can't put my hands over my ears. So I walk as fast as I can. But still I hear him.

"Sugar," he says. "You have to show some patience. That's all. You'll get your room. Sooner than you think, maybe."

It sounds like he means the war will soon be over. And I know that's wishful thinking, so I don't even bother to ask him what he actually means. When I get outside in the hall-way, I drop all my books. And when he comes out to help me, I tell him not to touch a thing. He just looks at me and shakes his head.

Paige and Polly's Room

None of us knows exactly what to do about Christmas. Back in November, Mama and Sallie made a huge fruitcake. Like always, they mixed it in the big blue enamel pan that Grandma says fruitcakes have to be mixed in. They kept the oven going all day, cooking it in the tin mold Grandma also says fruitcakes have to be cooked in. So, war or no war, it's waiting for us in the pantry, wrapped in cheesecloth soaked in brandy.   .

And back in the summer when Johnny and I were walking to the pasture one day to get the cows, we found a perfect cedar tree. He and I planned how we would cut it on Christmas Eve morning. At our house we always decorate the tree on Christmas Eve so it will stay fresh till New Year's Day.

But there is more waiting for us than the Christmas tree and the fruitcake. There's Edward R. Murrow and the news on the radio at night. There are the newspaper headlines every day. There's Tommy Gray and who knows how many other boys that are volunteering for the army. Almost every day we hear about somebody else.

But more than all this, there's Aunt Mary Lee and Courtney. Seeing them every day. And never knowing which days Uncle Walter is flying a mission to bomb German cities. Never knowing which day he possibly won't come back. Aunt Mary Lee is trying to make the best of it. She never looks sad or anything like that. And she and Mama have a good time talking and laughing. It's like old friends have finally gotten back together.

But Courtney. She acts like she knows everything about everything anybody reads in the newspaper. I just feel like I can't stand her another minute. Mama keeps reminding me that she's far away from her home and her friends and her daddy. "Put yourself in her place," Mama tells me. I try. I try to feel sorry for her, but I just can't. And it doesn't help that she's interfering with Bobby Holland and me. Lately it seems like every day Bobby and I have an argument, and it's all her fault. I don't guess you can actually have an argument without words, but it's at the dress rehearsal for the Christmas pageant that Bobby and I get really angry.

Mrs. Chapman has been directing the pageant ever since I can remember, and she's chosen Courtney to be the head angel. I don't actually want the part myself, but I don't want Courtney to have it either. She gets to speak the best lines in the entire play. And she is so beautiful in the costume Mama made for her. At the dress rehearsal she's standing there glittering like a Christmas ornament, and I'm sure I hear Bobby Holland in his shepherd's bathrobe doing a wolf whistle. I look at him real quick and he shrugs and holds both hands out palms up. So then I frown at him and he frowns back. I decide that Bobby Holland and I are not speaking.

Elizabeth is coming home from college on Friday, two days after our school gets out for the holiday. That Thursday morning, the day before she's supposed to come, I'm standing in the hall, wondering what to do with myself, when the phone rings. It's about ten o'clock.

"Elizabeth," I say so loud that Mama comes running from the kitchen. Mama is scared to death. People don't make long-distance calls unless there is an emergency. Something like a death in the family.

"I want to speak to Daddy," she says.

"He's at the barn," I tell her. "But Mama's standing right here."

"Go get Daddy" is all she'll say.

So Daddy comes running, out of breath, and all she has to tell him is that she wants him to drive the truck to meet her in Suffolk. I'm leaning against his ear, so I hear every word she says.

"I'm told it's not safe to leave your belongings here over the holiday, so I have to bring the trunk with me."

"Okay, sugar," Daddy says.

When he hangs up, he won't say another word about it. Not to me or Mama or even Grandma. But I can tell something extra is worrying him.

Grandma says Aunt Mary Lee and Courtney should be the ones to ride with Daddy to Suffolk.

"Since Elizabeth didn't get here for Thanksgiving, she hasn't even met them."

"How are you going to stuff Elizabeth in there with both of them?" I ask.

The minute the words are out of my mouth, I'm sorry. Getting Courtney out of the house for a minute is a great idea, but I can just imagine Elizabeth saying, "Oh, I'll ride home in the back of the truck. I have on my heavy coat." The weather has turned really cold. In fact, it's freezing outside. Besides, I don't like to think about Courtney getting to do another thing I can't do.

"Courtney can sit in her mother's lap on the way back. After all, the child hasn't seen anything of the countryside. Everybody's been working so hard getting in the crops. It will do them good to get out. Keep their minds off the war over there in England."

"But she . . ."

I'm just about to say that Courtney always gets to do things. She's the one who gets to spend the night in Smithfield with her new friend, Joanne Cox. She's the one who gets new skirts and dresses. My skirts have not one, not two, but three lines in them where the hems are let down. And she's the one who sits beside Daddy at meals. She's the one. . . . But I can hear Mama saying, "For me," even though she hasn't breathed a word. So I close my mouth.

The twins are excited because Elizabeth is going to sleep with them in their room. While the others have gone to Suffolk, they come with Johnny and me to get holly and running cedar from the woods behind the barn. Johnny shoots mistletoe out of a high branch of an oak tree. And then I take the rifle and I get a piece too. Mistletoe always grows up real high, where it's hard to reach. But Johnny can hit anything with a rifle. He's the one who taught me to shoot. Between Johnny and Daddy, we have squirrel for breakfast most any morning we want. Rabbit too. Johnny and I like squirrel best. It's Courtney who won't even taste it.

"I can't eat a wild animal," she says. "They're much too beautiful."

So when we get back, the twins pull a chair up to their bedroom door, put a stool on top of that, and stretch way tall to hang mistletoe on these two wooden pieces that Daddy says used to hold a shotgun when he was a boy. The twins say they want to be sure Elizabeth kisses them when she gets here.

As it turns out, Elizabeth doesn't kiss anybody. She walks into the front hall and stands right there and tells us she is going to marry Tommy Gray. Before he leaves for the army.

"Oh, Elizabeth," Mama says. "Married girls can't go to college."

"And I'm not going back to college either, Mama."

"What is this?" Grandma is standing on the stairs, looking down at us.

"Elizabeth says she's going to get married," I say, loud enough so everybody in the house will hear it and get it over with.

"Nonsense. I'm the one who paid good money to send you to college, Elizabeth Motley. You can't just walk off and get married and have it all go to waste."

Grandma seems to straighten and grow taller as she speaks. I think I would have fainted if I'd been Elizabeth.

"Grandma," Elizabeth is speaking just as calmly as if she were talking about the price of sugar, "if Tommy can give up everything to defend this country, I can surely give up an education. Besides, I know how to sew and cook better than any teacher in Farmville. And that's what I was aiming to do in life anyway. I never wanted to be a teacher. I just said that because I thought you wanted me to. I thought I could teach a few years and then marry Tommy and live up the road from Mama and Daddy. But now there's no time for all that. So Tommy and I are getting married as soon as we can get the license. And that's all I have to say about it."

At first I feel proud of Elizabeth. But then I feel scared. Elizabeth is so different. I don't know her anymore. Then Aunt Mary Lee speaks for all of us.

"Good for you, Elizabeth," Aunt Mary Lee says. "I'm all for education, mind you, but this war has changed everything."

"Yes," I say. "It surely has."

Daddy doesn't argue much with Elizabeth. Actually I think he understands how she feels. He didn't get married to Mama before he went to war, but that's because Mama was still a little girl then. Daddy is lots older than Mama.

Mama never argues with anybody. Besides which, she only went to college for one year before she quit to marry Daddy, so what could she say? But I do think she really wants somebody in our family to make it all the way through college and graduate.

Grandma has been mumbling all day long, but for the second time in my life I realize that nobody is listening to her. So late that afternoon when Mr. and Mrs. Gray and Tommy come over to visit, all dressed up on a weekday, everybody seems to agree that it will be all right for the marriage to go ahead. Tommy has brought twelve quail he shot and dressed, and Grandma loves fresh quail better than anything. She is smiling and patting Tommy on the shoulder and discussing crops and weather with Mr. Gray. After that you would have thought it was her idea for Elizabeth and Tommy to get married. There is definitely something strange going on with Grandma Motley.

The wedding has to be on Christmas Eve, because it will take that long to get a marriage license. Plus, we need time to do the cooking. Mama says the chicken salad can't be made until the day before or it won't be fresh, but we start right in on the ham, two cakes, and five different kinds of cookies.

With all this cooking, and the wedding, and Christmas, and the pageant at church, we're getting pretty excited. And then we get word about the air raid drill. That's on Sunday night, December 21. Our mailman, Mr. Loomer, has already been chosen to be the chief air raid warden for the county. On Thursday he drives to the house with the mail, right around twelve o'clock. Daddy is in the kitchen eating dinner, but he goes out back and he and Mr. Loomer talk for no more than five minutes. When Daddy comes back in to finish his slice of ham and turnip greens and biscuits, he's the air raid warden for the roads all around Isle of Wight Courthouse. He and Uncle Waverly Saunders.

It makes me nervous to think about practicing for an air raid. If you practice for something, it shows you expect it to happen. Like we're practicing for the Christmas entertainment at church because we know we'll perform it on Christmas Eve at seven o'clock at night. I don't like the idea that this drill might be the first step toward actually having an air raid.

As soon as it gets dark outside, Daddy puts on his overcoat to go out and start patrolling.

"I'll be back from time to time," he says. "Because we have to call in to headquarters every half hour."

"What do you mean, 'headquarters'?" I shout out the door after him. "What kind of headquarters?"

He doesn't stop to tell me, but Mama says she thinks the headquarters, at least for the time being, is the telephone office in Smithfield.

"I believe the telephone operators are doing a lot of the organizing of the signals and that sort of thing."

Sure enough, in about fifteen minutes we hear seven short rings on the telephone.

"Lights out," Grandma calls from the living room.

"Come on, everyone," Mama says. "That's the signal. Let's all go sit in the living room together. We can't do anything without lights, so let's go where we can talk."

Courtney and the twins are already there. And Tommy

and Elizabeth and Grandma and Aunt Mary Lee. I decide to slip off upstairs by myself. Because I am sure that whatever goes on in that living room, Courtney will be at the center. She and Grandma Motley. I can just hear Grandma saying something like: "Come on, Courtney, tell us a story." Or "Come on, Courtney, lead us in singing. Teach us some of those songs you sing in England."

I start for the stairs, but then I see how dark it is up there. And just at that moment I hear an airplane. We never hear airplanes flying at night. What if it is the Germans already?

Mama sticks her head around the door.

"Hurry, now, Margaret Ann. I have to get this light turned off. You know your daddy. He would report us just like anybody else if he happened to see a light on."

"I'm going to bed," I tell her.

"At this time of night? You can't possibly be sleepy."

"Yes, I am. Really, Mama. I need some extra sleep."

"All right, then. But hurry and get the light turned off."

"Okay. See you in the morning."

Of course I can't sleep. I keep imagining all sorts of things. And every once in a while I hear everybody in the living room laughing like they're having a party. After an hour or so, I see a light come on in the hallway, and Grandma Motley pops through the doorway. "Well, it's over," she says as she flips on the light. "You should have been downstairs with the rest of us."

"It sounded like you were having a party."

"A party? During an air raid? We were trying to keep your aunt Mary Lee and Courtney from thinking of the terrible things they saw in England."

"What do you mean?"

"I mean being in that bomb shelter before they left London."

"They were in a bomb shelter?"

Grandma starts to bat her eyes, and this time it goes on for so long I am really worried.

"Grandma? Grandma? Are you all right?"

She gives a little shudder and looks at me. "Of course I'm all right. Why wouldn't I be all right? Now, close your eyes so I can get undressed."

So then she never says another word about the air raid drill, or anything that happened that night. It's like her mind has been wiped clean and she remembers nothing.

The morning after the air raid drill we're so busy we hardly have time for breakfast. I eat a fried egg biscuit on my way to the dog pen to feed the dogs. By the time I get back I'm as hungry as if I hadn't eaten, but the dishes and pans are already washed and put away. Sallie is making rolls and Mama is making a cake. So I stay hungry right on through till lunch.

Grandma is walking all over the house, with the twins

holding tight to the handles of the same big blue enameled dish pan the fruitcake got mixed in. Only this time it's full of little snips of holly. Every year she puts a piece over every picture in the house. On top of the piano. All along the mantel beside the clock. On the buffet in the dining room.

"This year I want to put a little extra," she says. "For the wedding."

Elizabeth is sewing a beautiful blue wool dress. Grandma gets a bit huffy over that.

"I hope this blue color doesn't mean what I think it means," she says. "In my day a bride wore white for purity."

"Don't worry, Grandma," Elizabeth tells her. "I am pure as driven snow. I just don't have time to make two dresses. And Tommy wants me to wear blue for a going-away dress."

Nobody has time to make a new dress for me either. I guess I should be able to sew for myself, but I can't. I tried to make myself a nightgown once. It came apart in bed the first night I wore it. Besides that, the sewing machine is in constant use. So Mama and Elizabeth decide that I will wear a yellow wool dress that Aunt Janice had given Elizabeth several years before. The hem has to be let out, but Sallie can iron it so it looks like new.

Elizabeth says that we need every bit of space in the living room for the wedding guests and that I should help Aunt

Mary Lee put the tree up in the hallway beside the front door. I've always kept as far away from Aunt Mary Lee as possible, but I've been working with her for less than fifteen minutes when I realize I'm having a good time. She has an interesting story to tell about every ornament we pick up. She says things like, "Good Lord, look at this bear. I used to be so scared of this old thing."

"Really?"

"Yes indeed. When I was little, Mama put it on the tree to scare me away. I think she said I had broken some of her best ornaments one year. So ever after she put the bear on the tree. Even when I was grown, there it would be."

"It's always been there," I agree.

"You mean Emily Ruth uses it too?"

"Grandma says to."

I hadn't noticed it before, but Aunt Mary Lee's laugh sounds just like Elizabeth's. Do laughs run in the family like brown eyes and curly hair?

"Thank you, Margaret Ann, for making this so pleasant. I wasn't sure I would make it through Christmas."

"Well," I said, "I'm feeling pretty good too."

After the house is decorated, and Grandma goes upstairs to lie down, Courtney finally makes her appearance. "What a pretty Christmas tree," she says. "At home we had one so tall I had to look way, way up to see the top."

She swallows a couple of times and stares out of the window by the bottom of the stairs.

"Your ceilings must be higher than ours, then. This tree is as tall as you can get in here."

"I guess," she says.

I look back at the tree and realize it's not shaped as pretty as Johnny and I thought when we first saw it in the woods.

"Well," says Courtney, "what can I do?"

"Looks like we've pretty much finished, doesn't it?" I tell her.

"You should have called me."

It's an amazing thing, but at that very moment Mama really does call us.

"Sallie and I could use some help with this chicken salad if there's a free hand."

I smile at Courtney.

"I guess you got your wish."

Mama tells Courtney and me to cut celery while she and Aunt Mary Lee cut the chicken. We all get knives and bowls and start to work. This goes on for maybe five minutes and then Courtney shrieks like she's being murdered.

"Oh, Mother, look. I cut myself. I'm bleeding."

"Watch out for the celery," I say.

Mama and Sallie and Aunt Mary Lee cluster around her

like her fingers are falling off. It takes all three of them to walk her over to the sink. And then Aunt Mary Lee and Sallie hold her hand under the faucet while Mama runs to get gauze for a bandage. They swath that finger like it's baby Jesus in the manger.

"Here, sweetheart," Sallie says. "You just sit down and watch us. You'll be all right."

"I guess this means I have four stalks of celery to cut all by myself," I say.

Nobody even hears me. All they can talk about is whether to take Courtney to the doctor for stitches.

"Stitches?" I say. "That's ridiculous."

But they don't hear that either. When Grandma comes in they have to go over the whole thing again.

"She might need stitches," Aunt Mary Lee says. "What do you think, Mama?"

"I think if there's any doubt, you better take her to the doctor. Here, Emily Ruth, I'll take your place. You go get dressed so you can drive them."

Again, nobody says a word to me. They leave me standing there cutting celery. And they haven't got a mile down the road before Grandma Motley says she's feeling a little tired.

"I think I better go upstairs for a little nap."

"You just had one, Grandma."

"Indeed I have never closed my eyes today. What's the matter with you, Margaret Ann?"

A good question. What is the matter with me? I decide I must be an idiot to allow people to treat me like this. I put down my knife and go to the sink to wash my hands.

"What you doing, Margaret Ann?" Sallie asks.

My mouth is open to tell her that I am tired too when Elizabeth walks in.

"Where is everybody?" she asks.

"If you mean Mama and Aunt Mary Lee, they've gone to take Courtney to the doctor because she cut her finger and three drops of blood ran out."

"Now, you know it was more than that," Sallie says. "Your Aunt Mary Lee was afraid it would leave a scar since the cut was so jagged."

"Well, then," Elizabeth says, "that leaves the three of us to get this chicken salad finished."

I go back to the table and pick up my knife. I contemplate hacking one of my own fingers to see if I get such special care. But as the knife gets closer and closer, I decide I would rather cut up celery.

We are still cutting celery and chicken when they get back.

"Oh, Elizabeth, you shouldn't be doing this," Mama says. "You've got to finish your dress."

"It's finished. And Margaret Ann and Sallie can't do everything."

"Thank you," I say.

But again nobody hears me because Courtney comes walking in, wrapped up in gauze from her wrist to the ends of her fingers.

"Where are the aspirin, Emily Ruth?" Aunt Mary Lee asks. "The doctor said to give it to her as soon as possible."

I can't believe it. Courtney is stumbling around like she's been in the hard cider. And she's holding her hand tight to her chest like people do with a broken arm.

"Get me a chair," she says.

"Margaret Ann," Aunt Mary Lee says. "Bring that chair over here. Hurry."

"My hands are sticky."

"Then wash them. Quick."

I take as much time as possible just to see if she'll really fall. And she doesn't. That proves to me that there is nothing wrong with her in the first place. I have an overpowering longing to yank the chair out from under her. I think I might have done it except that Grandma Motley comes walking in and grabs the chair to steady it.

"What is this?" she says. "Has something happened to Courtney?"

"She cut her hand, Mama. You remember that. You told us to take her to the doctor and it's a good thing we did. He said there was a possibility of infection."

"Well, I never heard a word. You say she cut herself?"

So now Aunt Mary Lee knows about Grandma too. But

she doesn't know about her own daughter. Her own daughter
is a fraud.

By the time we finish the chicken salad, it's dusky dark.
Too late to cook supper, so everybody but Elizabeth and
Johnny eat ham sandwiches and a piece of fruit. Elizabeth
is eating with the Grays, and Johnny has a date. He won't
say with who, though. Courtney has her supper on a tray
in her bedroom. It seems the aspirin is making her too
sleepy to stay downstairs. But when I walk by the door on
my way to bed, I discover it doesn't make her too sleepy to
read one of my books. Which she never even asked if she
could borrow.

Before I can go to sleep, I absolutely have to get my hair
rolled up for the wedding. Elizabeth asked me if I would be
her attendant, and of course I said yes. She said I just had to
stand beside her and hold the ring that Tommy was giving
her until the preacher asked for it. And then I would have to
hold her flowers while Tommy put the ring on her finger.

"I can do that," I tell her.

But when Grandma gets finished telling stories about
people dropping the wedding ring, I am feeling nervous.

"I don't know if I would trust the child," Grandma says.

"I trust her," Elizabeth says. "There is absolutely nothing
to worry about."

Elizabeth takes my hand and squeezes. Her fingers are

so tiny to have such strength. I squeeze back.

"Thank you, Elizabeth. I'm really proud and I'll do my absolute best."

When I get to Grandma's room, she won't let me turn the light on.

"I need my rest," she says.

"But I need to roll up my hair for the wedding."

"You'll have to do it somewhere else. Try the bathroom."

Aunt Mary Lee is in there and Mama is next in line. So I go to Johnny's bedroom. He won't be home for hours. Of course he has a mirror about the size of a pinhead.

I have about half of my hair rolled when the light goes off. Just like that first time, it's Johnny.

"What are you doing home?"

"And what are you doing in my bedroom?"

"I'm here because Grandma won't let me turn on the light so I can roll my hair."

"Okay. But you'll have to hurry. I'm sleepy. Anybody in the bathroom?"

"Aunt Mary Lee. And then Mama is next."

"Well, I guess there's no need for you to hurry, then. I'm third in line."

Johnny takes off his class ring and his watch and puts them on the dresser. Then he loosens his shirt collar.

"Where have you been anyway?"

"I was invited to a family dinner at Charlotte Holland's house."

"Ah. Charlotte Holland, eh? Was the food good?"

"The food was great. But the company was even better. I think you would have enjoyed it too."

"Really?"

"I believe so. A mutual friend of ours was there."

"Bobby Holland?"

"Yep."

"Did you talk to him?"

"Sure did."

"Did he say anything about me?"

"Sure did."

"What did he say?"

"Not much. He just asked for your hand in marriage."

"He did not."

"Sure he did. I told him I thought it was a good idea. You could make it a double wedding tomorrow. Save Daddy a lot of money."

"Don't be silly, Johnny. Neither one of you said a word about me, I bet."

"That's true. But suppose he had asked me. How would you feel about it?"

"Stupid is how I'd feel about it."

I stick in my last bobby pin and get up to leave.

"It seems like Bobby Holland and I stay angry with each

other all the time. I wish I could be sure he still likes me."

"What do you mean? He's crazy about you."

"Are you sure?"

"I am sure."

"I wish I was," I say.

I blow Johnny a kiss.

"'Night," I say.

"Sleep tight."

Grandma is up at daybreak the next morning.

"Come on," she says. "Rise and shine, sleepyhead. It's Christmas Eve."

"It's too soon," I mumble. "I need one more hour of sleep."

I don't get it. Mama is knocking at the door before I can turn over.

"Margaret Ann, I need you. Here's a list of jobs for you to do today. Tomorrow I promise you can sleep as long as you want to."

"Who wants to sleep on Christmas Day?" I ask her.

She hands me the list and is out the door before I can read the first word. But when I do read it, I nearly faint. Bring in firewood and chips. Fill and cut the chicken salad sandwiches. Put doilies on the plates. Fold napkins. Supervise the twins' bath. See they wear the right dresses. I stop reading about halfway down. What does Mama think I am? I can't do all this.

I dress as quick as I can and go downstairs to tell her, but I can't catch her. She is all over the house, doing one job right after the other. I try to corner her. Behind the pantry door. In the closet under the stairs. Out on the back porch, where we keep the cooked hams. "I can't stop now, Margaret Ann." Over and over she keeps telling me this.

Courtney comes down to breakfast about ten o'clock. I have already cut bread and made three trays of sandwiches.

"I'm so sorry I can't help with the sandwiches," she says. "Mother says there is too much danger of infection."

"You look fine to me," I tell her.

"I feel fine. I'm looking forward to the wedding, but Mother and Grandma both say I must be careful."

"Yeah. Me too. I just need to be careful that I don't work myself completely to death."

"Poor Margaret. I'm so sorry I can't help you. You haven't even had time to take your hair down, have you? I guess I'm lucky having hair that doesn't need to be rolled."

Mama comes rushing through at just that minute which is probably a good thing since I have a knife in my hand.

"Hurry, Margaret Ann. It's getting late. The twins need to take their baths by noon in order to keep on schedule."

And she's gone. Good Lord. I have two more trays of sandwiches to go. Then baths for the twins. Then who knows what. I look over at Courtney. She's pouring herself a cup of tea.

"Would you like a cup, Margaret?"

"You know I don't like hot tea. But even if I did, I don't have three hands you know. The two I have are pretty busy."

"And I have only one."

She holds up the hand with the bandage like I've never seen it before.

"You're so lucky," she says. "I wish I had two hands. I'm sure I could cut the crusts more evenly than you're doing. Oh, well."

She breaks into a smile like a picture of the Virgin Mary. I'm sure I look more like the Devil himself.

I finish the list by three o'clock and the wedding is at four. I go upstairs and knock on the bathroom door, only to find that Elizabeth is in there. So I wash behind the closet door, using one of the antique bowl and pitcher sets. I hope I'm not too smelly.

I know Aunt Mary Lee has insisted that Elizabeth have her old room back to dress for the wedding, but it doesn't occur to me that she and Courtney need to dress in Grandma's room. I just get the yellow dress over my head when in comes Courtney, carrying a wire hanger with a brand-new dress on it in her good hand. That's the first I know about a new dress for Courtney.

"Can you take this?" she says. "I guess I shouldn't really have been carrying this hanger."

"Why ever not? You didn't cut that hand."

"Yes. But I'm still a bit woozy from all the aspirin I took yesterday."

"Good gosh, Courtney, you are really being foolish. I've cut my hand a dozen times and nobody ever even put Mercurochrome on it for me."

"Then I'm sure you weren't hurt as badly as I am."

I look at Grandma's clock and see it's almost fifteen minutes past three. I don't even have time for a fuss. I smooth my dress down and start removing the bobby pins in my hair.

"Oh, Margaret!" Courtney shrieks. Almost as bad as when she cut her hand. "I can see the lines where the hem has been let out."

"Imagine that," I say right back to her. "How kind of you to notice."

"Shall I call Sallie and have her bring up the ironing board?"

"Don't be stupid. Sallie doesn't have time to breathe, much less iron my dress again. Besides, it wouldn't do any good. I'm sure she did the best she could the first time she ironed it."

Aunt Mary Lee comes rushing through the door, out of breath and red in the face, carrying one of Mama's dresses.

"Hurry, girls," she says. "The Grays are here early. And Emily Ruth is still down in the kitchen with Sallie. And of course Elizabeth can't go down. She mustn't see the groom before the wedding. So the three of us are a welcoming committee."

"Where's Daddy?"

"He's down there. But he's not your mother's idea of a perfect host for the ladies. Hey, Margaret Ann, you look ready. Why don't you go down and help him entertain? We'll be along in a minute."

"Sure," I say.

I grab my hairbrush and rake it through the curls. It hurts like heck, but I keep going.

"You look fine," Aunt Mary Lee says. "Now go."

Once I get through the door, I start grinning. Saved by the Grays.

Everybody in the neighborhood is there for the wedding, mainly because almost everybody is kin to us or to the Grays. Joyce's mother is Tommy's aunt from his father's side, so all the Dardens are invited. And Tommy's mother was a Holland, so all the Hollands are here. And all the Grays, of course. And all the Saunderses. Somehow there aren't a lot of extra Motleys. Granddaddy Motley was an only child, and Grandma Motley's brother died young.

There are enough Grays to make up for it. Tommy has

three older brothers and one sister who are already married, and they all have lots of children. Paige and Polly latch on to a couple of Tommy's nieces and they start eating cookies before the wedding even begins. Johnny has at least three girlfriends here, which might be a challenge even to him.

Uncle Waverly and Aunt Janice and our Saunders cousins are dressed to the nines. Aunt Janice buys all their clothes ready-made, and they never let down hems to make do for another year. But they aren't near as pretty as Elizabeth.

As soon as Mama comes down, she says I should go back upstairs till the wedding starts, to be with Elizabeth. I'm on my way when I get a glimpse of Bobby Holland. He's standing beside the Christmas tree at the front door.

"Hey, Bobby," I say.

He waves and smiles. Bobby Holland looks good anytime, but whenever he wears his blue suit with a white shirt and that necktie his grandmother gave him, I just about lose my breath. I'm walking toward him to say hello when Grandma grabs my arm.

"Don't you know you're supposed to stand up with your sister?" she asks me.

"Of course. But I just want to say hello to Bobby."

"Child, you don't have time for such as that. Go upstairs right this minute. Elizabeth needs to explain what you're supposed to do."

"I know what to do, Grandma, and I'm going upstairs in just a minute."

I look back toward the door, but Bobby isn't there. I know he can't have gone far.

"It will only take a minute, Grandma."

"Do you see your sister at the top of the stairs?"

I turn to look, and there she is, motioning for me to come. I have to go to her.

We go over all the details, such as how I'm supposed to take the ring from Tommy and hold it very carefully until the preacher gets to that part of the ceremony. And then we practice handing the bouquet back and forth between us.

"Now, be careful about the ring," Elizabeth says. "Grandma Motley would faint if one of us dropped it."

"Oh, Elizabeth, I wish you hadn't said that. Grandma made me so nervous with those stories about people dropping wedding rings."

"I was kidding, Margaret Ann. Just calm down now."

"I'm trying."

Aunt Mary Lee sticks her head in the door.

"Time to start," she says. "Are you ready, Elizabeth?"

"I think so. Do I look okay?"

"You look beautiful. I love that color blue."

"Thanks, Aunt Mary Lee. And thanks for playing the wedding music."

"I'm happy to do it. I guess I better get started. Mama is downstairs about to explode."

As soon as we hear the music, Elizabeth and I start down the steps. I go first and she's right behind me. But where is Bobby Holland?

"Look in the living room and be sure Tommy is there," Elizabeth says as soon as we get to the bottom step.

I peep through the living room door. Tommy is standing beside the preacher with his oldest brother, Henry, right beside him. I nod to Elizabeth.

"How does Tommy look?" she says.

I go back to the door for another perusal.

"He has on a brand-new suit," I whisper when I get back. "But his shirt must be too tight at the collar. He keeps running his fingers around it like it's choking him."

"Okay, let's get started before he chokes to death. Tell Aunt Mary Lee I'm ready."

I stick my head around the door again and nod to Aunt Mary Lee. She starts playing the wedding march and Elizabeth and I start walking. Daddy meets us at the doorway and walks beside Elizabeth till we get to Mr. Kales, standing with his back to the fireplace. The room is so crowded I feel like I can't breathe. And I am so nervous about holding the wedding ring. If only Grandma hadn't told me all those stories.

The music stops as soon as we settle in our places.

Tommy takes the ring out of his pocket and reaches across to hand it to me. My hands are shaking so I can hardly hold it. I stick it tight on my thumb and try not to think about Grandma. But there's a particular story about a girl named Sara Lee Cofer. Grandma says she died one month after her wedding. And her ring was dropped during the service. That is so creepy.

I look across the room and there's Bobby Holland standing in the doorway. Joyce is on one side of him and Courtney on the other. I try sending thought messages to him. *Bobby Holland, look at me. Look at me.*

"Dearly beloved," Mr. Kales reads out of the prayer book, "we are gathered here today to join this man and this woman in holy matrimony. . . ."

Bobby Holland, will you be standing in Tommy's place one of these days? Will I be standing in Elizabeth's? Heck, he still isn't looking at me. I glance at Bobby's mother and she smiles. She's holding tight to Tommy's grandma. Old Mrs. Gray has some kind of sickness that makes her shake all the time. Bobby should be there to hold her other arm instead of standing between two girls.

Suddenly I hear Elizabeth's voice, high and squeaky like she's nervous, saying she will take Tommy to be her lawfully wedded husband. And then Tommy's voice, like it's coming out of a cellar, saying that he'll take Elizabeth to be his lawfully wedded wife "till death do us part."

Tommy reaches for the ring and I hold my breath. It's stuck so tight on the end of my thumb that he has to pull hard to get it away from me. But then it's on Elizabeth's finger and nothing sad is going to happen. Not in a month. Not ever.

Mr. Kales pronounces them man and wife and Aunt Mary Lee plays the recessional music that people usually walk out of the church to. But there's nowhere for us to go. We all stand in a jumble watching Tommy and Elizabeth kiss.

"Well, Margaret Ann, you've got a new brother," old Mr. Gray, Tommy's grandfather, tells me while he's waiting to kiss the bride.

"I guess so."

I just have to find Bobby Holland. I keep pushing at people and nodding and shaking hands until I get to the hall door. I take two steps into the hallway, and Grandma grabs me hard by the shoulder.

"Ask Joyce if she will help you serve the chicken salad sandwiches out here in the hall. We can't get everybody inside the dining room at one time."

"Why can't Courtney do it? I have something I really need to do, Grandma."

"You know Courtney's finger is hurt too badly for her to be carrying around these heavy trays. Now," Grandma says triumphantly, "here's Joyce. And I am sure she'll help you."

"Grandma, I really don't want to."

Grandma isn't listening. She hands us the trays and is off to the dining room before I know what's happening.

We pass three trays of chicken salad sandwiches. And then everybody is saying, "No, thank you," so we decide to go over to the stairs and eat the six little leftover sandwiches ourselves.

Well . . . when we get there, who should be sitting on the bottom step except Courtney and Bobby Holland? I am so stunned I nearly drop the tray. Courtney has her bandaged hand resting on Bobby's knee, and Bobby is leaning so far toward her he's almost touching her shoulder.

"What are you two doing here?"

I am so angry I feel like I'm spitting out little sparks of fire.

"We're talking," Courtney says just as calm as you please.

"I'm sure you're talking, Courtney, no matter where you are."

"Now, Margaret Ann," Joyce says quickly, "that's not a nice thing to say."

"It sure isn't," Bobby agrees.

"Nobody talks more than you do," Joyce tells me.

And Bobby Holland is nodding his head to that too.

"To everybody but me," he says.

"I would talk to you if I could ever find you."

"You found me. So sit down and talk."

"And where would you suggest I sit? It looks like the steps are pretty well taken."

It's Courtney's fault. I know she's the one who asked Bobby to sit with her, and not the other way around. But somehow I'm just as mad at Bobby Holland as I am at her. And then what she says next. That is the absolute end. She stands up and hugs me before I can pull away.

"Now, I won't hear another word. Margaret is my favorite cousin. And she is perfectly right. I do talk too much. Here, Margaret, you sit with Bobby for a while. I'll find Mother and have her take a look at this bandage."

"Courtney, there is nothing wrong with the bandage. I am so sick of hearing you talk about that tiny little cut on you finger. Honestly."

"Come on, Margaret Ann, that's a pretty nasty thing to say. Her hand has seven stitches," Bobby says.

"She told you that? And you believed her?"

"Why wouldn't I believe her?"

"Why ever not?" I say and start up the stairs. There is no way in the world I am going to sit down on those steps with Bobby Holland. For a while, Courtney says. As if she's sharing him for a few minutes and will be back to take him over later. I reach around, hand him the tray of sandwiches, and keep going.

"Come on, Joyce," I say.

But Joyce tells me no.

"I'll share the sandwiches with Bobby," she says.

"Suit yourself."

I run up the rest of the steps. The heels on my shoes are wedges and I sound like I'm hammering nails into each step. When I get to the top, I hear Elizabeth and Mama and Aunt Mary Lee in the front bedroom laughing. They're getting Elizabeth ready to go off on her wedding trip. Elizabeth is going to throw her bouquet as she comes down the steps, and I have so much looked forward to catching it. But not now. Not with Bobby Holland downstairs mushing around with Courtney. And Joyce too. My best friend in the world. I have to find a place to be alone. Johnny's room. I go in and lock the door. I cry and cry until I'm like Grandma. There's no more water to make tears.

I miss seeing Elizabeth and Tommy leave for their wedding trip. I miss catching the bouquet too. It's Courtney, cut hand and all, who grabs it.

That night we have to go to church for the Christmas pageant. I'm in no mood to be an angel, I can tell you. So I tell Mama I absolutely refuse to go. Then she tells Daddy and he says I absolutely have to. So that's all there is to that. What Daddy tells us to do, we do. But I don't think Mama wants to go either. She looks so tired. Some of the people stay until almost six o'clock. Then everything has to be cleaned up and put away. Sallie has two of her daughters with her to help out, but there's still a lot for all of us to do. Except Courtney, of course. All the dishes have to be washed and the floors swept and the furniture put back in place. It isn't anywhere near being finished when it's time to go to church.

"You go on now," Sallie tells Mama. "It's not often you get to see Margaret Ann be an angel."

I know Sallie is just teasing, just trying to make Mama laugh and stop thinking about Elizabeth. But I'm not so sure that going to the pageant will do that. Last year Elizabeth played the part of Mary, sitting beside the manger looking down at one of Polly's doll babies. And Tommy Gray was Joseph, standing right beside her. Mrs. Chapman was expecting them to act the same parts this year. Right till the last minute she kept talking to Mama about when Elizabeth would be home from college and how many rehearsals she would be able to attend.

And right up until the last minute she doesn't choose another Mary. Mrs. Chapman doesn't like a change. She says she always tries to follow tradition, but I think she just likes to have everything her own way. Like the way she has it in her head the Holland boys have to be shepherds. So there they are. All of them dressed in these ugly brown bathrobes. The same ones they wear every year. Bobby says the one he wears belonged to his granddaddy. Maybe these bathrobes are a tradition. I don't know. But thinking about the bathrobes makes me sad and angry at the same time. How could Bobby have talked to me like that?

All the time I'm climbing the steep stairs to the choir loft over the pulpit, I keep hearing what Bobby Holland said at the wedding. So, okay, I guess I sound rude sometimes. But what I said this afternoon is true. Courtney is using that cut hand to get what she wants. And it looks like what she wants is Bobby Holland. So let her have him. And she can have Joyce Darden, too, if she needs another friend so badly.

I'm the first one of the angels to step into the choir loft. I walk to the back and stick my arms up over my head. I can feel my wings bouncing around behind my shoulders. In the back row I won't be able to see Courtney down there in the pulpit, but I'm sure I'll be able to hear her. I always hear her. Like tonight when Grandma asks her if her hand hurts too badly to be in the program, and she says she thinks she can bear the pain.

"I wouldn't want to disappoint Mrs. Chapman," she says.

It is positively sickening to think of it.

The shepherds start down the aisle while Mrs. Kales, the preacher's wife, launches into "While Shepherds Watched Their Flocks by Night," and the five-year-olds, like Paige and Polly, sing. I look down at the Harris girls, swaying to the music and smiling like they know some wonderful secret. Maybe they do. Maybe all that confessing of their sins teaches them something. They look just as relaxed. Maybe I should try it. Maybe I should ask Bobby Holland to forgive me for all the things he thinks I've done. Even if I haven't done them.

In a few minutes I realize I'm relaxing in spite of myself. When Courtney says her speech, I really listen. Her voice is like a bell ringing. Clear and crisp.

"For unto you is born this day . . . in the city of David . . . a savior which is Christ the Lord."

Courtney's voice is beautiful. I look down into the audience again and see Mama and Daddy and Aunt Mary Lee and Grandma Motley. They all look so proud and happy.

"Fear not. For behold I bring you good tidings of great joy which shall be to all people."

I might even smile myself except that my arms and hands are going limp from holding them over my head so long. Think of something else, I tell myself. Think of the wedding and how I didn't drop the ring. Think of Elizabeth and how happy she is. Gosh, her name isn't Motley anymore. She's Elizabeth Gray. And she and Tommy are spending the night together in Suffolk in a hotel. And she's probably wearing this real thin, silky nightgown. And she and Tommy are kissing all they want to.

I lean forward so I can see Bobby Holland. He's looking

up at me too. But he isn't smiling. He looks just as angry as I was this afternoon. Oh, Lord, I just want this whole thing to be over. My arms are so tired. I don't think I can keep them up much longer.

Finally the three kings get there to worship the Christ child, and then the junior choir sings "Silent Night." It's time for Mrs. Chapman to turn the lights out, and that means the angels can take their arms down. Hallelujah.

All we can think of is getting out of these costumes. The girls go to one Sunday school room and the boys to the other. I get finished early and go back to meet Mama and Daddy in the church. I don't know how I'm going to do it, but I know I need to apologize to Bobby Holland. That is, if I can talk to him where nobody else can hear me.

But when Bobby comes back from taking off his shepherd's bathrobe, he walks just as straight as he can to where Courtney is standing. And then I'm not just mad at him, my heart is broken.

I don't see Bobby Holland anymore during the Christmas holidays. Courtney tells me she talks to him on the telephone, but I'm not sure it's true. I think she just likes to torture me. It works. I don't even try on the green sweater Mama and Daddy give me. I eat my raisins and my chocolate-covered cherries, but then I feel sick. I read my books, some of them over and over. Mostly I get my coat and walk down to the dog pen and talk to the hounds.

When Elizabeth and Tommy get home from Suffolk, they're smiling like they've won a gold medal. They look at each after every word they speak. Somehow it makes me feel embarrassed just to look at them. Sad, too. Elizabeth seems so different now. Not just her name, but her whole personality. You can look at her and see that Tommy is more important to her than any of us. As soon as possible, I'm back at the dog pen.

The rest of the holiday drags on and on. When Joanne Cox calls with an invitation for Courtney to go to a party at her house and to spend the night, I feel better. But Aunt Mary Lee says she can't go.

"If Joanne isn't polite enough to invite Margaret Ann too, then nobody goes."

"Please, Aunt Mary Lee," I say quickly. "You have to let Courtney go. I'll feel embarrassed at school if you don't." Which is only partly a lie. Joanne Cox can really make me feel like a country hick.

Just before she leaves to go to Smithfield, Courtney decides she can remove her bandage after all. Grandma agrees that it will be better to let air get to it. So they pack up a suitcase with a party dress and a nightgown and things like that. I'm counting the seconds till she's out the door. At the final second Courtney tells me that Bobby Holland is invited too. It's like she wants to make sure I don't enjoy the time at home without her.

When Courtney gets back home late on Friday afternoon, all she can talk about is Bobby Holland. When Aunt Mary Lee finally tells her she's heard enough about that, Courtney starts in on "the war effort."

"It seems that people forgot about the war during the holidays," she says. "When things settle down, each of us must find a way to do our part."

I know she's right, but I have no idea what I'm going to do. Courtney does, of course. She says she's been reading a lot about it in the newspaper at Joanne's. So I go out on the back porch in the cold and find last week's copy of the *Smithfield Times*.

Back in the kitchen I read all the ads from Delk's department store. Then I read about how Dot and B. T. motored to Smithfield from Battery Park on Tuesday to do a little Christmas shopping. I don't actually know who Dot and B. T. are, but I'm impressed to see their names in the paper.

Then I get down to brass tacks, as Grandma calls it. I read all about the air raid warning system that is being put into operation. The county is going to build towers in a number of locations, where people can watch for enemy airplanes. And there will be more blackout practices.

But the big thing is that on December 30, there's supposed

to be a registration day for volunteers. Everybody in the county—man, woman, or child—is supposed to sign up. And that day has already passed. I haven't registered either. I don't think anybody in this family has registered. But what can I possibly do anyway?

I read on down the page until this catches my eye. "By bomber, Isle of Wight County is between three and four minutes from Norfolk and Portsmouth."

Good Lord, that's where all the navy ships are. And the naval shipyard. Germans would surely want to bomb there.

"If they are attacked it is possible that many dogfights will take place in the air over our county."

I look across the kitchen at the window. German planes can fly over our fields, our yard, our house. I push my shoulders against the wooden back of the chair. It stops me from shivering for a few minutes. Until I read on.

"The enemy we face is ruthless, is smart, and is efficient. He has means and desire to attack us. We must be prepared. We must practice blackouts. We must prepare to see that no enemy troops parachute into the area unnoticed."

I look out across the field. What would it look like to see a parachute falling out of the air? How long would it take for a soldier to reach the ground once he has jumped out of a plane? Would we have time to lock all the doors? Would we have time to call the telephone operator? And what could she possibly do if we called her? I read on.

"We must be prepared to put out fires caused by falling planes and bombs."

I look back quickly at the peanut field. Airplanes and bombs are totally different from Yankee soldiers in our backyard, stealing our hams and sides of bacon.

"We must train our children to protect themselves," the newspaper says.

So maybe Courtney is right. Maybe we do need to march in formation during little recess at school. At least I'm a pretty good shot with a rifle. Johnny said I'm almost as good a shot as he is. And I beat Bobby Holland many a time when he and Johnny and I had target practice together. At least I can do that.

"We must train men and women to care for the injured. . . . You will be called upon to do your share. . . . You are expected to do your share."

Oh my gosh. I hate to think of it, but it seems that Courtney is right.

Johnny's Bedroom

Nothing gets any better between Bobby Holland and me after we start back to school in January. I feel like he ought to apologize to me and he never does. So I refuse to speak to him at all. But that doesn't mean I don't think about him. The very worst thing is that Tommy Gray doesn't tease me about him anymore. That makes everything seem so final.

The next draft lottery is going to be held on March 17, and since Tommy Gray has already volunteered, we figure he'll be called up. That means he'll go to boot camp right away for his training. Elizabeth says when it happens she's going wherever he is sent. But then Tommy finds out she can't see him at all until the training is over, so she decides to wait. She is still two miles away at the Gray house waiting to pack Tommy's suitcase and tell him good-bye.

Grandma complains all the time about the regular black-outs. She says she doesn't have enough time to read her Bible anymore. So when Mama hears that blackout curtains are available in town, she buys them for every window in the house.

I am as glad as Grandma about it. Because right after supper every night I go upstairs to Johnny's room to get away. Johnny doesn't mind because he stays downstairs anyway, listening to the news or talking to Aunt Mary Lee. I do my homework first, and then I read my library book until he comes up to bed. Then I sigh real loud and grumble my way down the hall to Grandma's room and try to sleep.

On the very first day of February, a Sunday, a scary thing happens up in Surry County, the next one over from us. Jack Hubbard is up there visiting his uncle Henry and he sees it all. He's still nervous on Monday morning when he gets to school. He doesn't even ask Miss Boswell for permission; he just starts telling the class about it.

"It was this here army pursuit plane from over at Langley Field," Jack says. "Me and my cousins heard the sound of the motor first. It was real loud. So we ran outside and looked up and it was doing tailspins and stuff. I don't know what you call some of it."

Jack stops talking for a second and looks at Miss Boswell.

"Why don't you come up front, Jack, where the whole class can hear you?"

"Yes, ma'am."

Jack is taller than anybody else in the class, but he's stoop shouldered and kind of lopes along. You can tell he has walked many a mile, chopping peanuts. When he gets to the front, he looks like he's losing his breath.

"Go on," Miss Boswell says.

"All right. Like I told you, we were standing there, looking, and the plane just came crashing right down in the road not far from Uncle Henry's place. We saw the pilot, too, when he jumped out the plane. And then the parachute opened, and he drifted down like he was a feather. I mean, he landed in a big clump of bushes, though, and he got a few scratches was all. But that airplane exploded when it hit the ground, parts of it flew down the road, and its motor was buried so deep in the ground, there's nothing in this world that's going to get it out. They sent this truck over from Langley to try. Couldn't do a thing. Not a thing."

"So what happened next?" Miss Boswell asks him.

"Nothing happened. I mean, if it did, we didn't know about it. Daddy said we had to go on home to feed up."

"What do you mean, 'feed up'?" Joanne Cox asks. "Didn't your uncle have anything to eat?"

"He had plenty to eat, but the mules we had to feed and the cows we had to milk weren't with us. So we had to go home to feed up. What's so hard to understand?"

"Exactly," I say. "What's so hard to understand?"

Jack Hubbard looks at me and smiles. Then he reaches inside his pocket and brings out a big hunk of metal.

"Y'all want to see it?" he asks. "I can pass it round."

Courtney raises her hand before anybody can move.

"I should think it would be against the law to keep any part of the plane. My father says that in the case of an accident it is important to retrieve every part of the airplane, no matter how small. In that way it is possible to reconstruct the accident and find out why it happened."

Everybody looks at Courtney first, then at Jack, and he gets red in the face. I feel sorry for him, actually.

"What do you mean?" he asks. "My cousin picked up a piece too. We didn't see how something small as this could matter."

"Calm down, Jack," Miss Boswell says. "I am sure Courtney is not suggesting that you meant to do wrong. But sometimes we do wrong without knowing it."

"It must be returned to the authorities," Courtney says. "That's the least you can do for men who are willing to give their lives for you."

Jack's face goes from red to purple. He keeps shaking his head and looking down at Courtney. Everybody in class is talking and nobody is listening. I turn my head and look back at Bobby Holland. I can tell by his eyes that he is looking straight at Courtney. He isn't smiling, but he isn't frowning either. I clear my throat as loud as I can, but I can't get his attention. He just keeps looking at Courtney.

When Miss Boswell calls the class to order and starts our history lesson, I write a note to Jack and send it off down the row to him. I tell him not to worry. If my stupid cousin Courtney says something, it's bound to be wrong.

Sending that note turns out to be one of the worst things I have ever done, because Jack Hubbard thinks it means I want him for a boyfriend. I can't get rid of him. Not even when I tell him plainly that I hate him.

"I know what that means," he says. "Hate means love, don't it?"

"No, it don't . . . I mean doesn't."

"You just as well love me," he says. "Bobby Holland don't love you no more. He loves your cousin."

"He does not!" I shout, even though I'm pretty sure it's true.

After that, my life just gets crazier and crazier, and Courtney is a big part of everything that happens. It isn't that she actually causes any of it, but just like before, she makes it worse. For example, on a Monday, February 9, at two in the morning, all the clocks in the whole country have to be set ahead one hour. That's a very simple matter, but Courtney talks about it and explains about it until I think I will lose my mind. Besides this, she brags constantly about the foreign stamps she gets off her daddy's letters. Particularly when she takes them to school for the stamp drive. A pound of already used stamps is worth thirty-nine cents. Miss Boswell says our class is going to make money to buy some extra books for the library.

Miss Boswell also talks to the class about buying defense stamps. Every Monday morning we're to bring as much money as we can get our hands on. She says she will have enough stamp books for everybody.

"I have my allowance," Joanne Cox says. "I'll take a part of that to buy my stamps."

I don't get an allowance. When I ask Daddy about it, he says he never heard of such.

"If you need something, Margaret Ann, your mother and I will buy it for you. All you have to do is tell me."

Grandma Motley says there's no need in the world to give me money every week because all I'll do is lose it. Which is simply not true.

I have to figure out a way to get some money for savings stamps. I can just imagine what Joanne Cox will say about it if I don't bring money at all. Besides which, it will be terrible not to be doing my part for the war effort.

So I wait till Daddy is in a good mood and isn't too tired. And I try to be real quiet, and I smile a lot. And I ask him.

"Of course, Margaret Ann. You know I want to support the war effort. How about a dollar a week?"

I can hardly believe my ears. I'm sure I'll have more money even than Joanne Cox.

"That's great, Daddy."

"And I tell you what. I'm going to give Courtney a dollar too. Your Aunt Mary Lee has no way on earth to get money over here from England. And half of this place will belong to her someday anyway."

"Half of this place? You mean this house? This farm?"

"Of course. Not that she will want to live here after the war. But it's hers if she does."

My heart sinks right down to my toes when I hear this. What will I do if Courtney never goes back to England? How can I stand it if I have to live my whole life stuck in the room with Grandma and with Courtney down the hall?

That first Monday when we buy the stamps, I get four of them to paste in my stamp book. Of course Courtney does too. There's a really interesting picture on the twenty-five-cent stamp. The soldier looks like he fought in the Great War, like Daddy. He's wearing tight boots up to his knees and a large brimmed hat, and he's carrying a gun almost as tall as he is.

"How many did you get?" I ask Joyce.

"I got two. But I don't know if I can get that many every week. Daddy says I might have to cut back till he gets the crops all planted. You know how much money you need in the spring for planting."

"That's okay, Joyce. I bet you can catch up next fall when the crops come in."

"I'll never catch up with Joanne Cox and them. They brought five dollars apiece. Five pages of stamps the very first day."

I look across the room at Joanne Cox and her friend Evelyn Stephens. I hope their tongues are stiff as boards from all that licking.

Another thing that happens at school is that the teachers give out rationing books for sugar. Mama comes to get ours. Everybody in our family, including Aunt Mary Lee and Courtney, gets twelve ounces of sugar a week. Mama has to measure out how much sugar we already have at home and then she gets a book with twenty eight tickets in it. It's supposed to last for twenty-eight weeks. After that nobody is sure what will happen. Maybe the war will be over. Maybe everything will be back like it always has been.

The very next week Courtney and Joanne Cox get all the girls in our class organized for marching. Miss Boswell says we're to do it for our physical education.

"Remember," Courtney tells us, "marching is good exercise. Heads up. Backs straight. Knees straight."

Day after day after day, we march. It's almost like she and Joanne want to keep the war going, just so they can tell everybody what to do. Courtney is captain and Joanne is the lieutenant. And the two of them decide what everyone else is supposed to be.

Courtney asks me to be the sergeant, but I say no. I don't want to be anything important in something Courtney has charge of. But when she asks Joyce to be the corporal, Joyce says yes. So there I am with all the other privates, marching around and around. From the tennis courts on one side of the street, down beside the school building, and then up and down the baseball diamond. I feel like a two-year-old.

"Attention," Courtney yells.

I am truly surprised that she can talk so loud. Usually she's so mousy. Anyway, standing at attention is pretty easy. We all get that.

"Forward, march."

That isn't too bad.

"Company . . . halt."

Half the girls don't, and so the ones behind bump into us, and step on our heels, and pull our shoes half off, and get mud all over our socks. It's a mess.

One day Joanne Cox's friend Evelyn Stephens, who agreed to be the sergeant, bumps me so hard I lose my balance and fall. So of course Courtney has to stop everything right there and walk all the way back to see if I'm hurt.

"No," I say. "I'm not hurt. People just ought to watch out where they're going, that's all."

That afternoon when we get home from school, I won't even speak to her.

"Margaret," she whispers in that funny voice of hers. Maybe she's hoarse from all the yelling. "I'm really sorry if I embarrassed you. But I felt I had to check on you. After all, I am captain. It is my duty to look after my troops."

"I'm not a troop, thank you very much. And I wouldn't have fallen if that stupid Evelyn Stephens hadn't bumped me."

"Oh, Margaret, how can you say such a thing? Evelyn is an awfully nice girl. Really she is. I'm sure she was sorry."

"Well, good for her," I say. Real loud. So that makes Mama stick her head out into the hallway to see what's going on.

"Margaret Ann," she says. "Are you being impolite to Courtney?"

"Yes, I am. Just as impolite as I can possibly be."

"Then you can go to your room. Right this minute. And don't come down until you can apologize."

I stomp upstairs to Johnny's room, holding tight to my books. I throw them down on the bed and walk to the window. I'm too mad to read, so I just stand there, and look out across the fields.

Gradually I can feel myself calming down. I love looking out of Johnny's windows. No matter what season of the year it is. No matter what work is going on. It's something Bobby Holland and I have in common. We know what is going on in every field on both our farms. Even though I don't have Bobby anymore, I still love looking in the Holland fields as we drive by in the school bus.

For about a week, Daddy and Johnny have been in this field, the one I can see from Johnny's window, doing the spring plowing. Some days seagulls fly in from the James River, all the way to our farm, and they swoop down just over Daddy's and Johnny's heads. It is really beautiful with the red tractors and the blue overalls, and the white birds in the sky. Just like the United States flag. Red, white, and blue.

Today there is nothing to look at. Not a tractor plowing, and not a seagull flying. I love it anyway. In a few minutes my stomach starts to growl and I realize how hungry I am. I miss the snack Sallie saves for me in the warming closet.

I think about going down to the kitchen, but that reminds me of how mad I am with Courtney. I decide I'm madder than I'm hungry. Besides which, Mama sent me up here. I can't go down until I'm ready to apologize to Courtney.

So I open my geography book and plop myself down on the bed. And then I push myself backward and fix the pillow against the headboard like I usually do.

But just as I'm leaning back, two envelopes drop out of the pillow and fall on the floor beside the bed. I reach down and pick them up. One is addressed to Mama and Daddy. And one is addressed to me. How in the world did they get here?

I settle myself and pull at the flap. It's sealed, but it isn't like a regular letter. There's no stamp on it. No postmark. Not even an address. Just, "To: Margaret Ann."

I tear it open and pull out a sheet of notebook paper. I look down at the signature right away and I can hardly believe my eyes. It's from Johnny. Why in the world is Johnny writing me a letter when he's probably right up the road at the Crumpler place plowing? The Crumplers haven't owned that land in a hundred years, but that's what people call it. There are two big fields and a lot of woods up there. It takes nearly a week to break up those fields.

I look back at the letter. And suddenly I feel all shivery, just like when I was reading the air raid article in the *Smithfield Times*. Just like when Jack Hubbard was telling about the airplane crash. Just like some nights when Edward R. Murrow is talking about the war. Clearly there is something wrong if my own brother is writing me a letter.

Dear Margaret Ann,

I need your help. And I know I can count on you. Because someone has to break this news to Mama and be really nice to her for a while afterward. And you might have to help explain all this to Daddy, too. And maybe help out around the farm if it comes to that.

Now, this is what I want you to do. Before you hand the other letter to Mama and Daddy, I want you to tell them what your letter says. I want you to tell them that I have decided to volunteer for the navy. I know Daddy needs me on the farm. But I have talked to the Darden boys and they have agreed to help out however they can. And then I have talked to Bobby Holland. I know he is only thirteen years old, but he can plow as good as any man in the county. And he said his daddy didn't really need him. His brothers can do all the work around the Holland farm. He said he would work for Daddy after school and on Saturdays till school is out and then full-time.

Also, tell Mama and Daddy that I couldn't stay here, with Tommy Gray and so many others going off to war. Not after all Courtney has told me was going on in England and all over Europe. In the Pacific, too. Somebody has to fight Hitler and Mussolini and Tojo. And I'm it.

Besides all this, Margaret Ann, if I'm gone, it means you can have a room to yourself. You'll like that. Tell Mama I said you are to sleep in my bedroom until I come home from the navy. I'm doing this for you. Because I love each and every one in this family. Even Grandma. But don't you let her see this letter. Don't let anybody see this

letter. Just remember what it says and tell Mama and
Daddy. But especially Mama.
Sincerely,
Your brother, John

I read the letter four times, so I'll remember every word
of it. But there are parts of it I wish I could forget. Especially
the part that says he's joining the navy for me. So I'll have a
bedroom all to myself.

I close my eyes and think about Johnny walking up and
down on a navy ship. It might be a battleship built in
Newport News. But it won't stay there. It'll go out in the
ocean where the waves get really rough. Way out where the
German submarines patrol. Where the Luftwaffe planes fly
back and forth.

"Oh, Johnny," I say, right out loud. "I never wanted a
bedroom as bad as all this."

Mama is so pitiful when I tell her about it. I guess I should
have waited to tell Mama and Daddy together. But Mama
comes up to see about me right after I read the letter for the
fourth time. Otherwise I probably would have read it a fifth
time.

Mama sits down on the bed beside me, plumps up the
pillow, puts it behind her back, and rests against the headboard.

"Margaret Ann," she says. "We have to get things straight. We just can't go on this way with you treating Courtney so badly. Courtney doesn't want to be here any more than you want her here. And your aunt Mary Lee is worried too. We just have to get together and talk this thing over."

"Oh, Mama," I say. "There's something worse than that to talk over. Really."

I start to hand her the other letter, but then I remember what Johnny said. That I'm to tell her first. So I blurt it out.

"Mama, Johnny's gone to join the navy."

"What? What do you mean? That's not possible. Johnny went to town this morning with one of the Holland boys to get a part for the tractor."

"And he's not back yet, is he?"

"I expect he is. He said he was going to take dinner at the Holland's. And then go straight to the field with the tractor part."

"Which field was he going to?"

"I don't know. You got me so upset I don't remember where your Daddy said he was going this afternoon. But I'm sure Johnny is somewhere in the fields plowing."

"No, Mama, he's not. And it's my fault. Or partly my fault. Some of it is Courtney's fault because she told him so much about the war in England."

"Margaret Ann, I think you're trying to change the subject. But we have to do something about the way you treat

Courtney. I've told you this before and you just don't listen. You need to try putting yourself in her place."

"Putting myself in her place? Well, I don't think Courtney would like that. I think she likes her place very well. But, Mama, listen to me. I really do need to change the subject. Here, read this, Mama, if you don't believe me."

And then I do the other thing Johnny asked me not to do. I give her my letter to read.

All the time she's reading, her eyes get wider and wider. And I can hear her breath coming in these short little gasps. All she says is, "No. No. No."

I don't come downstairs until I hear Daddy driving down the lane on the tractor late that afternoon. But the minute I step into the kitchen, I can tell that Mama hasn't told a soul about Johnny. Because everything is quiet. Mama and Sallie are poking around the stove. Courtney is probably doing her homework in her own bedroom. I heard her come upstairs right after Mama left. And Grandma and Aunt Mary Lee are probably drinking tea in the parlor. Grandma has become a tea drinker these days. I think it actually keeps her awake at night. She isn't snoring as loud as she used to. Which makes me think she's lying there, staring up at the ceiling. She always sleeps on her back, so at least I never have to turn over and look her right in the face.

When Daddy walks in the kitchen door, I notice that

Mama keeps her head turned away from him. He's so tired he doesn't look up. But I feel like this has to be done right away, so I give Daddy the letter.

"What's this?" he asks.

"It's a letter from Johnny. I think you should read it."

"Yes. I was wondering what was keeping him so long in town."

"He's not in town," I say.

"Well, over at the Holland's, then."

"He's not there, either."

"What do you mean? Where is he?"

"He's wherever you go to join the navy."

"Margaret Ann, what are you talking about?"

Daddy is starting to say something else when Mama interrupts.

"I think it's true, John. Go ahead and read the letter. I just didn't have the heart to after Margaret Ann let me read hers."

"You got a letter too?" Daddy asks.

I nod.

Daddy pulls out a chair from the table and sits down. Mama and Sallie are both standing in front of the stove. They're hardly breathing. And all I can think is that it is all my fault. Johnny would be right here in the kitchen washing his hands at the sink if I hadn't carried on so over wanting a bedroom.

Daddy reads the letter, then looks up.

"Aye, Lord," he says.

Then Mama says the strangest thing. At first I can't believe my ears.

"If it were you in the same place, John, you would go. You know you would."

Daddy just stares at Mama for the longest time.

"What do you mean?" I ask. "Are you saying it's okay for Johnny to go in the navy and maybe have his ship get blown up?"

"Margaret Ann, what is the matter with you? How can you stand there and say such as that in front of your mother? She's trying to make the best of it. I'm trying too. And you're not helping the process one bit."

"I'm sorry. I'm sorry I said anything. I'm sorry I made Johnny join the navy in the first place. Because I did. The whole thing is my fault."

I don't wait to hear them say I'm right or wrong. I run upstairs, and all the way to Johnny's room, which is now my room. And I don't want it. I really don't want it.

In spite of all the sadness, I learn a lot in the first few days after Johnny joined the navy. I learn that just because Mama is quiet and calm, it doesn't mean she's not a strong person. Because after that first little while, after she sat on Johnny's bed saying, "No. No. No," you would think Johnny going was her idea. All she tells everybody who will listen is that she's proud of her son.

"This war was not our idea. That's true. But something has to be done. It will take good boys to go out there and fight this war. Just pray for him every night. That's all I ask."

Another thing I learn is that Grandma is as glad for me to move out of her bedroom as I am to go. That very first night, Grandma insists that I sleep in Johnny's bedroom.

"Here, let me carry your socks and underwear," she says, all the time eyeing the insides of the dresser drawer like she can already see her own bloomers and silk hose and her Sunday corset tucked up inside it.

But even Grandma gets quiet when she steps inside the door to Johnny's bedroom.

"Here," she says. "You take them. Put your things wherever you want to."

And out she goes.

It isn't so bad while I'm putting my things away in the dresser drawers and hanging my dresses in the closet. As long as the light is on, things are fine. But later, after I have gone to bed, I feel awful.

I try to remember that wonderful night right after Elizabeth went away to college. About how good her sheets felt with the initials E. E. M. rubbing against my chin. Now I'm sleeping on sheets Johnny slept on last night. Nobody had time to change them. It's enough that Mama moved all Johnny's things down into the big bottom drawer of the dresser. So I told Mama I don't mind. "Johnny's cleaner than I am," I said.

But when I lie down and pull the sheets up and the blanket up, I get a little smell that's just like him. Not a bad smell. Just what he smells like. A little bit of leftover shaving lotion. A little bit of soap odor. And a tiny little whiff that smells like his feet after he has been plowing all day.

Just at dark the March wind picked up and now it's roaring through the maple trees out front. I know I'm going to have a hard time getting to sleep. Because what I finally think about is this: We don't really know where Johnny is. Daddy says he thinks boys go to Richmond to volunteer for the navy, just like they do for the army. But after that, where? And what if he doesn't call us or write us to say? What if the navy doesn't allow him to say? Joyce says her cousin in the army has whole sentences cut out of his letters sometimes. Daddy says it's true. If a boy writes something home to his family that might be dangerous if the enemy found it out, well, then, somebody somewhere takes scissors and clips it out of the letter. Or inks it out.

I turn toward the door and listen. The wind is getting louder and louder. The windowpanes are rattling, and the wind is whistling like a live person. Grandma will have to snore mighty loud to be heard over all this. Anyway, I bet she's lying there on her bed wide-awake from all that tea. Maybe she's thinking about Johnny too. Maybe Mama's awake. And Daddy. Maybe the whole house is awake, just waiting to hear where in the world Johnny is.

The next morning Grandma doesn't come down for breakfast. She sends word by the twins that she isn't hungry. I'm not either. Every time I look at a biscuit, I think Johnny ought to be here to eat it. Even the oatmeal makes me think of him, and Johnny doesn't like oatmeal. Sitting across the table from Courtney doesn't help. I push the bowl away and start to get up.

"What's the matter with you, Margaret Ann?" Sallie asks.

"I'm not hungry."

"You better get used to eating without your brother, because this business is not going to be over anytime soon."

"What do you mean?"

"She means," Courtney says, "we're fighting two powers at the same time. That's hard. If it was easy, the war in Europe would have been over long ago."

"Exactly," says Sallie.

I feel like I am smothering. I have to get outside. So I pick up my books and my lunch, and I start for the front door.

"Wait for me," Courtney calls out.

I keep walking. I don't try to find Mama to tell her goodbye. I just walk.

Courtney catches up with me halfway down the lane. The school bus is nowhere in sight, so we stand there. I don't look in Courtney's direction, but I can hear her humming. When the bus finally gets there, Mr. Jones opens the door and smiles and claps his hands.

"There's Miss Courtney," he says. "Prettiest smile in Isle of Wight County. Am I right, boys?"

The whole busload starts yelling and whistling.

"Come on, Miss Courtney, take your seat."

So Courtney gets on first and goes to sit with Joyce Darden. That means I have to sit on the aisle instead of in the middle, like I usually do. And before I can say a word about Johnny and how horrible last night was, Courtney and Joyce are having a great discussion about a history test I didn't even know we were having today.

I try to ask about the test, but Courtney is going full tilt. She and Joyce don't even look in my direction. I still haven't said a word when the bus stops at the Holland farm and Bobby gets on. He slouches into the seat in front of us and grins.

"Morning," he says. "Y'all talking about our history test?"

"I'm not," I say quickly. "I didn't even know we had a test today."

"I guess you weren't listening, then," Courtney says. "Miss Boswell made it very clear. Didn't she, Joyce?"

"I thought so."

"Well, I didn't," I tell them.

"We'll be glad to help you, Margaret," Courtney says. "Here, let me ask you some questions."

"No, thank you. I'll take my chances on my own."

The three of them talk about the history questions all the way to town. I turn to face this girl named Frances Lowe, who sits across the aisle from us. She's in the eleventh grade, and everybody says she lets boys touch her breasts and maybe more than that. I heard Daddy tell Johnny one day that he better not hear of him taking Frances Lowe home from church or anywhere else. But she seems friendly enough to me. She's telling me about a movie magazine her sister buys every month, and how all the starlets' dresses are so short and slinky.

"I'm going to get me one like that," she says.

I keep nodding, trying to hear everything she has to say. But what I really want is not to hear Courtney and Joyce and Bobby Holland.

When we get to school, we have to wait in line to get off the bus. Like always. It goes row by row, with the right-hand side getting off first and then the left. That makes five people between me and Bobby Holland. But he waits for me and starts walking beside me toward the school.

"I'll be getting off at your place this afternoon, Margaret Ann," he says.

"Why is that?"

For a minute I can't remember what Johnny said in his letter.

"You know. Because I promised Johnny I would."

And then he just stands there, staring at me, waiting for me to say how glad I am. Probably he thinks I'm grateful to him. Just like maybe I'm grateful to Courtney for telling Johnny so much about the war in Europe. And most of all, grateful to myself for wanting his bedroom. I'm already mad at myself and Courtney, and now I add Bobby Holland to the list.

"If you hadn't promised him you'd work for him, he'd still be home in the field plowing."

I'm getting ready to say all the other stuff too. About how it's my fault and Courtney's fault, but he breaks in before I can say another word.

"So you think it's my fault," he says.

I nod my head, and he turns and walks away.

I follow and try to tell him that it isn't just his fault. That it's Courtney's, and most of all mine. But he won't listen to me. "I don't want to hear it," he says every time I open my mouth. I decide it isn't worth making a fool of myself over it.

That afternoon when the three of us get off the bus, Bobby is carrying Courtney's books along with his. Behind me I can hear two of the older boys whistling and yelling.

"Bobby, I see you got a new girlfriend."

I turn around and look up at the bus to see who's yelling. So I'm staring right in Tommy Pierce's face when he says it.

"Courtney took your boyfriend away from you, Margaret Ann."

"He's not my boyfriend," I yell back. "He never was."

I grab my books tight across my chest, and I start to run. When I pass Bobby and Courtney, I don't even look at them. I get to the house long before they do. I run up to Johnny's room. And I don't come downstairs until I see Daddy drive Bobby home.

That same night, right after supper, we get a call from Johnny. I'm walking through the hall, on my way upstairs to my bedroom, when the telephone rings. I grab the receiver before anyone else can get there. At first there's a lot of scratching, and then I can hear Johnny's voice. It sounds like he's on the other side of the world.

"Johnny, is this you?" I say. "This is Margaret Ann, and I have been so worried. If you haven't already joined the navy, then please don't. I can sleep with Grandma. Really I can."

"Margaret Ann, I don't have long to talk. Get Daddy."

"Okay, but first tell me if you're already in the navy."

"There's no time for all this, Margaret Ann. Just get Daddy."

"Not until you tell me if you're really in the navy, and where you are too."

"Okay, then. I'm in the navy, and I'm at a place called Bainbridge, Maryland. Now, get Daddy."

I put the telephone down and I get Daddy quick. But I stand close beside him with my head resting on his. Except for when he's pushing me away. Johnny says he rode to Smithfield with the Holland boys and took a bus to Richmond.

"The Navy took me," he says, "and I'm here at Bainbridge, Maryland, for six weeks."

Daddy pushes me away real hard about then, so all I can hear is Daddy saying, "Okay, son. Okay. Well, be sure to write as soon as you can. When we get your address, your mama will write. Okay. Good-bye."

"Aren't you even going to let Mama hear his voice?" I ask after the phone is already hung up.

"No, Margaret Ann. Your mama is strong, but not that strong," he says.

Daddy walks back down the hall to the kitchen. He looks so tired. If I'd been a boy, it might make things better. But I'm not and that's that. Grandma Motley says the women in her family don't work in the field. So there's nothing to do but go up to Johnny's room and study. Miss Boswell said I could take the history test over since I've never failed a test before.

. . .

I can't sleep that night either. I keep seeing Bobby Holland staring at me like he did this morning, and hearing myself tell him what I should have been saying to myself. Bobby has nothing to do with Johnny joining the navy. I'm the one who caused it. And Courtney. But mostly me.

I keep hearing what Tommy Pierce said too. "Courtney took your boyfriend away from you." And I have to admit that Courtney didn't do that either. Again, it's me. I served him up to her on a platter.

Getting Used to Johnny's Bedroom

I t's just like we thought it would be. Tommy Gray leaves
for boot camp on March 17. He is sent to Camp
Wheeler, Georgia, for his basic training. That lasts six
weeks. By the middle of May, Tommy finds Elizabeth a place
to stay and writes a letter telling her to come down as soon
as possible. She gets on a bus the very next day with one suitcase, a hatbox, and a paper bag filled with two sandwiches
and peppermints. Daddy wants to drive her down there, but
he can't because of gas rationing. It's just like sugar. You have
a book of coupons and you only get five gallons a week.
Grandma says he ought to take some of the extra allotment
he gets for the tractors and go. Daddy says that's dishonest.

"You take honesty too far, John Motley," she says.

It's amazing, but more and more, Daddy refuses to do
what Grandma says. Maybe it's the war. Or maybe it's having
Aunt Mary Lee around to take his side. Anyway Grandma

gets huffy and fusses for a day or two, and then she forgets it. Every time Grandma has one of those spells where she blinks her eyes and stares, she forgets everything. Mama says it's natural for old people to be forgetful, but I think this is more than that.

We're all happy when Elizabeth calls and says she arrived safely. And that the room Tommy found is with a widow woman who serves meals right there in the house.

"I don't have a thing to do," Elizabeth says. "Good thing I brought my knitting. All I do is take walks and hope Tommy gets an overnight pass."

Later on we discover that Tommy gets quite a few overnight passes. Because one day Elizabeth calls and her voice is trembling.

"Get Mama," she says.

It is surely a funny thing that my brother and sister never want to speak a word to me. It's always, "Get Mama," or "Get Daddy." This time I don't even try to listen in. It's the end of the school year and I'm studying my head off for exams, but Mama comes upstairs to tell me about it. I'm sitting on my bed reading my history book, and she sits down beside me like she always does.

"Margaret Ann," she says. "You're going to have to help me with this. I just don't know how to go about it."

"What do you mean, Mama?"

"Look, you'll be thirteen years old next month. Girls

thirteen used to be old enough to get married."

"What, Mama? You want me to get married?" I giggle.

"Of course not. I just want you to understand about Elizabeth . . . and be . . . more thoughtful of others."

"Okay, Mama. I'll try. But what do you mean? Is there something wrong with Elizabeth?"

"In a way."

"What? Is she sick? Is she hurt? Mama, you know I would do anything for Elizabeth."

"We all might have to. What she called to tell us is that Tommy is going to be sent off to some kind of a school to learn about land mines and ammunition. And then . . . he'll be shipped overseas. Right after."

"You mean where there's fighting?"

"Yes. At least that's what Elizabeth thinks. Nobody tells them anything for sure."

I think of those posters in the post office. A girl with her fingers at her lips, saying, "Sh-h-h." You're supposed to imagine that the enemy is listening.

"All she knows for sure is that he's going to be shipped overseas within the next couple of months."

"What's she going to do?"

"She's coming home. But not till after he leaves for that school."

"She can have this bedroom, Mama. I mean, if that's what you're asking me."

"No, Margaret Ann. It's not as simple as that. She still insists that she's going to stay at the Grays' like Tommy wants her to. But we've got to be there for her."

"Be there? You don't mean I have to live at the Grays', do you?"

"Of course not. But we'll all have a lot to do. Because Elizabeth thinks she's going to have a baby."

"A baby?"

All I can think of is baby Jesus in the manger with Elizabeth and Tommy looking down at it. But this will be a real baby. And Tommy won't be around to help watch over it until after the war.

"Well, Mama, I have to be honest with you," I say. "I've never cared much for babies. But if it's Elizabeth's, then . . . Good Lord . . . that means I'll be Aunt Margaret Ann."

"Indeed you will. And I'll be Grandma Motley."

"No, Mama. You'll never be Grandma Motley."

"It looks like I will."

"You sure don't look like a grandma, but you raised us, so I guess you can do anything. And I'll help," I say. "Whatever it takes, I'll do it."

"Thank you, Margaret Ann."

"So . . . what do you want me to do now?"

"I want you to be with me when I tell your grandma Motley."

"What do you mean?"

"I mean that Grandma is funny about babies. She loves them after they get here, but while you're expecting, she acts like it's some kind of a disgrace."

"You're kidding."

"No, I'm not. So we have to tell her right away, so she'll be over it by the time Elizabeth gets here. Elizabeth doesn't need anything more than the worry she already has."

So we get up that very minute and find Grandma sitting in the living room drinking tea with Aunt Mary Lee and Courtney.

"Who was that on the telephone, Emily Ruth?" she asks the minute she lays eyes on us.

"That was Elizabeth," I say before Mama can get her mouth open. "She's expecting a baby, and soon as Tommy goes to this school to learn about land mines, he's going overseas. So we have to help Elizabeth and not make her feel bad because she's expecting the baby."

"Margaret Ann," Mama says. "Not so fast."

"What?" says Grandma. "What foolishness is this child saying? Emily Ruth, I have been telling you this for a long time, and now you can see for yourself it's true. Something has got to be done about Margaret Ann. If you and John won't punish her, then I will. You just go to your room, young lady, and wait till I get up there. I will not have this kind of talk in my house."

• • •

I go to my room and I stay there. But it's Aunt Mary Lee who comes up and not Grandma.

"Margaret Ann," she says.

I'm sitting on the bed where she can't see me unless she comes all the way into the room.

"May I come in?"

"Yes, ma'am."

She sits down on the bed across from me and smiles.

"Your grandma was always mad at me when I was your age," she says. "I couldn't seem to keep my mouth shut. And she never understood that I was just like her. She can't keep her mouth shut either. And now she's getting really old . . . and the world is changing all around her . . . and she can't seem to keep up."

"But why does she think it's bad for Elizabeth and Tommy to have a baby?"

"She doesn't, really. But when she was young, you didn't talk about things like that. And you couldn't go out of the house from the time you started to show until the baby was actually born. That's the way she thinks it should be."

"Oh. You mean she doesn't think Elizabeth should be riding the bus."

"I guess that's part of it."

"Okay then, I understand about Grandma, but what about Mama? She asked me to tell her, you know."

"Margaret Ann, your mother is the kindest, gentlest person

I have ever known. But she has one fault: She can't stand up to your grandma. She has lived her whole married life here, doing what your grandma wanted her to do. Or what your daddy wanted her to do. But underneath all that, she's strong. You just wait and see. She'll surprise us all."

"So what am I supposed to do now?"

"Talk to your grandma for a start. Listen to her and then explain to her how you feel about things. She's a good person underneath all her sternness. And don't forget she's getting old. You know her problems as well as I do."

"You mean when she blinks her eyes and forgets everything?"

"Exactly. I have no idea what it means and she won't see a doctor. We'll just have to wait and see what happens."

We talk for a while and when Aunt Mary Lee gets up to leave, I really don't want her to go. It's like the day we decorated the Christmas tree together. I can feel us getting closer, and yet there's that one thing standing between us. Courtney. I don't see how we can ever work that out.

I try to talk to Grandma, but everything is so busy, and besides, Aunt Mary Lee is right. It does seem that Grandma has forgotten about it. The one time I really try to say the words, "I'm sorry," she looks at me like she has left the world for a while and doesn't see me, or hear me, or anything.

We get through exams at the end of school. Courtney

gets 100 on every one of hers. Of course, I get 97 on two of mine, and 98 on the others. But nobody ever talks about that. It's always those straight 100s that are such a marvel.

The last day of school we have a party and get to leave school early. Bobby Holland comes home with us as usual and has all afternoon to work with Daddy. From then on Daddy picks him up every morning, and they stay in the field till dark. He takes dinner with us every day at twelve o'clock. And Courtney sits beside him while we eat and takes up every second of his time.

My birthday is on June 14, but I don't expect any kind of party or presents, not with all the rationing, and getting ready for Elizabeth. Sallie will probably just bake a cake for dinner.

First thing that morning I'm down at the dog pen by the old barn. In the summer I usually feed the hounds every day. It isn't hard. You just have to bring the buckets of mush and table scraps and pour it in the trough. The only hard thing is keeping the large dogs from eating it all before the young ones get anything.

I'm just fixing to give a good pop to Zeke, one of the young males, when Bobby Holland walks up to the fence and calls me. I haven't said three words to him since we got out of school, and there he is staring at me like I might vanish into thin air.

"Margaret Ann, I need to talk to you."

"In a minute."

I try to sound like I don't have time or don't want to. I don't look at him, but I can feel his eyes staring right at me. When I can't find anything else to do, I set the bucket down and look back at him. He smiles, but it's not his usual. It's more like it's being forced out through a meat grinder.

"I'm listening," I say.

"Well . . . first of all, happy birthday."

"Very kind of you to remember. Thank you."

"You're welcome. But I have to tell you something else. And I'm really sorry about it."

I turn my head and look back at the dogs pushing and growling at the trough.

"Margaret Ann, look at me. I'm having a hard time here."

"Well, I'm sorry, but I've been having a hard time for quite a while."

"You never act like it."

"How would you know? You don't even bother to ask whether I'm okay or not."

"That's not true, and you know it."

"Okay. Okay. That's enough about that. Say what you want to say. I'm looking at you."

"I ought to just walk away and not tell you one word about it. If I didn't care so much about you, I guess I would."

I don't know what to say to that. I reach down and pick

up the empty bucket without ever taking my eyes off his face. After that I don't move a muscle. I'm like a statue.

"Okay, then . . . this is what happened. Soon as I got here this morning I was looking for you because I brought you one of Princess's puppies for your birthday."

"Oh, Bobby, did you? Male or female? Is it black like Princess? Where is it?"

"I'm trying to tell you."

"Well, go on."

"As I said, I was looking for you. And instead of you, I found Courtney . . . and she said something like, "'Oh, what a pretty puppy . . . Is it for me?'"

"Well? I hope you told her it wasn't."

"Margaret Ann, it wasn't that easy. Your grandma came out on the steps and then she called your Aunt Mary Lee. And both of them were thanking me for being so nice to Courtney. I didn't have the chance to say anything."

"Well, I have never."

"Look, Margaret Ann, I'll ask my daddy if I can have another one. It might not be as pretty as this one, but I think they're all pretty."

"You think they're all pretty, huh?"

"Yeah, I do."

"And don't you care what I think?"

I turn my head because I suspect there's a tear or two getting ready to run out of both my eyes.

"Margaret Ann, I'm sorry."

I shake my head and feel one of the tears loosen and start to roll. And there is nothing under heaven that will make me look at Bobby Holland with a tear galloping down my cheek.

"I've told you I'm sorry and that's all I can say. If I can't make you understand, I'm finished. I know I've said that a hundred times, but I mean it. Ever since I can remember, you've acted like you can rule the world."

"Me?" I holler. "Me rule the world?"

But I can't turn to look at him, so off he walks and that's the end of that.

I don't go back to the house until I'm sure everybody except maybe Sallie has left the kitchen. Just the second I step through the screen door onto the porch, she hears me.

"Come here, sugar," she says. "I know all about it."

"About what?"

"Come here. Come here. You know well as I do."

I take a few steps, then Sallie does, and soon she's hugging me and patting me.

"I know that dog was for you. I'm sure your mama and daddy know too. Who wouldn't know it? Your thirteenth birthday. And Bobby Holland always been sweet on you."

"Well, I'm not sweet on Bobby Holland. Courtney's welcome to him. But I do want my dog."

"Give it time, Margaret Ann. Courtney's not a dog kind

of person. Besides which, soon as this war is over, she'll go home and leave it. Mary Lee knows that. She'll handle it."

"But I want it now."

"There's an old saying, Margaret Ann. Your mama would say it wasn't polite, but in my life it's been true more than once."

"What is it?"

"You're old enough for your wants not to hurt you."

"Sallie . . . that's terrible. Don't you love me anymore?"

"You know better than that. I love everyone in this family. But right now, your aunt Mary Lee don't need another worry."

"But—"

"And your sister Elizabeth don't need another worry, and your mama don't need another worry. How about it? You think you can keep quiet about this puppy dog?"

I shake my head no, that I can't, but somehow my eyes close for a second while I'm doing it, and I get a picture of Elizabeth, right behind my eyelids. And then Mama saying, "For me," like she does. And then Aunt Mary Lee. All three of them flash by like one of these searchlights for spotting airplanes. I look back at Sallie. Her head is kind of nodding, like she used to do when Paige and Polly were first learning to talk.

"I'll try."

"I'll make you a birthday cake if you do."

"You'd make me one anyway. Even if I screamed and cried,

you'd get out the batter bowl and mix a cake and cook it."

"I guess I would. But please think of your aunt Mary Lee. I been watching you. You like her, don't you?"

I nod and reach over to the stove behind Sallie and pick up a leftover biscuit.

"Okay. I won't say anything about the dog. But I'm not going to feed it. If Courtney is going to get my dog, she's got to feed it and do everything. That's as far as I can go."

"That's as far as you need to go. Now, hand me that biscuit so I can put butter and strawberry preserves on it, just the way you like it."

Elizabeth comes home a week after my birthday, and by that time I'm able to look at the puppy without feeling like I want to scream. She remembers to bring me a present too. It's wrapped in white tissue paper with a pink bow tied at the top.

"Gosh, Elizabeth, what is it?" I ask her.

Then I really look at her, and boy does she look skinny. Those beautiful bones in her face that are so like Mama's are almost sticking through her skin.

"Haven't you been eating?" I ask her. "I thought you said that widow woman was a good cook."

"Open your present, Margaret Ann. I'm perfectly all right."

So I open my present, but all the time I'm untying the bow I'm sneaking little glimpses of Elizabeth's stomach. It's flat as a pancake. Maybe there's no baby after all and I'm not going to be Aunt Margaret Ann.

"I have never seen it take anybody so long to open a package. Just tear the paper."

"What are you saying, Emily Elizabeth Mot—um—Gray? Grandma would have my head if I tore it. She'll ask Sallie to iron it this very afternoon, and then she'll put it away for Christmas. You know that."

"Well, hurry, then. We'll be here all day."

"I'd like that, Elizabeth. It's been so long since we've had time to talk."

"I know. But we'll have lots of time now. Too much time."

I know what she means, but still it doesn't sound right. It sounds like she doesn't want time to talk to any of us. It sounds like the only thing she wants is to be with Tommy Gray. I fumble at the ribbon until finally the knot comes undone, and then the paper falls away all by itself.

"Oh, Elizabeth, I love it."

It's a little china figure of a dog. It looks near as anything like one of Daddy's fox hounds.

"I'll put it in my bedroom if that's okay with you."

"Of course. It's yours. You can do anything you like with it."

"Thank you, Elizabeth. And thank Tommy, too, when you write him."

Elizabeth looks sad just hearing Tommy's name. I'll have to remember that.

"Hey," I say. "Want to go upstairs and see my bedroom? I'm in Johnny's room now, you know."

"Poor Johnny," Elizabeth says. "So far from home. A year ago I never would have thought all this could be happening."

"I know. But I don't think Johnny or Tommy would want us to be sad all the time."

"If you can help yourself," Elizabeth says. "But I know what you mean. Look at Aunt Mary Lee. She has more than I do to be sad about. Uncle Walter is already in the fighting."

"That's true. And maybe the war will be over before Johnny finishes his training and gets sent off on a ship. And before Tommy gets finished too. It can't last long."

"I wish I could believe that. But I know you're right. For the sake of the baby I should try to be calm and happy. People say that influences the baby, you know."

"Ah," I say.

What I know about babies can fit in a thimble, but I don't let on. I'm so glad to be talking to my big sister.

"Come on, then," I say. "We need to make that baby happy. Let's go see my new bedroom."

Elizabeth stays with us all afternoon. We eat the last slivers of my birthday cake at about four o'clock. It's a tea party, Aunt Mary Lee says.

"Come on, Margaret Ann, try a cup of tea," she says. "You'll love it."

I drink it. Swallow by swallow with tiny bites of cake.

"Isn't it lovely?" Courtney asks. "I knew you would love tea if you tried it."

If I answer her, I'll hurt Aunt Mary Lee's feelings, so she has me. I'm a hostage. But one of these days, I'll find a way to let Miss Courtney Liveley know just how I feel about tea, and Bobby Holland, and everything else. Meanwhile I sit in my chair and rock. And smile. Like I could bite ten-penny nails in two.

Mama takes the plates and cups and saucers to the kitchen. She insists the rest of us sit right there on the front porch, rocking or swinging and talking.

"I need something to do," Elizabeth says. "If Mama can find some old cloth somewhere in one of the trunks, I would be glad to make some pillows for your bed, Margaret Ann. I could make new curtains, too, if there's enough left over."

"I would love it," I say. "What about yellow flowers? Would that be good?"

"Back home I had yellow flowered curtains, didn't I, Mother?" Courtney asks.

"You did," Aunt Mary Lee says. And then she gets a sad look in her eyes too. Just like Elizabeth. And like me whenever I think about Bobby Holland and the dog that's supposed to be mine.

When Daddy takes Bobby Holland home, he takes Elizabeth to the Grays'. I really don't think she wants to go. But Mama manages to make her smile. Mama can always make Elizabeth smile.

"I tell you what," Mama says. "Maybe you can spend the weekend with us. Margaret Ann would be glad to have a roommate. At least temporarily."

"I would. I would. Say you'll come."

"I would love to."

Elizabeth is still smiling as Daddy drives out of the yard. Of course, I only look at her. I don't even glance in the direction of Bobby Holland in the back seat.

On Saturday morning Mama, Aunt Mary Lee, and I drive to town to buy a few groceries and to pick up Courtney, who spent the night with Joanne Cox. Again. We stop to see if Elizabeth wants to ride with us or if she wants us to pick her up on the way back.

"You run up and see if she wants to go," Mama tells me.

Mama is talking over some things with Mrs. Gray. All about rationing books and how in the world the town people can keep from starving. On the farm we have lots to eat because we grow it. But town people have next to nothing of butter and meat and stuff like that. So I go upstairs, walking kind of slow because I have never been upstairs at the Gray house before.

"Elizabeth," I whisper.

When she doesn't answer, I say it louder. And still louder until I hear a pitiful-sounding voice from down the hallway. I open the door just a crack and peep in. There is Elizabeth lying in bed with the sheet pulled up to her chin. There's a big china bowl beside her.

"What's the matter?" I ask her. "People don't have the flu in June."

"It's not the flu."

Elizabeth sounds angry. Or something.

"Is Mama here?"

"Of course she's here. You don't think I walked all the way to the Grays', do you? She's downstairs talking to Mrs. Gray about rationing books."

"Tell her to come here. I need her."

"Your room's pretty," I say. "I see you've made pillows and curtains already."

"Go," she says.

I'm hardly out the door before I hear her gagging and coughing. Like she's being sick.

"Elizabeth?"

"Go," she says.

. . .

We're late getting to town. And all the way there, Mama and Aunt Mary Lee discuss Elizabeth and the baby. I learn more on that one ride to town than I have ever wanted to know before about having a family. They say some people throw up for three months. Good Lord, how can you stand it?

"I don't think it's worth it," I say.

"Of course it is, Margaret Ann," Mama says.

"Maybe," says Aunt Mary Lee.

We laugh for a couple of miles. No doubt about it, Aunt Mary Lee is a great human being. The question is, how can she have a daughter who is so stuck-up?

Daddy always says it's a good growing year if we have toma-toes in the garden by the fourth of July. And there they are, growing bigger and bigger, sure to be red and luscious by the big day. The fields on each side of the house are planted in corn. It's growing so tall it makes me feel like I'm suffocating. I like the years Daddy plants peanuts in the home fields. Then you can look out and see all the way down to the crossroads.

Courtney spends most of every morning lolling around on the front porch, playing with her dog. Every time I walk around the house and see them, or hear her talking baby talk to it, I think I'm going to scream. I know she's watching for Bobby Holland. She doesn't seem to understand that dogs and people both have jobs to do. They don't just spend mornings lolling around. But Mama says Courtney doesn't have to help pick peas and beans and tomatoes out of the garden. I guess everybody thinks she'll hurt herself, like she did when she was cutting celery for the wedding. Besides which, she always picks the flat pods with no beans in them. And she doesn't seem to understand that a tomato needs to be red. And that squash and cucumbers need to measure longer than three inches.

In the afternoon all of us sit on the front porch. It's cooler there than anywhere else on the farm. Grandma likes the glider. And she likes to have the twins sitting beside her to keep it moving. Then she stretches her feet out straight in front of her and gets a little smile on her face. And she hums all these old songs like "Camptown Races," and "Polly Wolly Doodle," and "Sweet and Low."

Aunt Mary Lee likes the swing at the other end of the porch. She and Courtney sit there. I sit in one rocking chair and Mama sits in another. Sometimes we have pans of peas to shell. Or butter beans. Even Paige and Polly can shell. Each of them has a little pan, and every half hour or so they dump the shelled peas in Mama's pan and grab out some in the hulls. But not Courtney. She shells one pea, then stops to look for her puppy, only she's really looking for Bobby Holland. Sometimes Daddy sends him to the house to get oil for the tractor or water for the men to drink. It's something to see Courtney's face whenever he comes walking through the yard.

But some afternoons we don't have anything to do, and so we fan and talk and drink ice water. It's a hot summer, one of the worst I can ever remember.

"I'm hot," I mumble.

"We're all hot, Margaret Ann," Grandma says. "But I've seen heat waves to beat this one. Mary Lee, do you remember the year you were twelve years old? Not a drop of rain during the whole month of July. Peanuts drying up in the fields. Corn stalks with not a sign of an ear of corn. You children have no idea of what I have seen on this place."

When Grandma gets like this, my mind starts to wander. And no matter where it starts it always ends up seeing Courtney smiling up at Bobby Holland like he's a movie star. He's handsome as one. Particularly when he smiles. Which I haven't seen much of these last few days. He never says a word at the dinner table. He looks down at his plate. Even if Daddy is talking directly to him, he doesn't look up. Maybe he doesn't want to see Courtney. Or maybe he doesn't want to see me.

Courtney talks to Joanne Cox on the telephone every day. She always knows what's going on in town. So when Grandma stops talking and drops off to sleep, Courtney gives her report, word for word, every item Joanne has told her.

"Joanne says that since her father is the president of the bank and can take off whatever hours he likes from his job, well, he was the first person in town to sign up to be a plane spotter."

"Daddy signed up too," I say. "And furthermore I intend to be a plane spotter myself. After all, I can see just as well as anybody. And I know how to use a telephone. So all I have to do is memorize all the sheets of paper with the different airplanes and which are ours and which are the Germans'."

"You're not old enough," Courtney says.

"How do you know?"

"Because Joanne says so."

"And what does she know?"

"Please," Aunt Mary Lee says.

I turn my head quickly and look at Aunt Mary Lee. She looks absolutely miserable. I don't want to do this to her. So I stand up quickly and start for the steps.

"I just remembered something I have to do," I say over my shoulder. And I keep walking. I walk past the cedars, wondering what's going on back on the porch. Wondering how I get myself into things like this. Should I just close my lips and never speak again in my own house? I just can't stand it.

When I get to the road, I turn right and start toward town. Hey, maybe I'll walk as far as the Grays'. Or I might stop off to visit Bobby Holland's mother.

I haven't walked half a mile when I look up and see

Bobby Holland driving Daddy's truck. Right down the main road. He brakes and stops when he gets even with me.

"What's the matter?" he asks.

"Nothing. What's the matter with you?"

"Nothing."

"Then why are you driving the truck right down the main road? You don't have a driver's license."

"I can drive, though. Good as anybody."

"Who says?"

"Your daddy, that's who. He sent me home for some water for the hands. You want a ride somewhere?"

"I guess so. I guess I might as well go home."

"Get in, then."

As soon as I slide into the seat, I can feel Bobby Holland's eyes right on my face. I turn my head just a little bit and I look at him too. He's smiling at me.

"Margaret Ann," he says, "I can't stay mad at you. I mean, look, I was wrong about that puppy, and I'm sorry. I'm sorry about everything. But if you could just smile at me once in a while . . . I mean. . . ."

Bobby Holland's face is so reddish tan from the sun every day in the fields, I wouldn't have thought anything could make it go redder. But it does. Bobby Holland is blushing.

"Margaret Ann, I'm really sorry. What I want is for things to be like they used to be."

"And how was that?" I ask.

"I think you know. Don't you?"

I look straight ahead at the road. Because I'm pretty sure I know what he means, but I don't want to read more into it than he means to be saying.

"Don't you?"

"I think so."

Bobby reaches over and takes my hand. He squeezes it and then I squeeze his back. We ride all the way home like that. And every time I turn my head and look at him, he's already looking at me. It sure is a good thing we don't meet any cars on the way home.

All the rest of that day, I catch myself smiling. And I remember the feel of Bobby Holland's fingers. They're so strong. And rough against my skin. I have the feeling that I will never let anything come between us again. He says he wants things to be like they used to be. But I'm thinking they're going to be better than ever.

Sharing with Paige and Polly

In the middle of July, my brother and Tommy Gray are both home on leave at the same time, which is kind of a strange thing. Johnny comes home first. He calls from Bainbridge, Maryland, to say he'll be on the three o'clock bus in Smithfield the very next day. Daddy is too busy in the field to go, so Mama drives to town that Thursday afternoon to get him. I'm afraid she'll want Johnny all to herself, but she invites me to go without my having to ask.

We get there early and the bus is late, so we're hot enough to fry by the time Johnny steps down those two steps onto the sidewalk. It's funny to see my own brother looking like a recruitment poster. His legs are already long, but in those white bell-bottom trousers, it looks like they stretch up forever. And he's wearing the navy flat hat, which isn't exactly flattering. But when it falls off while he's hugging Mama, I can't believe it.

"Gosh, Johnny, what did they do to you?" I ask him. His hair is cut off almost to the scalp.

"Well, Margaret Ann, I have missed you. Nobody can keep me in my place like you do."

"Yeah," I say. "That's just what you need. Somebody to keep you in your place."

I wonder what Charlotte Holland and the other girls will think of his haircut.

I don't know who goes to get Tommy Gray, but the next Saturday morning he and Elizabeth come riding up in Mr. Gray's car. They stay for dinner and Johnny and Tommy talk a lot about boot camp.

"The food's terrible," Johnny says about navy food.

"Not as bad as the army, though. I tell you, army food is so bad I bet you Grandma Motley could do better."

Grandma frowns for a few minutes, but then she smiles and nods and reminds Tommy how she won a prize at the county fair one year for her peach cobbler.

Tommy and Elizabeth don't stay any nights with us, but they go to church with us and spend a whole Sunday afternoon. And they eat supper with us several times. Actually it's good they don't spend the night, because our house is pretty crowded. When I start to move my things back to Grandma's room, she stops me.

"Leave everything right where it is. Johnny won't mind. And you can sleep in the room with Paige and Polly."

"You don't want me to sleep with you?" I ask.

"Well, since you put such a fine point on the matter, I don't. You used to keep me awake of a night."

"Me? Keep you awake?"

"Yes, you did. I never saw a child so fidgety in my life. Never slept a wink in all the years I had to keep you with me."

"Grandma, that's not fair. The reason I was fidgety was because you snored so loud."

"Me? Snore? I never heard of such a thing."

So I don't move my things out of Johnny's bedroom. He says I can come in any time he's not in there dressing. When it's bedtime I try to sleep with Paige and Polly. Which is just as bad as sleeping with Grandma. It feels like I have about six inches of space. Five times during the night I get up, walk around the bed and get in on the other side. I wake up as sleepy as the farmers who man the plane spotters' posts at night and then work all day in the fields. I might not have made it through the two weeks Johnny was home except that I start sleeping on the floor. Grandma says it's lowlife, or lowbrow, or something like that for people to sleep on the floor, but I don't care. I need the rest.

Everybody is working hard during this time. Johnny is helping Daddy plow peanuts, and Tommy is working most days over at the Gray farm. And since none of the farmers have enough help, nobody is quite sure how they'll get the crops harvested. Daddy says he's really lucky to have Bobby Holland to help him. And every time he says it, I can feel my cheeks getting pink.

Not that anybody thinks anything different about us. In fact, Grandma still thinks he's Courtney's boyfriend. But I know better. At dinner each day, I don't mind that I sit across the table from him instead of beside him. He's still quiet and Courtney still tries to get most of his time, but every once in a while he catches my eye, and I know what he's saying even though he doesn't use words.

There's also plenty of canning to take care of and when all our canning jars get filled, Mama buys more. She wants to give some to Aunt Janice. Aunt Janice is like Uncle Waverly. She doesn't do any work either. Mama thinks they might starve due to the rationing, so she works longer hours to make sure there's enough food. Aunt Mary Lee helps too, but there's no hope for Courtney. It's clear to me that she will never be a farmer's wife.

When it's time for Johnny to leave, it's worse than the first time. Because the first time we didn't know it was coming. But now we count off the days and say, "In three more days Johnny won't be here." When we eat breakfast four days from now, Sallie won't need to cook those six extra slices of bacon and fry those extra three eggs. Of course, none of us say it out loud. But I'm sure we're all thinking it.

Johnny has to leave on a Tuesday and Tommy leaves on Thursday. So on Monday we have a big going-away dinner. We invite Charlotte Holland and all the Grays, including Elizabeth and Tommy. Mama and Sallie fry six chickens and boil butter beans, and cook peas with little dumplings, and mash potatoes.

"This house is too hot to draw a good breath in," Grandma says. "I say this calls for a picnic."

So she sends Courtney and me to the washhouse to get this old table that has been used for everything imaginable. As you might guess, Courtney gets a splinter in her finger before we even get it through the doorway.

"I'm so sorry, Margaret, but I have to find Mother so she can get the splinter out."

"Good gosh, Courtney, let me see. I can pull a splinter out. I take care of the twins all the time when they get splinters."

"Thank you, but no. I wouldn't want to get an infection."

I drag the table all the way around the house all by myself and situate it under the maple closest to the side yard before Courtney gets back.

"I guess I shouldn't help you wash the table," Courtney

says. "It could have all kinds of germs left over from the hog killing last January."

So I wash the table, and then Aunt Mary Lee and I together cover it with a couple of white tablecloths. It looks good.

Then everybody helps take the food outside. There's everything Johnny likes best. Even a big chocolate cake and a freezer of vanilla ice cream. The rest of us won't have so much as a spoon of sugar for the next three months. Because we use all our ration coupons.

Johnny and Tommy are the guests of honor. All of us look at them and see to their needs in a way we never did before. I get the feeling there's something new between them too. When they look at each other, it's like they know something the rest of us don't. I guess it's all about killing. They both have been to schools to learn how to kill and how to keep from being killed. Of course, Daddy knows. Maybe he knows more than they do, because he's been in battles where people are alive one minute and dead the next. Maybe he actually killed a man. He would never tell.

Wouldn't it be sad if Tommy and Johnny had to kill somebody? But wouldn't it be a whole lot worse if somebody killed them? I guess that's why we're all looking at them so intently. We're studying their faces so we can remember them if we never see them again. I get so choked up I can't eat a bite.

"What's the matter with you, Margaret Ann?" Grandma says. "I've never seen you when you weren't hungry."

I shake my head and try to smile, but I can't say a word. Then the funniest thing happens. Courtney speaks right up.

"I think Margaret feels exactly as I do. We're both thinking of all the people in the world who don't have food like this."

"No, I'm not," I manage to croak out.

"Well, perhaps not," Courtney says.

She looks down at her plate and it seems almost like she's going to cry too. I'm sorry I disagreed with her like that. For once Courtney is trying to take my side. And I won't let her. So what does that make me?

Later on, just before dark, when the lightning bugs are starting to glitter across the yard from us, Courtney's dog comes running up and starts jumping on everybody and barking and generally making a nuisance of himself.

"Margaret Ann," Tommy calls out to me, "can't you do something with your dog?"

"It's not my dog," I say.

"Looks like it ought to be. Ain't this one of Princess's puppies? I thought Bobby Holland must have given it to you."

"No. He didn't. He gave it to Courtney. You can blame her for the way it's acting."

"Blame me," Aunt Mary Lee says. "I know how to train a dog. And I just haven't done it. So don't blame Courtney."

"Of course you shouldn't blame Courtney," Grandma says.

"I don't see there's blame for anyone," Mama says. "Here, won't anyone have more iced tea?"

As soon as no one is looking at me, I get up and walk down to the barn. I am so miserable. I know I'm the worst person who ever lived on earth. I don't deserve to have Bobby Holland love me, although I know for sure he does. Mainly, I'm sorry I upset Aunt Mary Lee like that. I really love her. I love being with her. We had so much fun fixing the tables.

I spoiled Johnny's last night at home too. I don't deserve to have a good brother like Johnny. But please, God, don't take him away from me. From us. Please let him come home again from being in the navy.

The next morning at breakfast everybody is so busy they seem to have forgotten all about how I acted at the picnic. I guess they're used to my being that way. Anyway, I'm helping Sallie butter the biscuits she takes out of the oven. Mama is packing Johnny a lunch. Aunt Mary Lee is getting out clean napkins and folding them. And, of all things, Courtney is setting the table in the dining room.

Just as Sallie is taking the last pan of biscuits out of the oven, Courtney walks through the kitchen door, shaking her head.

"Mother," she says. "Look what I've done."

She's holding a broken cup. And it's a piece of Grandma Motley's good china.

"Oh, no, Courtney," Aunt Mary Lee says. "However did you do such a thing?"

"I was reaching for the extra coffee cups, and my hand hit against one of Grandma's best china ones. I tried to catch it, but that seemed to make it fall faster. Oh, Grandma, I am so sorry."

I watch Grandma's face. Her eyes kind of blink a couple of times, and her lips tighten. I know exactly what she's going to say, because I remember what she said to me the day I was five years old and it happened to me. Boy, am I shocked. Because she smiles.

"Don't let that worry you, child. I have learned in this world and you should learn it too. People are more important than things."

"Well," I say. "I wish you had learned it a few years back."

The minute I say it I'm sorry. Grandma looks at me like she has no idea what I'm talking about. I'm sure she doesn't. But Aunt Mary Lee understands exactly what I mean.

Nobody eats much except Johnny. He's grinning and actually seems excited. He's going across the country to meet a ship. That's all we know. But we all think Johnny will be seeing active duty in the Pacific fairly soon. Daddy is staring down at his plate of eggs. Grandma is holding tight to her coffee cup. Mama is the only one besides Johnny who is laughing.

"Don't you bring home some girl from out there in California, now," Daddy says finally. "Charlotte Holland suits us just fine."

"But does she suit me?" Johnny asks.

This time we all laugh. After that it's like it's our duty to laugh, to fill every minute. Silence is the enemy. Silence causes us to lose control. "Go to pieces" is how Grandma says it.

I feel like I want to grab hold of time and not let it go by. But it does. And then Daddy and Johnny are getting in the car to go to town and catch the bus. I don't even ask if I can go with them. It's bad enough to hug Johnny in our front yard knowing I might not see him again. Riding back home in the car with Daddy is not something I can do. But Aunt Mary Lee speaks up.

"John, would you like some company? I could ride along with you."

"Thank you, Mary Lee. I'd like that."

We stand under the maple trees and wave as long as we can see the car. And then everybody starts mumbling about someplace we have to go or something we have to do. And

Courtney has to pick this time to ask me to help her start training her dog.

"He is getting too large to be as rough as he is."

"Not now" is all I can say.

Courtney shakes her head and walks away. I know I should say something more, maybe even apologize, but I can't. I head for Johnny's bedroom. Mama says I have to change the sheets and get the room cleaned so I can move back in. Just as I round the corner of the house, I look back at her. She's standing there, staring at the dog, still shaking her head.

Two days later we have to tell Tommy Gray good-bye. We know he'll be going overseas immediately. Of course, we don't know the exact day and hour. "Loose lips sink ships." That's the slogan. So there's a lot that families don't know. But Elizabeth knows it's her last chance to see him for a long, long time.

On Wednesday night the Grays have all of us over to their house for a big meal. Only thing is, they eat inside the house, the grown-ups in the dining room and the children in the kitchen. Courtney and I aren't exactly children, but we're given the job of looking after the others while the grown-ups are enjoying themselves. There's still a fire in the wood stove and it's so hot we have perspiration running down out of our hair and big wet spots right in the middle of our backs.

Mama says to pay particular attention to Paige and Polly and be sure they mind their manners. But there are so many little Gray children that I can't always tell who's misbehaving. The noise is getting really bad and some of the little boys are having a fight over the last chicken leg.

"Children," Courtney says softly.

There's no way she's going to be heard over all the noise. I can hardly hear her myself and I'm sitting next to her.

"Children, listen now. How many of you would like to hear a story?"

Paige and Polly say yes immediately. And then all the little Gray girls say yes. And so she starts. By the time she says ten words, the boys stop fighting and are listening too.

It's a story about a lady who is queen for a week. Her name is Lady Jane Gray, and of course that interests the little Gray children.

"A lady with a name just like ours was the queen of England," one of the boys says.

All through the rest of the meal, Courtney tells the story. You can hear a pin drop. After dessert, when the children go out to play, I ask her more about it.

"You're very good at making up stories," I say. "Where did you get the idea of a lady with the same name as the children?"

"I didn't make it up," she says. "It's straight from English history. There really was a Lady Jane Grey who really was queen for a week. We learn about it in school the way you learn about Jamestown and Williamsburg."

"You did a good job of calming them down," I say. "Some of the little Gray boys are pretty rough."

"I wish I could do the same with Gladwin."

"Who's Gladwin?"

"Gladwin is the dog Bobby Holland gave me."

"I didn't even know you named him. Anyway, if you get tired of having a dog, you can give him to me. Bobby Holland didn't intend to give the dog to you, you know. He brought him to me as a birthday present, but everybody misunderstood."

Courtney's reaction was instant. She gasped.

"Margaret Motley. How can you say such a thing? You're jealous, that's all. You've been jealous of me every second since I've been here. So it isn't just because Bobby likes me better than he likes you. You never did like me. You wish I were somewhere, anywhere but here. And I wish so too. I just have better manners than you do, or I would have told you this long ago."

"Well," I say. "I'm glad you got around to telling me. Because every word you say is true . . . except one. Bobby Holland does not like you better than he likes me. Just ask him. See what he says."

"Very well, then, I will. Tomorrow I'll ask him. And I'll be sure to do it where you can hear him too. Then you'll find out."

. . .

I am so nervous that night I can hardly sleep. It isn't that I
don't believe Bobby likes me best. I'm sure he does. But he
has never actually said the word "love." Nothing like that.

The next morning, very early, I hear a knock on my bedroom door. I sit up and listen. The roosters are still crowing.
What on earth is happening? The knock sounds louder.

"Who is it?"

"Courtney."

"At this hour of the morning? You're up?"

"Of course. You better hurry, Margaret. We'll miss Bobby
if you don't."

"Oh my gosh."

It's my last thought before I finally get to sleep. But this
is too early in the morning to remember it. I start grabbing
bobby pins out of my hair as fast as I can.

"We might have to wait till twelve o'clock. I don't even
have my hair combed."

Courtney opens the door and walks in.

"But I do," she says. "And I have on my good white blouse
too. What are you going to wear?"

"I have no idea. But, look, Courtney, I've been thinking,
and I don't want to do this."

"Why, Margaret? Is it because you know what I say is true?"

"No, that's not why I don't want to do it. I'm still half-asleep
for one thing. And I'm not dressed and my hair looks horrible."

"Is that so unusual?"

When she says that, I kind of lose my mind, I guess. I jump up, put on my dirty dress from the day before and brush through my hair a total of five times. Then I'm at the door staring bullets at my cousin Courtney.

"Okay," I say. "Let's find Bobby Holland."

"Are you sure you want to wear that dress?" Courtney asks. "And maybe you should comb your hair."

"It's okay," I say. "Let's go."

We go down the back stairs together. Neither of us will let the other get ahead. In the kitchen Sallie is frying ham slices.

"What is this?" she says. "You two girls up at five o'clock?"

"We have something important to do," I say.

"Well, it must be important for Courtney to be up."

We go out the door, across the porch and down to the barn. Bobby Holland is standing by the dog pen. He's watching Daddy work on the tractor motor. We can't hear what they're saying.

"Do you plan to ask him in front of Daddy?" I say.

"Of course not. I've got it all planned. I'll ask Bobby if he can help us with something."

"What, for instance?"

"I won't need to say exactly what. Bobby will be quite happy to help me with anything. I am very sure of that."

"Well, I'm not so sure. Daddy is paying him good money,

and I don't think he'll do anything unless Daddy tells him to."

"Well, then. There's no problem."

Daddy looks up from the tractor motor.

"What are you two doing up so early?" he asks.

But then he goes right back to his work. I don't think he expects an answer.

"Uncle John," Courtney says sweetly. Sickeningly might be a better way to put it.

"Yes, Courtney?"

"Could we borrow Bobby just for a moment? Margaret and I can't lift this . . . basket, and we need his help."

"Sure. He can't do anything until I get this tractor fixed."

Bobby looks puzzled, but he follows us over to the washhouse without a word.

"Come inside," Courtney says.

I go in first and then Courtney and then Bobby. He's looking around for the basket, I guess.

"Where is it?" he asks.

"Nowhere," Courtney tells him. "We just said that to get you over here."

Bobby looks at me, still puzzled. And then he looks again and starts laughing.

"What have you done to your hair, Margaret Ann? It looks like ghosts and goblins got loose in your room last night."

"It does look strange," Courtney says.

She steps closer to Bobby and touches him on the shoulder. He steps away from her.

"What is this?" he asks.

I refuse to answer. Let Courtney take care of it.

"Margaret and I have a difference of opinion on something. And you're the only one who can decide which of us is right."

"Look, I don't want to get between two cousins. I mean, you two will have to work this out. I got to go see what Mr. Motley's doing."

"Not till you tell us one thing."

"Look, I'm being paid. I don't want Mr. Motley to think I don't give him a day's work."

"Okay. Okay," Courtney says. "Just tell us which one of us you love best."

Bobby puts his hands over his face.

"Good Lord," he says. "Margaret Ann, how could you do this?"

"I didn't do it. It was Courtney's idea. She woke me up at five o'clock in the morning to get things settled. So, let's settle it. Tell her which one of us you care about."

"Oh, God."

He takes his hands down and looks at me.

"Margaret Ann, you tell her. You know."

"I surely think I do. But maybe she knows something I don't know."

"No, Margaret Ann. No. You tell her. You know how I feel."

Daddy sticks his head in the door.

"You girls through with Bobby?"

"I think so," I say, smiling across at Courtney.

"Okay. I got this tractor ready to roll. We need to be in the field."

Bobby walks straight to the door and jumps over the two steps to the ground.

"See you," he calls back to us.

I wait until I'm sure they're out of earshot, and then I tell her.

"I guess that settles that."

"Indeed it does. Bobby likes me better than you."

"How can you say such a thing? Didn't you hear what he told me?"

"Of course. He said you know how he feels about me."

"He did not."

"Look, Margaret. I know what I know. And now that I am absolutely sure of it, I don't want to discuss it with you. Just think about it. Think about Gladwin. Gladwin makes a real bond between the two of us."

"Gladwin? A bond? You are crazy, Courtney Liveley."

"And you are jealous as you can be."

I walk about five steps behind her all the way to the house. Nobody is in the kitchen except Sallie.

"I'm going back to bed," Courtney says. "My job is done."

"I'm too wide awake to go back to bed. I guess I'll eat breakfast if there is any."

"You know there's plenty of breakfast, Margaret Ann," Sallie says. "But you might want to go on and feed the dogs while this next batch of biscuits is cooking."

"Good idea."

Both tractors are gone when I go back outside. It's still cool and the air smells sweet. Maybe I'll get up every morning at five. Maybe I'll meet Bobby Holland at the barn just as he's going to work. I look back toward the house just in time to see Mama come out on the porch.

"What on earth are you doing up at this time of morning?" she asks.

I sincerely hope she will never know.

Johnny calls on the telephone the night before his ship leaves port in California. Each of us gets to talk to him for a minute, and then Daddy talks for a long time. Johnny says he'll write as often as he can. But not to worry if we don't hear for a while.

"No news is good news," Grandma says.

Tommy Gray's ship leaves out of Hampton Roads, but Elizabeth doesn't get to see him again. He tells her not to try to come over to Newport News. I think he just can't stand to tell her good-bye again. We know he's going to be sent either to England or to Scotland, so Aunt Mary Lee gives him names and addresses of Uncle Walter's family. Just in case he has time to go see them.

"I know Grandmother Liveley would be glad to have him," Courtney says. "It's so beautiful at Grandmother's house."

I'm dying to know about her grandmother's house. But I won't ask. Not about London, or Windsor Castle, or the white cliffs of Dover. But I want to know if there are really bluebirds there like in the song. And has the war stopped them from flying? I decide I never want to know if I have to ask Courtney.

It's quiet for these first weeks in August. Hot and dry and not much to do. Courtney spends a whole week in town with Joanne Cox. And while she's gone, Mama lets me have Joyce over to spend the night. But it's too hot to do much. We just sit around and talk about the same things over and over. I will surely be glad when it's time to go back to school. At least then there will be something to do.

It's on the twenty-first of August that it happens. For the first time I can ever remember, somebody in our house gets a telegram.

"Oh, Mary Lee," Mama says when she puts down the telephone.

The operator insists on reading the telegram to someone

other than the wife of the missing person. And so poor Mama has to tell Aunt Mary Lee.

"The International Red Cross has been advised to tell you that . . . Walter . . . didn't return with his squadron. He is . . . missing in action."

Aunt Mary Lee sits right down on the first chair she can get to. And it's like she can't take her eyes off Mama's face.

"Walter?" she says. "Did you say Walter?"

"Yes, Mary Lee. . . . I am so sorry. But it doesn't mean he won't come back later."

"How? How the hell can he?"

Grandma walks into the hallway just about the same minute Aunt Mary Lee says "hell."

"What is this?" Grandma asks. "What is all this ugly talk about?"

"It's Walter," Mama says. "He's missing in action."

"Oh, no," Grandma says. "Mary Lee."

I don't believe my eyes or my ears. Grandma walks right up to the chair where Aunt Mary Lee is sitting, rocking back and forth and staring straight ahead like she doesn't even see us. And Grandma leans down and puts her arms around Aunt Mary Lee, and she's rocking too.

Daddy has to go to town to get Courtney. Mama calls ahead to say that she's needed at home, but she doesn't say what's the matter. When Daddy and Courtney get home, before they come inside the house, Mama goes out front, and she and Daddy tell her about Uncle Walter. Oh my Lord, it's awful. I'm trying to take care of Paige and Polly and keep them quiet, but it's awful. And all I can think of is that this might be only the first of three telegrams we get. There's Tommy Gray . . . and there's Johnny. Aunt Mary Lee is right. This war is hell.

Part Two

A Roommate in Johnny's Room

School starts on September 1, and even with all our troubles I'm still excited to be going into the eighth grade. Our classes are upstairs on the second floor of the same building, but we get a different teacher for every subject. On the first day everybody dresses up, almost like going to church, and I see all the people I haven't seen since June, Jack Hubbard included.

Paige and Polly start to school this year. They're so excited even Mama is about to lose her temper. They're dressed up in matching pink dresses, dancing all over the kitchen. That makes four lunches to pack. I help Sallie as much as I can, grabbing out lunch boxes and flapping slices of ham on white bread.

"I want a biscuit," Paige is yelling.

"Me too," says Polly.

"Mama," I say. "I will not go to school with little sisters

who carry biscuits in their lunch box. People will think we're poor and pitiful if they carry biscuits."

"What is this?" Grandma says, looking up from her coffee.

"Nobody but poor people carry biscuits in their lunch," I say.

"Margaret Ann, I am surprised at you. I have never heard you say such a thing before in your life. You know well that people can't help it if they're poor. Emily Ruth, stop what you're doing and talk to this child."

Mama looks over at Grandma and nods. That's all she has time for. Because all at the same time she's braiding Paige's and Polly's hair, checking to see if their ears are clean and explaining to them that they have to sit where I tell them to on the school bus.

"In a minute, Mrs. Motley," she says.

"It's okay, Mama. I know you don't have time. And anyway, I'm sorry. If the twins want biscuits, I'll give them biscuits. Grandma's right. Joanne Cox and them are going to laugh at me anyway. And I'd rather be friends with poor children than with those town girls."

Courtney looks up at me for a second, then stares at her scrambled egg. It takes her a very long time to eat her breakfast these days. She's still sitting there beside Grandma, chewing and staring off toward the window. And of course, the whole sad feeling comes right back to me. How can I forget, even for a moment about Uncle

Walter? I shouldn't be saying bad things about her friends.

In my heart I know Courtney is trying to be brave. It makes me feel even worse that I still don't like her. I feel sorry for her, but that's as far as I can go.

After we're back in school for a few weeks, I know there's something really wrong with Courtney. Lessons in the eighth grade are harder than grade school. We know that. Each one of the four teachers acts like she's the only one who gives us homework. It takes hours to get it all done. But that shouldn't make a difference to Courtney. She's always been so far ahead of us. Now she never knows the answer to a single question. And she never raises her hand either. One day Miss Timberlake, our history teacher, asks her the simplest question, and Courtney just stutters and mumbles. Miss Timberlake says she's not paying attention, and that's exactly what it is. Paige and Polly are learning to read in their *Dick and Jane* books, and I'm working on a big report for extra credit in history. It's like we're leaving Courtney way behind.

One afternoon I'm sitting on my bed, reading out of some old pamphlets that Grandma bought on a trip to Richmond, when I hear a knock on the bedroom door.

"Who is it?" I ask, even though I know it's Paige or Polly or both at once. They love to read their pages to anybody who will listen. I'm really surprised when I hear Courtney's voice.

"I need to talk," she says.

"Okay."

I get up off the bed and go to the door.

"May I come in?" she asks.

Her eyes are red.

"Sure," I tell her.

She walks past me and I close the door and go back to sit on the bed.

"Where shall I sit?" she asks.

"Anywhere. I mean . . . you can sit in either chair you like."

"Can't I sit on the bed beside you?" What's going on here? Is this Courtney or is it an imposter in Courtney's dress? "I need to ask you something, but I must whisper."

"Sure," I say, and move further back against the pillows.

Courtney sits down real close to me and leans even closer than that. She looks terrible. Her face is splotchy and her hair is hanging down across her face.

"I think you're going to have to speak louder, Courtney."

"Very well, but I don't want Mother to hear. Oh God, it's difficult to ask you this, but I simply must. And I suppose I need to start at the beginning. All right?"

I nod.

"Okay, then. It's like what I told you that night at the Grays'. Remember? From the moment I arrived in this house, I knew you didn't like me. And I couldn't understand why. I thought you were a lovely girl, and Mother had been telling me all the way down on the train that we would be such friends. You and I, I mean."

She stops then and all I can think of to say is "Okay."

"But we weren't friends. I think you could say we became enemies, wouldn't you?"

"And I guess you're trying to say it's all my fault."

"No. It's my fault too. But no matter whose fault it is, I have to ask a favor. Even if you don't like me. Even if I don't like you. Because there's nothing else I can do. I can't bother Mother with it."

"Look, Courtney—"

"Don't say it, Margaret. Please. Give me a chance."

"It won't do any good."

"It has to. You see, I've failed all three of the tests we've had since school started. And the problem is that I simply can't hold my eyes open in class to listen. I feel like I'm dropping off to sleep all the time. And yet I can't sleep at night. When Mother turns the lights out, all I can think of is Father. And I start to wonder what will become of us. I really don't feel comfortable here. I want to go home."

I open my mouth to tell her she doesn't want to go home any more than I want her to, but something stops me. Mama, I guess. Yes, it's Mama's face smiling at me and whispering that terrible sound. "For me. Please."

"I hope that doesn't sound ungrateful to Uncle John and Aunt Emily. I don't mean that actually."

"Then what do you mean?"

"I don't know. I don't know anything except that I can't sleep at night, because Mother is lying there beside me, crying. She won't show her true feelings in front of any of you. And, of course, she thinks I'm asleep. But that's the real reason I failed those tests. I never get any sleep. And I don't know what to do."

"Well, Courtney, I don't see what I can do about it."

"But someone has to. Mother and I can't go on this way."

I know it's true. Mama tells me all the time that Aunt Mary Lee won't eat. You can look at her and see that her dresses are hanging on her. But I don't see how anyone can make her happy until Uncle Walter comes back.

"There's a very simple solution, Margaret. Tell Grandma and Aunt Emily and Mother that you want me to move in with you."

"What do you mean? Move in this bedroom? Be here with me all the time?"

"Yes, Margaret, that's exactly what I mean. It's not that I am so anxious for your company. I just want a good night's sleep."

I have to look away from her so I can speak. Because she does look so pitiful. And I start to think how I would feel if Daddy were missing in action and maybe dead. But I won't let myself do it. Courtney has taken too much away from me already.

"I'm sorry, Courtney. You'll have to find somewhere else. I have wanted a bedroom by myself since I was ten years old. You took the best one in the house from me no more than a month after I got it. I can't let you take this one."

And just like that, Courtney starts to cry. Her nose gets all bubbly and her eyes are leaking like crazy. I take my handkerchief out of my pocket and give it to her.

"Take this," I say. "But don't expect any sympathy from me. You think you can get everything you want by getting people's sympathy. Don't think I haven't noticed. Like last Christmas when you cut your hand on purpose so you wouldn't have to help with the work for Elizabeth's wedding. Your finger didn't hurt you. You just wanted sympathy."

She stops crying instantly and looks up at me.

"So that's what you think, is it?"

"That and a whole lot more. I've heard how you talk about me to Joanne Cox. Hey, maybe you should get a room at Joanne's house. You stay there enough. But this time I can tell you, you won't have Bobby Holland coming over there to parties."

"Margaret . . . I don't know how you can say such things. I wish I'd never seen you. I wish you weren't my cousin."

"But not half as much as I wish it."

I watch her go. And for a few minutes I feel good. I take a deep breath and it reminds me of the way you feel on a cold winter morning. Or like when it snows, which isn't very often around here, and you've been outside having a snowball fight. All clean inside and kind of empty. This will be the end of all my troubles with Courtney because I know she'll never speak to me again. Good riddance, I say.

And then it occurs to me. Courtney will go straight downstairs and tell Mama. And Mama will tell Daddy. And he'll tell Aunt Mary Lee. And Grandma Motley will find out from one or the other of them. Maybe I ought to go downstairs right now and tell Mama myself. But somehow I can't. I can't stand to see her face looking so disappointed at me. At what I've done.

So I wait. And nothing happens. That night at supper everything is just like it always is. Nobody says much. Nobody but the twins and me seem to eat much. But slowly it comes to me. She isn't going to tell. Nobody will ever know. But that makes me feel really bad. I push my plate away and ask to be excused. And I go upstairs to my bedroom. All alone.

For three days I just worry and do nothing. Courtney looks worse each day, and the thing I wonder about is why nobody but me seems to notice. Or maybe they do notice and don't know what to do about it. The thing is that I do know what to do about it. But somehow I can't do it.

The fourth day is the worst of all. In our history class, the last period of the day, Miss Timberlake makes Courtney go to the blackboard to take a little test. She is supposed to write the answers to three questions and then go sit down. The first one is the easiest thing in the world. I could have answered it when I was in the fourth grade. But Courtney can't.

"Courtney, do you mean to tell me you don't know who said 'Give me liberty or give me death'?"

"No, Miss Timberlake," Courtney whispers.

"Then you not only have not read your homework assignment, you must have been asleep for most of your life."

I raise my hand to tell Miss Timberlake that Courtney has lived most of her life in England where that isn't an important quotation, but she doesn't even look at me. Courtney does, though. Her eyes are kind of pleading. So I form the words with my lips. Courtney shakes her head. She doesn't understand. So I whisper, but she doesn't hear me.

Bobby Holland puts his head down on his desk just as Courtney starts to cry. I guess he can't stand to look at her. Tears are rolling off her cheeks and plopping down on her print dress that Mama made her out of feed bags.

"Don't expect to get sympathy from me, young lady," Miss Timberlake says. "You have done nothing in this class since school started. I simply won't have it. Now think about it. What is the answer to that first question?"

"Oh, for heaven's sake," I say. "It's Patrick Henry."

"Margaret Ann Motley, you and Courtney stay after class. Now go sit down, Courtney. Joanne, I am sure you know these answers, don't you?"

"Of course," Joanne Cox says.

I put my head down too, expecting every second for Miss Timberlake to yell at me to sit up straight. But I just feel too bad to care.

When class is over I rush up to Miss Timberlake's desk and explain to her that we can't stay after class because we'll miss the bus.

"Nobody gets to drive to town more than once a week," I tell her, "unless one of the tractors breaks down. There's not enough gas. So you'll have to tell us quick."

"I had planned, Margaret Ann, to have you write 'I must not interrupt' five hundred times. But you can make it a thousand. Courtney, you can write 'Patrick Henry said Give me liberty or give me death' five hundred times."

"That's a terrible waste of paper," I say.

"Make that two thousand times."

I'm about to speak again when Bobby Holland walks up behind me and puts his hand over my mouth.

"Miss Timberlake," he says. "The bus driver says he can't wait much longer."

"Then go. But I want to see a difference in your behavior tomorrow, girls. You're cousins, aren't you?"

"Yes, ma'am," we say together. Then we grab our books and run for the bus.

Courtney sits as far away from Bobby and me as she can get. I don't blame her actually. But from time to time Bobby turns his head and smiles at her. I want to, but I can't.

"Bobby," I say as soon as the bus is out of town and driving down the highway. "How could Miss Timberlake do such a thing? Doesn't she know Courtney's father is missing in action? I would think all the teachers would know a thing like that."

Bobby just looks at me. I can feel my face getting red. In a few seconds I feel like a plum. Because I know what he is thinking. "Don't you know too, Margaret Ann?" Bobby would never say such a thing to me, but he must be thinking it. Because I'm thinking it too. I know I have to do something. And I know what that something is.

As soon as we get home from school, Courtney just seems to disappear. I get my snack and talk to Sallie for a while and then I start to look for Courtney. She isn't anywhere around the house, upstairs or down. I ask Aunt Mary Lee and Grandma and the twins, but nobody knows where she is. And I guess it does seem strange for me to be looking for her.

So I go outside and I look across the front yard, then around the back. Finally I give up and go to the barn to see if I can find Bobby Holland. There's nobody there either except a few of Daddy's hounds. I sit on the step and things get quiet and then I hear Courtney and Gladwin behind the barn. I walk around the barn and there they are. Courtney has a stick in her hand and she throws it just as I get close. Of course Gladwin comes running to me instead of in the direction of the stick.

"I'm sorry, Courtney. I didn't mean to break into your training session."

She doesn't say anything and Gladwin just stands beside me licking at my fingers. I shake my hand at him to shoo him away, but it excites him and he jumps on me and then I have to speak firmly to make him quiet down. Courtney just shakes her head when she sees how I'm able to control him. I can feel tears coming to my eyes as I watch her.

"Courtney, I'm sorry for what happened at school today. Miss Timberlake was really cruel."

Courtney looks at me. "I thought you agreed with her."

"No. Really. Did you think that?"

"What else could I think? When you said the answer, I could tell you thought I was a dope."

"Not at all. I know how much you know about British history. But this is American history and you haven't had that like we have. You couldn't be expected to know it."

"I guess I can't be expected to know how to train a dog either."

"That's not true. It's just that I walked around here and broke his concentration. Gladwin is doing very well."

"No, he's not. I might as well give it up."

"For now maybe," I say. "Because I really want to talk to you."

"You want to talk to me after all you said. . . ."

"I do, Courtney. And I'm really sorry. I mean . . . what I want to say . . . what I mean actually is . . . will you be my roommate? Starting right now?"

Courtney looks at me. She doesn't smile. She doesn't speak. She just stares.

"Come on, Courtney. You said yourself that you had to do something. And I really feel bad. I mean . . . when Miss Timberlake said that about not having any sympathy for you, all I could think of was when I said that. And I thought about your father . . . and Aunt Mary Lee. And I was so sad and so sorry. Please try to forgive me."

"I don't know," she says.

"Just think how happy it would make your mother. Just think about getting a good night's sleep."

She shakes her head.

"Look, Courtney, let's go upstairs to my bedroom and we'll talk about how we can make it ours. Okay?"

She doesn't speak, but she throws the stick she's holding as far as she can and turns with me to walk back to the house.

. . .

As we walk into the doorway, I stand for a minute looking from one end of the room to the other. My bedroom. My chairs. My bookcase. My closet. There's empty space everywhere. More than enough room for Courtney's few possessions. But still there's a way in which I want it all for myself. I just have to concentrate on remembering what Miss Timberlake said and the way she said it. And I know I don't want to be like that.

"What about it, Courtney?"

"If I could only feel that you really wanted me to. I don't know. I'm just thinking that you can't have changed so quickly."

"I know what you mean. I don't understand it either. But I guess I just don't want to be the kind of person who would go to bed each night knowing there was someone in the next room who was miserable. And there's Aunt Mary Lee too. I really love your mother. And if I can do anything to make her happy, I'll do it."

"Me, too," Courtney said.

"Then you'll move in with me?"

"Yes, thank you. I will."

"Good," I say, even though I have this strange feeling I can't really describe. I know I better hurry or I'll change my mind. "Let's go tell Mama and Aunt Mary Lee and Grandma."

• • •

Mama and Aunt Mary Lee look at us a bit strangely when we find them on the front porch. Grandma obviously hasn't recovered enough to understand. She just looks up at us and blinks a couple of times.

"I wonder how you folks would feel about Courtney moving in my bedroom with me," I say.

"You two be roommates?" Aunt Mary Lee says immediately. "I think that would be splendid."

"Good idea," says Grandma. "You should have done this long ago. Anybody knows two cousins, both thirteen years old, ought to be sharing a bedroom."

"I won't be thirteen till next month," Courtney says.

"Then we'll have a big party," says Mama. "We'll all save our sugar and Sallie can make you a cake."

"My front teeth have been begging me for a cake," Grandma says. "This sugar allotment is not big enough for me. Though I don't suppose I should complain."

I expect Courtney to start in with one of her speeches about the war effort. Instead she looks at me and smiles. And this time she isn't so smug. Maybe those three Fs are doing her some good.

That night after we go to bed, Courtney is quiet for a long time. I can't seem to get to sleep, so I fume and sigh and turn back and forth about fifteen times. Just as I feel myself dropping off, I hear her whispering.

"Are you asleep, Margaret?"

"Not really. I think I was about to go."

"I'm sorry. But I really need to talk to you."

"Sure," I say, trying to make my voice sound warm and friendly. Maybe this is what Mama does. Maybe this is how she always seems so comforting.

"I have to tell you that I knew all along that Bobby Holland liked you better than me. I just wanted to think he liked me because Joanne Cox and Evelyn and all those girls like him so much. I guess I thought it would make me important."

"But you already were important."

"Not really. I was just new. And different. It was the war that made me special. But now that father is missing, I think it makes the girls uncomfortable to be around me. They don't know what to say."

"I hadn't noticed that."

"The thing is, you don't like people to completely overlook it. I mean, you want them to say they hope your father gets back soon. Or something."

"I guess so. I mean if Johnny was missing, I'd want people to tell me they would pray for him."

"I don't know much about prayer. We never went to church at home. But if you think it might help, then I would appreciate your praying for Father."

"I don't know as much as I should about prayer either, but maybe this would be a good time to learn."

She doesn't say anything else for a long time. Then I hear her whisper.

"Thank you, Margaret. And let me say one more thing: If I do something you don't like, let's talk about it. That may have been our problem all along."

I'm not so sure that talking will change things. But I decide to keep it to myself. My feelings are too complicated. I'm not always sure what they are. So I'll try hard to follow Mama's advice. There are many things in life that are better left unsaid.

The next morning I'm really glad I didn't say anything. Because Aunt Mary Lee actually smiles at breakfast when Mama is talking about the new roommates and how bright and shining they look this morning.

"Yes," Courtney says. "I slept very well."

So then I feel like I have to say how well I slept too. In a few minutes Grandma comes in and says she's so pleased this morning, though I don't think she has any idea what she's pleased about. And Paige and Polly are bouncing back and forth between Courtney and me and laughing and telling little jokes.

When Mama hands me my lunch box, she hugs me and whispers real softly.

"Thank you, Margaret Ann."

I'm afraid she doesn't really have much to thank me for. But once again, I leave that unsaid.

October 2 is Courtney's birthday. So we celebrate the twins' birthday and hers at a dinner halfway between the two days. I don't have anything else to give Courtney for a present, so I give her my stamp dollar for this week. She has two dollars for stamps on Monday, but I don't mind as much as I thought I would.

Then, when our homeroom teacher, Miss Joyner, asks me what happened that I don't have even a quarter to buy one stamp, Courtney raises her hand and tells her.

"Miss Joyner, it's because Margaret gave me her stamp dollar for a present."

Miss Joyner looks puzzled. And Joanne and Evelyn look at each other like they know something nobody else knows.

"That's very nice, Margaret Ann," Miss Joyner says. "But why did you do that?"

"I did it because it was Courtney's birthday and I didn't have anything else to give her."

Joanne and Evelyn laugh out loud at that. Like not having extra money is something even worse than your little sisters bringing biscuits to school. Later on at recess, they walk right past Courtney on the way to the lunchroom. So

Joyce and I make a place for her at our table. Then Bobby Holland comes over to sit with us. And Jack Hubbard and Tommy Pierce. Joanne Cox is so jealous she can't even eat her piece of chocolate cake.

But what really makes Courtney and me friends is when the town boys and girls sign up and come out to our farm to pick cotton. All the schools in the county let out for two weeks so the farm boys can work the fields. Bobby Holland comes every morning at sunup and works till after dark. But still there's not enough help to get the crops in. Somebody gets the idea that the town children can pick cotton. Daddy doesn't much want them to come, but he says the only other choice is to leave the crop in the fields to rot.

So he signs up to take twenty boys and girls from the seventh and eighth grades. He feels like it will be better to put them in the home fields. That way Mama and Aunt Mary Lee can help keep an eye on them.

On the last Monday in October, the school bus drives into our gate loaded with people from our grade at school and a few from the grade behind us. You can hear the noise all the way down the lane.

Grandma comes out to the side yard waving her handkerchief and smiling. She greets each boy as he gets off, but she looks kind of angry at the girls.

"On behalf of the Motley family, I want to welcome you here this morning. However I want to make myself perfectly clear about one thing. I do not approve of girls working in the field. If it were not for this terrible war, I would never let my own granddaughters near one."

Everybody laughs at that, but then the bus driver says, "Ya'll listen now," and they get quiet.

"Indeed, you will do well to listen," Grandma goes on. "Before this morning is over, you will have need of this announcement. If you will look in the direction I am point- ing, you will see a small alleyway between two buildings. At the end of that alleyway, you will find an outhouse. Feel free to use it if nature calls. Also, you may use the spigot at the horse trough if you want water. It is perfectly clean and pure. Everything else besides the cotton field will be off limits. Is that understood?"

I guess Grandma thinks laughing is a way of saying yes. Because that's what everybody does. Just laughs at the top of their lungs. And yells out all kind of things I don't think Grandma can hear. Because if she could, those people would be back on the bus and out of there in five minutes.

The first day nothing too bad happens. Except for all the jokes about country people using outhouses. At first I tell everybody that we have a perfectly good bathroom inside the house. But all they do is laugh and say things like "Yeah, I just bet you do." And "Who gets to use it? The cows?" So I give up and let them think whatever they want to think.

The first words out of Joanne Cox's and Evelyn Stephens's mouths are "Where's Bobby Holland? We heard he was working for your father."

"He is working for Daddy," I say. "But he's really working. Not playing around picking cotton."

After that they don't say another word to me, but they're back being friends with Courtney. They won't take a step unless she's right there beside them.

Courtney and the twins and I picked cotton the week before, so we feel like we know what we're doing. When Daddy gives out the big white bags, we start off down the first row. Only there's Joanne and Evelyn right behind us. Courtney teaches them how to reach into the prickly bolls and pull the cotton out and stuff it in the bag without dropping any of it in the dirt. And she shows them how to be careful so the tip ends of the dried bolls don't prick their fingers. Plus, a few of the bolls aren't quite open, and you have to slit them with your fingernail right along the four little lines that hold the bolls together.

"Why don't you just leave it if it's not ready?" Evelyn asks angrily after she breaks a fingernail.

"Because nobody has time to go back the next day and find it," I tell her. "It's hard enough to pick over the fields once."

"Who used to do the picking?" she asks. "Before the war, I mean. Where have they all gone?"

"Different places. To the army. The navy. To the ship-yard in Newport News. Some folks work in the hospital now. Things like that."

We pick on down the row.

"I'm hungry," Joanne Cox says. "I think I'll eat my lunch now. Come on, Courtney. You and Evelyn and I can have a picnic under those shade trees in front of the house."

"Grandma said not to," I tell them, Courtney included. But it's like I haven't opened my mouth.

"That doesn't mean Courtney's friends," Joanne says. "Right, Courtney?"

"I guess."

So off they go. And furthermore, not only does Grandma see them sitting there on the tree roots having their picnic, she gets Sallie to take lemonade out to them. In good glasses. And then she tells Courtney to take the girls back to the dog pen so they can see Gladwin.

That night when everybody weighs their cotton, gets paid, and leaves, I am so mad I can't speak to Courtney. But when it's time to go to bed, there we are, side by side, nowhere else to go, nothing else to do, and just like before, I'm drifting off to sleep, and Courtney decides it's time to talk.

"Margaret, I have the feeling you're angry with me again. And I see no reason why you should be."

"Oh, no," I say. "No earthly reason. Not even because you choose to be friends with those town girls who won't have anything to do with me."

"Now, that's not true. You know you didn't want to eat with them. You practically said so."

"I didn't say a word about eating. Anyway, did you hear them invite me when they got ready to waltz out to our shade trees and have a picnic?"

"But it's our house. We should have invited them."

"So now it's our house, is it? I thought you were ashamed of living out here in the country six miles from anywhere."

"Margaret Motley, I should get up this minute and walk out of this room and never speak to you again. And I would do it if it weren't for Mother and Grandma . . . and Aunt Emily. I won't worry them more than they're already worried. So we're going to get up and get this thing settled."

"Why do we have to get up? And what is there to settle? You like Joanne and Evelyn more than you like me. That's the whole thing. Last week at school they weren't having much to do with you, so you sat with Joyce and me. But today, when it suited them to be friends with you, back you went."

"Oh, Margaret, is that what you think?"

"What else can I think?"

Courtney goes very quiet for a while, and then she whispers so softly I can barely make out the words.

"You're right, Margaret. I'm not thinking. I guess I'm walking in a daze since Father went missing. I don't notice things around me. Since everything is so strange, I accept everything as it looks to me. Not the way it looks to others."

Another long pause.

"I can't ask you to forgive me. You've already done that too many times. All I can say is that I'll do my best to show you how I feel about you and this family. And maybe . . . if I don't make too many mistakes from now on, I won't need to ask."

"Maybe."

And that's all I can make myself say.

The next day Courtney sticks to me tight as a weevil to a cotton boll. At mid-morning Joanne suggests another picnic.

"I can't," says Courtney.

"Why ever not?" Joanne asks.

"Because you haven't invited Margaret."

"Why should I invite her at her own home? Besides, she doesn't want to eat with us. She doesn't like us."

I manage to get far enough away from them not to see

them while they're talking, but I can hear every word they say. And it's all true. It is my house. And . . . I don't like them. But whose fault is that? Ever since we started in the second grade and it snowed and they laughed at Joyce's boots because they had been her brother's, I've known they'd feel the same way about me. Because if Mama hadn't been up all night with the twins having croup, she would've made me wear an old pair of Johnny's boots. In a way they were laughing at me too.

"All the same," I hear Courtney saying. "Thank you very much, but I'm not hungry yet. I'll stay and eat when Margaret does."

As soon as I hear Joanne and Evelyn leaving, I slow down and let Courtney catch up with me. She doesn't say a word. I guess she's busy adding up things to make me change my mind about her.

In the afternoon something happens that makes Daddy madder than I have ever seen him in my whole life. It's about four o'clock, I think, when Billy Chapman, a boy in our grade, starts yelling.

"Apples," he says. "Look at those trees."

The orchard runs along the main road and is bounded by the front yard on one side and by the cotton field on the other two. It's fenced off with a tall wire fence to keep out any large animals. One side of it has a grapevine running along the length. I guess that's why they don't see the apples immediately.

"Come on," Billy yells. "Let's go get 'em."

Everybody in the field hears him at the same time, and they drop their bags of cotton wherever they are and run toward the wire fence. It looks like they all get there at the same time too. And they all start climbing at once. The wire fence sags, but they keep on climbing. So then the fence rips away from the fence posts and down it falls in the orchard with all the boys and girls laid out on top of it.

Aunt Mary Lee and Mama come out to see if anybody is hurt. Daddy drives in from the Crumpler place about that time, and he says he hopes they are hurt. Every one of them.

"And people try to tell me it's country folks with no brains," he says.

He makes them come out of the field right then and weigh up their cotton. Then they have to sit under the trees out front until the bus driver gets there. At first Daddy says they can't come back, but then Mama begs him.

"They're just children," she says. "They didn't know what would happen."

"Didn't know if twenty people hop up on a wire fence all at the same time what will happen?"

"It looks like they didn't. You can tell they're sorry by the way they look."

"Sorry is what they look, all right. Good and sorry."

"Look, John," Aunt Mary Lee breaks in. "There's only two more days. And you'll embarrass the girls if you say their friends can't come back."

"Yes, John," Mama agrees.

I don't agree, though. I know something else will happen if they come back. I know they aren't a bit sorry. But I also know nobody will listen to me. Besides which Courtney whispers to me, "No, Margaret. Not now."

The other thing that happens waits till the last day. And it isn't anything that gets broken. Daddy says it's stealing. And he's beyond mad. He says if the war lasts another year, he won't plant a single row of cotton, because he will never have these town children in his fields again.

What happens is that Daddy catches a boy from our own class at school pouring water on his bag of cotton. He suspects it two days in a row, because some of the cotton is damp when he mixes it all together after it's weighed. He watches carefully on Thursday afternoon. It's wet again. So Friday he stands behind the screen door to the back porch and watches the spigot at the horse trough. It's about four-thirty in the afternoon, a half hour before we stop picking. Jerry Andrews comes out of the field to get a drink of water. And Daddy sees him do it. He sticks his bag of cotton under the spigot and lets it run all down into the bag. And then he squeezes the bag until the water stops dripping out of it.

Daddy doesn't say a word then, but while he's weighing up the bags of cotton on these big scales in the barn, he grabs that bag of cotton and he squeezes so hard a few more drops of water run out.

"What's this?" he says. "You cheating me?"

Everybody turns around to look.

"What's your name, son?"

"Uh . . . Jerry Andrews. But I didn't do nothing. I just been picking cotton all day. I just picked a lot of it. That's why mine weighs more."

"Don't make it worse by lying. I saw you. I was standing right there on the porch and saw you pour water in your bag. Now. Who's your daddy? Do I know him?"

"He's Mr. James Andrews."

"You want to tell him or should I do it?"

"I'll tell him, sir."

"You sure of that?"

"Yes, sir."

"You better. Otherwise it's no telling where you'll end up. This is no joke, son. This is stealing."

I walk back to the house as fast as I can. I know I'm wrong to feel this way, but I'm so embarrassed about what Daddy says. Jerry Andrews is the best baseball player in our grade. He's even better than Bobby Holland.

That night at supper when Daddy says he wishes he'd never let the boys and girls come, I nod my head. It's another way that everything is changing. It's another way that things will never be the same again. I've learned that somebody I actually know will cheat and steal.

Still Roommates

When we go back to school in November, Joanne Cox and Evelyn Stephens don't speak to me or to Courtney. But it doesn't stop them from talking to Bobby Holland. He's too polite not to answer back.

"Look," he says when I ask him about it. "Mama has always taught me to be polite to everybody. That's all it is. Being polite."

"Yeah. Well, don't be too polite."

"Maybe you ought to try being a little bit polite, Margaret Ann."

"Bobby Holland, you are ridiculous."

He laughs and pokes me on the arm.

"Just kidding," he says. "I like you just like you are. You know that."

So then I don't care at all what Joanne and Evelyn do.

. . .

As the days go by, I get the feeling that everybody has forgotten about Johnny. I include me in that too. Courtney and Bobby Holland and I have so much homework and so many tests at school that we never catch up. Being in the eighth grade is hard. But studying with Courtney is a big help. We ask each other questions to be sure we know all the answers for the tests. And we help Bobby Holland as much as we can. He's working in the fields till past dark most every night.

When one of Johnny's V-Mail letters arrives, it's like we reinvent him, and all we can do is talk about what Johnny says. Which isn't a lot actually. We know he's on a ship named the USS *O'Neil*. And we know the *O'Neil* is a destroyer. A tin can is what Johnny calls it. We know it has just been built in a shipyard on the West Coast, and sometimes it seems like Johnny is in port and sometimes at sea. Like maybe they don't do a good job on certain parts of the ship, and they have to go back to the shipyard for repairs. But you can't be sure. The way they make the V-Mail—by taking a picture of the letter and shrinking it so it won't take as much space—well, the boys know for sure that somebody in Washington or somewhere is reading every word of it. Mama keeps all Johnny's letters in a basket on the piano in the living room. And anytime she can find a minute to sit down, she reads them.

When we don't have a test at school the next day,

Courtney and I go to the living room after supper to listen to the *CBS World News Roundup*. Some nights Daddy doesn't get in from the fields till long after it's over. But then he somehow holds his eyes open to read every word of the Norfolk *Virginian Pilot* newspaper. If he sees any mention of a navy ship, whether it's Johnny's or not, he reads it out loud to us. If there's a map of the Pacific Ocean, he passes it around the room. In addition to that, I look and look at the maps in last year's geography book. I memorize the names of all the islands so I'll know where they are if Johnny ever does mention one of them.

Sometimes on the weekend Elizabeth reads us letters from Tommy Gray. His letters don't say much either. She reads us something like "The weather is nice here" or "It's been raining a lot"—stuff like that. And then she gets to a part where she says, "Ummm . . . well, this is just something for me to read." Courtney and I really want to hear that part, but she won't read us a word.

"You're much too young," she says. We don't agree.

It's funny to see skinny Elizabeth with her stomach poking out. It reminds me of when she was twelve and I was six or so. I actually remember looking at her one day and realizing she had breasts like Mama. "You'll get them too," she told me. "When you're my age." And so I have. But they're nothing to write home about. I guess Motleys don't get the kind Frances Lowe has.

. . .

At school Miss Timberlake spends a lot of time talking about the war news instead of reading our history book. Every Monday we bring in a current event to share with the class. There's nothing in any of our schoolbooks as important as the war news, she says. One Friday afternoon she invites Joanne Cox's daddy to talk to us about the war effort. First he tells us a lot of things we already know. And then he tells us things he says the government won't let newspaper reporters tell us. Things like German submarines are being sighted just off the coast of Virginia and North Carolina.

I raise my hand and ask him how in the world he knows this. But he won't answer. He just smiles like Joanne does when she thinks she knows more than the rest of the class. Miss Timberlake frowns at me, and Mr. Cox goes right on talking about how the Germans under General Rommel are winning in North Africa.

But he comes back a couple of weeks later and says the tide has turned, that the British are winning. He says there must be a new offensive, either in Europe or in North Africa. He says to prepare for more British casualties. I look at Courtney, and I can see her shoulders slump. I raise my hand to tell Mr. Cox that our classroom is no place for remarks like this, but Miss Timberlake frowns at me like she did before and motions for me to put my hand down. So we have to sit there and listen while he tells us that this time there will be American casualties as well.

Mr. Cox is right too. We get the news a week later.

I'm not sure about the way things actually happen, because I'm not there at the time. Plus, I get bits and pieces of the story from different people. And most of these people aren't there either. But it happens at the Grays' house on a Wednesday morning while Courtney and I are at school.

Florence, the Grays' cook, tells Sallie that the whole thing starts when she hears knocking at the front door. She waits for somebody to answer it, but nobody does, so she goes herself. There's an army officer standing there with a paper in his hand. Florence says she gets a bad feeling the minute she looks at him. She says he stares at the door right over her head and never smiles.

"May I come in?" he asks.

So she takes him through to the living room and offers him a chair. And then he asks to speak to Mrs. Gray. So of course she goes upstairs and finds Tommy Gray's mother in her bedroom sewing. But it's Elizabeth the officer is looking for, and Florence has to go back upstairs to get her.

Nobody tells me what Elizabeth looks like, but I know

my sister. She always seems to do exactly the right thing. I can just see how she walks into the living room and shakes the officer's hand. She probably asks if he'd like a cup of coffee.

And then—I learn the next part from Mama—because Elizabeth tells her word for word what the officer says.

"Mrs. Gray, I'm sorry to tell you that your husband, Private Thomas Henry Gray, has been killed in action in the fighting at Oran in North Africa."

Nobody can seem to tell me what happens after that. But I always imagine Elizabeth saying, "No. No." Maybe because that's all I can think when Grandma Motley tells us, standing there in the kitchen.

But even before I was told about Tommy, I got a funny feeling. To begin with, Mama and Aunt Mary Lee are gone when we get home from school, and they're always home when we get there. Sallie is standing in front of the stove like she's pretending to cook. She's waiting for Grandma, because she can't bear to say these words. Tommy Gray is killed in Oran in North Africa. Before we really ask about it, Grandma comes downstairs, and she tells us, and I keep thinking, *No. No.* But I can't say a word either.

Of course Grandma doesn't have any tears to cry with. And I don't cry either. I feel terrible that I can't cry a tear about Tommy Gray. I just keep thinking, *No. No.* That's all that's inside my mind. And I can't speak a word.

By the time Daddy drives Courtney and me over to the Grays' Elizabeth has cried all the tears out of her whole body. She's like Grandma.

"I wish we could have a funeral," she keeps saying. "I wish I could know he was right there in the parlor closed up in a coffin. Even if I can never see him again, I just wish he was here."

"You'll see his baby," I say.

I don't even think about whether it's the right thing to say. It just slips right out.

I'm really surprised when we get home and Mama tells me, "Thank you, Margaret Ann, for knowing just what to say to Elizabeth. Nothing I told her had helped a bit. But when you reminded her of the baby, I could see a peace settle over her."

"Good gosh, Mama. That's the first time I ever said anything right—to anybody."

"Maybe this is the beginning of something new," Mama says. "Maybe this means you're becoming a young lady."

A young lady. I'm not sure I want to be one. But maybe I don't have a choice. I'm wearing silk hose to church now. And I plan to ask for some Evening in Paris perfume for Christmas. Courtney and I trade skirts and blouses so we'll have more outfits to wear. And we have pocketbooks and hats and shoes to match. Sometimes we spend ten minutes putting on our hose. The seams have to be straight up and down our legs. But does that make us young ladies? And does growing up matter anymore now that Tommy Gray is dead? Sometimes I feel like I can hear his voice saying, "How's things over at the Holland place, Margaret Ann?" How can Elizabeth possibly stand it? And Aunt Mary Lee and Courtney. How can they manage with Uncle Walter missing and now presumed dead? And all the rest of us. How do we manage with Johnny out there in the Pacific? With the Japs and their kamikaze planes that fly straight into a ship and set it afire.

I finally begin to understand Courtney. Whenever I hear somebody complain about not having enough gasoline, or rubber for new ties, or silk hose, or sugar for making a fruit-cake for Christmas, I remind them of the war effort. And I remember Tommy Gray and Uncle Walter. And I pray that Johnny doesn't join the list.

We listen to the news every night after supper, just like we always have, but somehow it doesn't seem like enough is happening. It's as if the army had to fight and get Tommy Gray killed, and now they're sitting around waiting, trying to decide where to go next. Why didn't they wait before Tommy got killed? Before Uncle Walter's plane got shot down?

. . .

At Thanksgiving, Elizabeth agrees to come stay with us.
Aunt Mary Lee says she and Elizabeth will be roommates.

The whole time Elizabeth is with us, from Thursday
morning till late Sunday afternoon, is the saddest time
I've ever seen. Elizabeth is trying so hard to act normal
and she just can't. She doesn't eat. She doesn't comb her
hair. She tells Aunt Mary Lee she can't get the strength to
roll her hair up and stick in the bobby pins. And she
doesn't put on lipstick. Even when I ask her a question,
she just stares at me. "I don't know, Margaret Ann," she
says. Or sometimes she just shakes her head and doesn't
answer at all.

I hear her talking to Aunt Mary Lee on Sunday morning
before breakfast.

"I dread going to church each Sunday, but I go because I
know I should. But the hymns all seem so sad. And I can't
seem to pray anymore. What is there to ask for? What is
there to be thankful for?"

Aunt Mary Lee nods and says she understands. In a way
I understand too. On the other hand, I think Elizabeth
should be thinking more about the baby. That baby is all
she has left of Tommy Gray. She needs to look after herself. There's an article in a magazine Elizabeth has that
says mothers are responsible for the future health and
intelligence of their babies. I tell Mama about this and she

says I shouldn't mention it to Elizabeth. She says Elizabeth is doing the best she can. So I bite my tongue and don't tell her. The real thing I wonder, though, is how I can get through Christmas without saying something wrong.

A Real Roommate

We decide to set up the Christmas tree early again this year. Mama says it will cheer everybody up. The very morning after we get out of school for the holidays, Daddy brings the two big boxes of decorations down from the attic. Then he takes Courtney and me and the twins out to look for a perfect tree.

By the time we get back it's ten o'clock and Mama and Sallie are busy in the kitchen. Grandma insists she needs the twins upstairs to help wrap presents, so that leaves Aunt Mary Lee, Courtney, and me to decorate the tree. The telephone rings three times while we're clipping on the lights and hanging the balls and, of course, finding the right spot for the bear.

I answer it the first time, and it's Uncle Waverly Saunders asking what size socks all of us children wear. Guess that means Aunt Janice is buying us socks again this year.

The second time it's Joyce Darden's deaf grandma. She gave the operator the wrong number. Anyway, she thinks I'm Joyce. Over and over I keep saying, "This is Margaret Ann Motley, Mrs. Darden." Finally I make her understand me, and then she apologizes for about ten minutes. I tell her not to worry, and finally we both say Merry Christmas and hang up.

We're finishing the lights and the balls, and starting with the tinsel, when the phone rings again. Aunt Mary Lee says she'll get it this time. She walks out in the hall with her hands full of tinsel, still laughing about Joyce's grandma.

Courtney and I have our hands full too. We're standing on opposite sides of the tree, carefully hanging a silver strand on each branch so it drapes down long like a real icicle.

"Where's Mother?" Courtney asks in a few minutes.

"I don't know," I say. "Let's go see."

So we get to the hall door just in time to see Aunt Mary Lee throw a handful of tinsel high up in the air over her head. It comes floating down like a snowstorm while she dances around the room, twirling till her skirts are hiked up above her knees.

"Oh, Courtney," she says, laughing so much we can hardly understand her. "It was a telegram about your father. He's alive. He's a prisoner in a German prisoner of war camp, but he's alive."

"Just in time for Christmas," Courtney says.

We dance all over the tinsel, and it gets twisted up and torn to pieces, but nobody cares. Except maybe Grandma. She spends the afternoon straightening it out. But she never actually says what we all know she's thinking. It's a source of great pride to her that we've been using the same strands of tinsel for the last ten years. Now they're gone, but I think it's a small price to pay for getting Uncle Walter back.

Later that afternoon down at the dog pen, where Aunt Mary Lee won't know he says it, Daddy shakes his head and looks me straight in the eye.

"Aye, Lord. I think I might rather be dead. But don't you tell your aunt Mary Lee I said so."

I tell him I won't say a word. But actually I wish he hadn't told me either. Everything is so wonderful until I start thinking about what it's like to be a prisoner of war. I gave a current event in history class about prisoner of war camps. There's a tall wire fence all around the area where the prisoners are kept. Like a dog pen, maybe, except it has barbed wire around the top. And there are watchtowers and searchlights and sentries on guard night and day. There's little if any chance of escape, because if somebody makes it over the barbed wire one dark night, the searchlights will sweep across the area and the guards shoot to kill.

• • •

That night after Courtney and I go to bed and everything is quiet, I can't stop thinking about Uncle Walter. I wonder if it's clean inside the barracks. . . . And what kind of a bunk does he sleep on? . . . And are there clean sheets? . . . And does he have a blanket?

"How cold is it in Germany in the winter, Courtney?" I ask.

"It's cold," she says. "Actually I was just thinking about that. I was wondering what Father will eat for Christmas dinner. I hope I don't sound ungrateful, but the more I think about his being a prisoner, the worse it seems."

"You're not being ungrateful, Courtney. You're just being normal. Anybody would feel this way."

"So you've been thinking about these things too?"

"Well . . . yes."

"Then I guess Mother will think about them too. How can she help it?"

"Probably she can't. But Aunt Mary Lee is a strong person. She'll be okay."

Courtney doesn't answer, so I say good night and pull the covers tight under my chin.

"Good night, Margaret. Except . . . I have one more thing to say. Thank you for all you do. I think what I like best about you is that you always say what you really mean. It makes me know I can trust you. Sometimes I think about it and I really don't know what we would do without you."

Neither of us says anything after that. But I feel good, even though I know I'm probably being really selfish.

There isn't much to do on Christmas Eve morning. The tree is decorated and there's a sprig of holly over every picture, and all along the mantel, and on the piano, and everywhere else that can hold one. I think about last Christmas Eve, with all the excitement of the wedding. About how busy we all were.

"Want to play Uncle Wiggley?" Paige (or Polly) asks.

I look at Courtney and she nods yes.

"Okay," I say. "But the game has to be over by twelve o'clock. Is that clear?"

Actually I'm glad to have something to do. Otherwise I'll be walking from window to window looking for Bobby.

It's late in the afternoon when Bobby Holland drives down the lane in his daddy's truck. I watch from the bedroom window and see him park under the largest maple tree. He sits for the longest time, looking toward the front door. I've stopped telling him he's breaking the law, because I know he can drive as well as anybody with a license. Daddy says so too.

Anyway, I leave Courtney sitting in our bedroom, reading, and run downstairs. Grandma comes out of the back hall ahead of me, so she gets to the door first. She invites Bobby to come in for a cup of eggnog, but he says he can't stay.

"I just wanted to see Margaret Ann for a few minutes," he says.

"You want to see Margaret Ann?" Grandma asks him. "Now, why in the world do you want to see her instead of Courtney?"

Bobby blushes and turns his head so he can look straight at me. I hold my breath and wait.

"Mrs. Motley, I thought you would know I wanted to see Margaret Ann," he finally says. "She's been my girlfriend since I was five years old."

Grandma looks at him with her face all pinched up.

"Well," she says after a long, long time. "Does Courtney know this?"

"Yes, ma'am. She does," Bobby says.

And then he smiles. There is nobody in the world who can smile like Bobby Holland.

"I hope Margaret Ann knows it too," he says. "I think she does."

"Well," says Grandma. "There's no accounting for taste."

Grandma excuses herself and goes down the hall toward the kitchen, which leaves Bobby and me alone.

"Can you come out on the porch a minute?" he asks me.

"Sure. Let me get a coat."

"I can't stay long enough for that. I got to feed your daddy's cows. But I need to see you right now by yourself."

As soon as we close the front door, Bobby reaches into his coat pocket and pulls out a little box.

"I brought you something," he says.

"Gosh. Thank you. But I don't have anything for you."

"That's okay. My brothers say girls don't give boys presents. But I wanted you to have this. Mama wrapped it in some paper from when she and Daddy were first married. It's real old, and I wanted it for your present."

"Oh, Bobby, thank you."

I'm shivering with the cold and with excitement, too, I guess. I look behind me at the living room windows to see if Grandma is looking. I can't see anything.

"Come on, Margaret Ann, open it. I want to see if you like it."

Of course I don't tear the paper. Anything as old as this should be treasured, and I know I'll get Sallie to iron it and I'll save it in one of my bureau drawers. I get Bobby to hold the red ribbon while I carefully remove the seals. When the paper comes loose, I get him to hold that too. And I open the box.

"Bobby," I say, almost whispering. "It's beautiful. An identification bracelet."

"It's got your name on one side of it."

"Margaret Ann Motley," I say, like I don't know my own name. "Oh, Bobby, thank you. It's beautiful."

"You like it? It's got my name on the other side."

I turn it over to look. And there's a plus sign, and then . . . BOBBY HOLLAND.

"Oh, Bobby, I love it. You ought to come inside so I can put in on my wrist and show everybody."

"No, I can't. I really got to go," Bobby says. "But I have one more thing to give you."

"Another present?" I ask him.

"Yeah."

He reaches in his other coat pocket and brings out a little piece of green stuff. Then he holds that over my head and leans way down. He seems taller than ever before. I see him every day, but being this close to him is somehow different. I guess I'm a little flustered so I don't catch on to what he's doing. I turn my head and kind of swat at him, and his lips brush past my cheek and bounce off.

"Good Lord, Margaret Ann, don't you know what mistletoe is for?"

"I know what mistletoe is for, but I didn't know that's what you had in your hand. I thought you were trying to scratch me with a holly leaf."

"Have I ever scratched you with a holly leaf?"

"No. But there's always a first time."

"And that's what I wanted this to be. So now that you know it's mistletoe, can I try again?"

"Absolutely."

I shiver with the cold and that's all it is, but he laughs at me just as he leans down to kiss me.

"So go ahead," I say.

His lips hover over mine. I can feel his breath inside my mouth. And then the door opens behind me.

"Margaret Ann, it's too cold for you to be outside without a coat," Grandma Motley says. "Either come in, Bobby Holland, or go on and do your jobs."

"Yes, ma'am. I have to feed the cows," he says. "It is mighty cold out here."

So we say good-bye with Grandma watching us like a hawk. And then Bobby jumps down across the steps and way past the first of the tree roots and is almost at the truck.

"Thank you," I call after him.

And then we both wave and holler "Merry Christmas." I get away from Grandma Motley as fast as I can and go upstairs to tell Courtney all about it. I put the paper in my dresser drawer. I decide I don't even trust Sallie to iron something as precious as this.

There's no Christmas entertainment at church this year, because we don't have blackout curtains big enough for the windows. Besides that, people only have enough gas to get to church and back on Sunday morning. So we pull down our own blackout curtains like we do every night. And we sit around the Christmas tree singing carols. But really we're thinking about Johnny and Uncle Walter, and Tommy Gray.

I try not to look down at my wrist too often. And I try not to smile too much. I remember the first time Tommy

Gray gave Elizabeth a Christmas present. A pen and pencil set. And Elizabeth wrote letters all Christmas Day. She wrote to every cousin and uncle and aunt we have. She wrote to Daddy and Mama. And Johnny. And me. Put a stamp on the letters and mailed them the next day. We got them back in the mailbox two days later.

I think Bobby's present is much better than a pen and pencil set. But suppose I lose it? That's the first word Grandma says after we get back in the house.

"Try not to lose it like you did the last one."

And Courtney answers right quickly.

"Oh no, Grandma. Margaret won't lose this one. This one is too important."

"Thank you, Courtney," I say.

And I smile at her. Just like I want to be smiling at Elizabeth but can't because she's so sad.

Unfortunately there is nothing we can do to keep Paige and Polly from showing how excited they are. This morning they give up looking at the Sears Roebuck catalog, but they have it all memorized anyway.

"What do you want, Courtney?" one of them asks.

And then they ask me what I want, and Grandma what she wants, and on around the room. When they get to Elizabeth, it's just more than she can stand. She gets up from the sofa as best she can and is out the door with Mama behind her.

"What's the matter?" one of the twins says.

So then we have to spoil their Christmas too.

"It's Tommy Gray," Courtney tells them. "All she wants is Tommy Gray and she can't have him."

"That's true," I tell them. "But listen to this. How about if Courtney and I play another game of Uncle Wiggley with you? Just till your bedtime. Would you like that?"

"Good idea," says Aunt Mary Lee, and then she goes off to find Mama and Elizabeth.

So we get through Christmas. And then through New Year's. And Elizabeth goes back to the Grays'. The baby is supposed to be born on January 22, so Mama calls over to the Grays' at least four times a day. Most days she even stops by to visit.

"Leave the child alone," Grandma says to Mama every time she picks up the car keys to go.

Mama won't listen to Grandma, though.

"Elizabeth is alone," she tells her one day. "So alone that I don't see how she will get through this whole thing. If I neglect the rest of you for a while, you'll have to get used to it. Right now Elizabeth is what matters."

Courtney and I are glad to finally go back to school after the Christmas break, because every time Mama goes over to see Elizabeth, Grandma grumbles the whole time she's gone about how many women in the history of the world have babies and manage fine. And when Mama gets back, she and

Aunt Mary Lee end up arguing with Grandma about it. But Grandma makes two in any quarrel, so the sides are even.

One day I hear Daddy say he's had about enough of strong-willed women. But I know he doesn't mean that. He's just worried about Elizabeth, because she won't go to the hospital to have the baby. She says she knows the baby is a boy and will grow up to be the president of the United States, so he needs to be born in Isle of Wight County. Daddy says he's never heard of such foolishness. He uses a cuss word too. Right between "such" and "foolishness." And right in front of Grandma Motley.

The thing I learn about babies when Elizabeth has hers is that the doctor might as well not bother to give a date concerning when it will be born. I fully expect to be awakened on the night of January 22, around midnight, give or take a little, and hear that whatever its name is has arrived. So I'm amazed beyond anything when Courtney and Paige and Polly and I get home from school on the tenth of January.

"Come in here, children," Sallie calls out as soon as we open the front door. "I made us a party to celebrate."

"Celebrate what?" I yell back down the hall. "Where did you get the sugar?"

"I didn't use sugar. Not sugar out the bag. I found some old strawberry preserves in the back of the pantry. I guess you could say it's turned back to sugar. So I made us a batch of cookies."

"That sounds great. So what are we celebrating?"

We all four drop our books and coats in the front hall and are standing around Sallie at the cookstove.

"Where are they? Where are they?" the twins are yelling.

"Look here," Sallie says. "Just calm yourselves. You want to hear the news, or do you just want to stand around calling for cookies?"

"Come on, Sallie," I say. "You know we want to hear. What is it?"

"You four girls got a new relation today. A little boy. Didn't weigh nothing hardly, but they say he's real strong."

"What? You mean Elizabeth had her baby? But it's too early. It's not even close to the twenty-second."

"Thomas Henry Gray, Jr., didn't feel like waiting."

"Thomas Henry Gray, Jr.?" I ask.

"What a lovely name," says Courtney.

"It won't be necessary to use the junior," Grandma Motley says.

We look over at the door to the stairway and there she is.

"I sent word to Elizabeth there was no need for it. A boy is only a junior until his father dies. The baby has no father, so it will just sound peculiar to those who know what's right to do."

"Grandma," I say, "do you think this is the time to remind Elizabeth that Tommy Gray is dead? Or do you think she doesn't already know it?"

"You know nothing about this, Margaret Ann. You may

think you're a grown-up, but you're only fourteen years old. Don't let me hear another word about this whole matter."

Courtney reaches out and gives me a punch on the arm.

"Wait," she whispers.

"For what?" I whisper back. But Courtney is right. Grandma has forgotten all about it.

"Give the children their tea party, Sallie," she says. "And bring me mine in the parlor. It has been a taxing day. Besides which, as soon as John Motley gets back, I have something I want to tell him. Now, what was it? Oh, well, I'll remember."

As soon as she was out the door, Sallie whispers to us.

"Miss Margaret's not herself today. This morning I thought sure she was having a stroke. She stood there staring and batting her eyelids."

"That's been happening for ages, Sallie," I say.

"Don't you think I know that? This is different though. It's not just that she doesn't remember things. She was white as a sheet. And she wouldn't eat a bite. She's some better now, though."

"I hope so," I say. "It would be terrible if she went over to see the baby and said things like that to Elizabeth."

"You're right. You and Courtney better keep your eyes on her. She's near 'bout eighty years old, and I'm afraid something bad is about to happen to your grandma."

"What else *can* happen to us, Sallie?" I ask.

"Plenty more can happen, Margaret Ann. But don't let it ruin this day. Now . . . where do you girls want your party? You better eat right now, because we're all going to see that baby soon as your daddy gets home. No telling when we'll get supper."

Daddy takes Grandma and Sallie over in the truck first, and when he brings them back he's driving the car.

"Soon as I get a few things settled at the barn, I'll take you girls over," he says.

We walk the floor and look out of windows and fuss until it's nearly dark. We just about give up hope of seeing the baby at all today, but then Daddy rushes in the back door, saying, "Come on, come on, your mama's going to be worried sick we haven't been over to see the baby." Like it's our fault.

So when we get to the Grays', the lights are on all over the house. Nobody has even thought to pull down the blackout curtains. Elizabeth is lying in bed with the baby on one arm and she is smiling. Really smiling for the first time since we got the news about Tommy Gray.

"Here you are," Elizabeth says. "What do you think of him?"

"Oh my gosh, Elizabeth, he's red," one of the twins blurts out.

"He's all wrinkled," says the other, like she's talking about a dead weasel or something.

"He's beautiful," I say quickly. "Isn't he, Courtney?"

We say every nice thing it's possible to say about a baby

that has his face all screwed up screaming and crying. But he is red. And he is wrinkled. And his head is too big for his body. And we can't see his eyes because they're all scrunched up.

"Come here to Grandma Motley," Mama says.

She reaches down and picks him out of Elizabeth's arms and starts to walk back and forth from the bed to the window, holding his wobbly head up so all of us can see him.

"Isn't he beautiful?" Mama says. "I think he looks a little bit like Elizabeth, but mostly like Tommy."

Elizabeth doesn't even cry when she hears Tommy Gray's name.

"Which of you girls wants to hold him first?" Mama asks.

"I'd like to try," Courtney says. "I've never held a baby before."

So she sits down in the rocking chair by the window and Mama places him carefully in her lap. All I can think of is how he'll look if he grows up to be president of the United States. I can see him wearing those pinch-on glasses like President Roosevelt, with a long cigarette holder in his fingers.

"Isn't he beautiful, Courtney?" Elizabeth asks.

"Oh, yes," she says.

I walk closer. His wrinkles are starting to smooth out since he's stopped crying.

"What about it, Aunt Paige? Aunt Polly?" Elizabeth asks. "Isn't he beautiful?"

"Oh, yes. Isn't he, Paige?" Polly says.

"Oh, yes. I think I really like him."

"Me too. We both like him. You don't have to worry, Elizabeth, we're going to be real nice to him. We're going to play games with him, like Margaret Ann and Courtney play with us."

Then Elizabeth looks at me. She keeps looking until I know I have to say something.

"Well, Elizabeth . . . of course he's beautiful. And I was just thinking . . . he looks smart too. I bet he really will grow up to be the president of the United States."

We all laugh, but I can tell you I feel strange. I tell a lie to keep from hurting Elizabeth's feelings. If this keeps up, I'll soon be a real Southern lady.

On January 22 we all expect a quiet day since little Tommy is already with us. And in just that short a time he's stopped being red and wrinkled, and he really is beautiful. I decide that makes me less of a liar. Maybe I'd seen into the future.

At bedtime, just as we're all listening to the ending of the *World News Roundup* on the radio, the telephone rings. Mama jumps up.

"It must be Elizabeth," she says.

But it's Johnny. And boy, does he have news.

"John," Mama calls from the hallway.

Her voice sounds strange, like there's something she needs to have explained to her. We all jump up and run to see what's the matter.

"Hello?" Daddy says into the telephone. "You what? Say that over again. I think I misunderstood you. This is not a very good connection."

We hold our breath. We're waiting for Daddy to say something else, but he just stands there listening with this worried look on his face. Finally he nods once, like he thinks Johnny will hear that or something. And then he says, "Certainly." And his voice changes completely.

"Hello there. Well, it's nice to meet you too. Even on the telephone. Yes, I look forward to seeing you one day too. Would you like to speak to my wife?"

That sounds so funny. Daddy never says things like "my wife" or how he looks forward to meeting somebody.

"Emily Ruth," he says, and hands her the telephone.

When he's out of earshot of the telephone, he shakes his head and says, "Aye, Lord." So we know something really is the matter.

I'm scared to ask. I just look at Courtney and try to imagine what might have happened.

"What is it, John?" Aunt Mary Lee asks. "Is it Johnny?"

Daddy nods his head yes. Then he goes over to the sofa and sits down. Daddy never sits on the sofa.

"The boy's married," he says.

"Married? How can he be married?" I ask. "He doesn't even love anybody."

"He thinks he does," Daddy says. "Lord, this is something. I sure hate to think of tomorrow morning when I have to tell Mama. She's going right through the roof. And this time I don't think I blame her."

"Now, John, you don't know anything about the girl," Aunt Mary Lee says.

"Exactly. I don't know a thing about the girl or her family. I don't know if she'll like the farm. What am I supposed to do if Johnny gives up on farming?"

"You've got Bobby Holland," Courtney says. "He and Margaret will always be here."

I blush, but I don't mind a bit that she says it. Because it's the truth. I will always be here on this farm, no matter what happens to anybody else. And I have a feeling that if I'm here, Bobby Holland will be somewhere close by.

We sit up so late that night talking about Johnny's new wife that we miss the school bus and Mama has to take us to town. Mama says she sounds real nice, but Courtney and I know that doesn't mean a thing. Mama thinks everybody is nice.

"If Johnny is happy," she keeps saying.

And Daddy always says, "Yeah. If?"

Grandma Motley is so astounded that morning when they tell her that she refuses to eat breakfast.

"Foolishness," she keeps saying. "Complete and utter foolishness."

Courtney and I decide not to tell anyone at school. Not even Joyce. So when we get home from school we're bursting to talk about it. Paige and Polly have lots of questions too.

"What's her name?" they ask. I realize then that I don't even know.

"What is it, Aunt Mary Lee?" I ask as she hurries into the kitchen.

"You mean Johnny's wife?"

"That sounds so funny, Aunt Mary Lee, for Johnny to have a wife."

"But he does," she says. "And nobody can know better than I how much you long to have that fact accepted. But, in answer to your question, her name is Vivian. Johnny says she's very pretty, with bright blond hair and blue eyes. He says he'll send a picture in a few days. Perhaps when he ships out, she will pay us a visit."

"Really? She'll come here?"

I am so confused. That night after Courtney and I go to bed, we talk for a long time.

"I sure thought Johnny would marry Charlotte Holland. Or, one of the girls from church," I say. "Not one of the Harris girls. They pray too much. But somebody close by."

"He would have if the war hadn't come. Just as I would never have met you and been your friend."

"And your daddy wouldn't be a German prisoner."

"And Tommy Gray wouldn't have been killed."

"Yes. Everything has changed, hasn't it?"

"Yes, Margaret, it has. And will keep on changing. I keep thinking about my schoolwork. I'm learning American history, not English. If I stay here much longer, how will I manage at university? And Grandmother Liveley is getting older, just as Grandma Motley is. And Father . . ."

Courtney stays quiet for a while. I can hear her swallowing hard, like she's trying not to cry.

"He'll be okay, Courtney. I'm sure he will."

"But think how I have grown since he last saw me. And think of Mother with the years passing too. They won't be young when they finally see each other again."

"That's true, Courtney. I never thought about that. I never really think that you and Aunt Mary Lee can't be truly happy here. And it's not your fault."

"But it's not your fault either. I shouldn't have said anything."

"That's okay."

We both get quiet. And then I go to sleep and I dream that a picture of Vivian Motley arrives in the mail and she looks just like Betty Grable. All that next day I keep picturing Betty Grable sitting under the maple trees, drinking lemonade.

Traveling Pallets

Grandma Motley says that people can get used to anything. Aunt Mary Lee agrees. I think I do too. From the minute the picture of Johnny's wife comes in the mail, I begin to think we might have to. She doesn't look like us. She's wearing tons of makeup. And she has on this skimpy little dress that shows off her legs and her breasts. And from the color of her hair you absolutely know she uses peroxide on it. It's this bright yellow that puts your eyes out. Daddy looks at the picture and he just shakes his head. Then he says what he always does in moments like this. "Aye, Lord."

But . . . in the middle of July, when it's as hot as it can stick, she calls us and says she's moving to our house because Johnny is at sea and she's expecting a baby in September. She says Johnny wants her where Mama can look after her. Poor Mama. How can she look after another person? For just a minute after she hangs up the telephone, I read that in her eyes. But then, you know Mama, soon she's smiling and saying how much she's looking forward to another grand-child.

"A playmate for little Tommy," she says.

Grandma says exactly what I think she will.

"Anybody with hair like that is not welcome in my house. She may bear the name of Motley, but she'll never be one. Besides, I don't want to see anybody that has little sense enough to ride from California to Virginia on a Greyhound bus. She's been using all kinds of strange bathrooms and eating who knows what kind of food. I will say it one final time. She is not welcome in this house."

And this time, this final time, she doesn't change her mind.

Nobody much wants to ride with Daddy to meet Vivian, so I say I'll do it. And when I look up at her climbing down the bus steps with her peroxide hair and her too short dress, I know what else Grandma is going to say.

Courtney and I are sleeping on pallets on the floor in Aunt Mary Lee's bedroom so that Vivian can have Johnny's room. Just until we decide what else to do.

"I don't want to put you to trouble," Vivian says that night at supper. "It's just that I don't have any family of my own. And I wouldn't have come all this way except that Johnny wanted me to."

"You're most welcome," Mama says.

"Indeed, you are," echoes Aunt Mary Lee. "And you will be looked after too. My daughter, Courtney, and I have been here since early in the war. I know you're going to love it."

"Oh, yes," Vivian says. "At least for a little while. But I don't think I could live on a farm for very long."

"You don't?" I say. "Then how is Johnny going to be a farmer?"

"He's not going to," she says. "He likes California as much as I do. We're going to live there."

I am surely glad that Grandma Motley is in her bedroom eating hot buttered toast. As it is, Daddy has to excuse himself from the table and go out to the barn. And Mama looks like she's going to faint. She wipes her lips with her napkin, then sets it down beside her plate. And she doesn't eat another mouthful of her supper.

Later Grandma comes out of her bedroom. She never speaks one word to Vivian. Not a syllable. At dinner, she keeps her head turned in the opposite direction, and once when Vivian asks her a direct question, Grandma pretends to get choked. She covers her mouth and nose and even her eyes with her napkin. And she keeps it there until somebody changes the subject.

. . .

The next day Vivian invites Courtney and me into her bedroom and offers to put makeup on us. Courtney and I wear lipstick when we go out somewhere, but that's about it.

"I don't know," I say. "What do you think, Courtney?"

"Oh, please," Vivian says. "I'm so bored out here. It would give me something fun to do."

So we both say okay. She starts on me first. She puts eyebrow pencil on my scraggly eyebrows. And then gets out a rectangular red box of stuff for my eyelashes She dips a tiny brush that comes with it into a glass of water, rubs the brush across the black stuff, and starts toward my eyelashes.

"Hold still, now," she says. "You wouldn't want to get this stuff in your eyes." I tense up and sit like a statue while she brushes it on. Then comes rouge on my cheeks. And powder over that. And then she takes the cutest little tube of lipstick with a flip top to it, and she paints my lips.

"Oh, Margaret Ann," she says. "You look beautiful. Do you have a boyfriend?"

"Yes, she does," Courtney says before I can loosen my lips to speak. "She has the handsomest boyfriend in the whole school."

"He'll love you even more when he sees you in makeup, Margaret Ann. Here, look in the mirror."

She runs over to the suitcase she still hasn't unpacked and takes out this real pretty silver-backed looking glass. It's

amazing how many things she's got packed in that one suitcase. But then I guess that's everything she has in the world.
Imagine having to pack up everything you own in one suitcase. For a minute I look straight in her face, wondering
where she comes from in the first place. Wondering how
she ever met Johnny. Wondering how she can know she
loves him when she never saw him till two weeks before the
wedding. But she doesn't look at me. She keeps her eyes on
the looking glass she sticks in front of my face.

"Now. What do you think?" she asks.

I can't believe my eyes. I do look good. You can notice
my eyes more than usual. And my nose doesn't look nearly
as big.

"Hey, I look good," I say.

"Go get your hairbrush and brush your hair while I do
Courtney," she tells me.

When I go to the other bedroom to get my hairbrush,
I'm glad Aunt Mary Lee isn't there. Because when I look in
the big glass over the dresser, I'm not so sure about this. I
know Grandma Motley would be horrified. And Daddy
would tell me to wash my face. I look again. I turn from one
side to the other. And it isn't a movie starlet I look like. It's
Frances Lowe. I brush my hair quickly so I can see what
Vivian is doing to Courtney.

"Come in here, Margaret Ann, and look at Courtney,"
Vivian says. "She's the prettiest girl I ever saw. She really

does look like a movie star. You better watch out, Margaret Ann. She's going to take your boyfriend away from you."

"No," Courtney says. "Nobody could ever take Bobby from Margaret. I tried. Before Margaret and I became best friends. Isn't that true?"

She looks at me and smiles.

"What? Is it true that we're best friends or that you can't take Bobby Holland?"

"Both."

"Well, it's true we're best friends," I say, and I mean it.

"Then what are you going to do when the war is over?" Vivian asks.

It strikes me for the first time. What am I going to do? Joyce has another best friend now, Mary Anna Jordan. And anyway, nobody's like Courtney. She knows all about geography, and history, and paintings, and music. Nobody else has been to all those places in France and Germany and Spain. And nobody else will be my roommate, whether we sleep on a pallet on the floor or in Johnny's bed, or wherever.

"Gosh, Courtney, what are we going to do? When the war's over, I mean."

"You'll come to see me in London. And I will come back here. Maybe every year. In the summertime."

"Oh, gosh," I say.

I don't think I'm really crying. Anyway, I don't think anybody would have noticed except for the makeup on my eyes. But I end up with black streaks running down my cheeks. It takes me half an hour to get enough of Vivian's cold cream on my face to take it all off.

Vivian seems to like Courtney and me better than anybody else in the family. She's always calling us into her bedroom for something. She shows us all her copies of *Movie Mirror* and magazines that have the words of all the popular songs. Courtney and I sit on the bed, and Vivian stands in front of the window and sings and sometimes does some dance steps. I'm afraid she's jiggling the baby too much, but she says it's okay.

Courtney and I don't ask her any questions. I think we're scared of what we might find out. But gradually she tells us everything.

"You see," she says, "I just knew I could be a movie star. I'm pretty. And I can sing. And I just love dancing. So . . . now, don't you girls tell a single soul. Not even Johnny knows this. But I ran off from home. I grew up in a small town in Kansas. And I promised myself I would never live in a small town again."

"So, then, maybe you should try living on a farm. I wouldn't want to live in town, large or small," I say.

Just then I hear a tractor motor and I walk to the window to see who it is. I'm beginning to think a tractor motor sounds different when Bobby Holland is driving it. Or maybe I just feel different when he's close by.

"I want to live on a farm," I say. "For the rest of my life. With dogs and books. And I'll be happy as a lark."

"Well, I won't. And I'm not going to do it. I told Johnny Motley the first day I saw him that farming was out."

"You mean you knew you were going to get married the first day you met him?" I ask.

"Oh, yes. It was so romantic. I was entertaining at a USO dance. I'll never forget it. I was singing 'Somewhere over the Rainbow,' and Johnny came up to the bandstand and just stood there looking at me. I never felt that way before or since. I just knew he was the man I would love forever."

I look at Courtney, and both of us have to fight real hard to keep from laughing.

"So when I finished the song, I walked right over to him and introduced myself. And that was it. An hour later he proposed and I accepted."

"You did?" Courtney says. "I cannot imagine such a thing."

I can't either, but I don't trust myself to talk. And just as soon as we can manage, we excuse ourselves and go downstairs.

"Dog pen," I whisper.

And we take off. I'm sure all the dogs think we're crazy. But we laugh and shriek for ten minutes before we can stop.

. . .

When September comes and we start back to school, it's a glorious day. We're so glad to get away from home. Because no matter where we go in the house, Vivian finds us and says she's bored. Then she invites us up to her bedroom, and we feel obligated to go. And once she gets us inside with the door closed, she starts telling us all about the further adventures of Vivian and Johnny. If Mama and Aunt Mary Lee had known some of the stuff she told us, they would have fainted.

So the days go by, and Vivian still hasn't had the baby, and she's still asking us into her bedroom every afternoon the minute we get home from school. Mama and Aunt Mary Lee are getting worried. Of course Vivian has already said she wants to have the baby in a hospital, so that's all planned out. But when on earth is she going to have it?

Every few days she starts with these terrible pains that last no more than twenty minutes. Then she's dancing again.

Grandma Motley still hasn't spoken a word to Vivian, but says plenty when she's not around. Usually it's in the kitchen, where she corners Mama and cuts loose.

"There's something wrong with that girl. I knew it from the moment I saw her. All I can say is that I hope she hasn't fooled our Johnny. He's a good boy, but he tends to be a bit gullible. Believes everything he's told. I have always noticed that."

Mama just stands and looks at her, not saying a word. It's Elizabeth who finally comes to the rescue.

"Grandma, there is nothing wrong with Vivian. She's a very kind person. It's just a different world we live in nowadays. People don't do things the way they used to. You'll have to get used to it."

"Indeed I do not have to get used to it. I have no intention of changing my actions or my feelings."

"Well, heaven knows I've had to change. And I might as well take this time to tell you my news: I'm getting a job in Smithfield. And I'll probably move to town and get an apartment as soon as I save up some money. Mrs. Gray says she'll be glad to keep little Tommy till he's old enough to go to school. All I have to do is drive him out here every morning before I go to work."

"You mean to tell me you're going to wake that child up at the crack of dawn and drive him five miles out in the country to spend the day where he ought to be living already? I have never heard of such a thing."

"Grandma, I have to think of my future and little Tommy's future. I need to be able to support myself . . . and him."

"Well, I hope you don't starve to death is all I can say. As to living in an apartment in Smithfield, where would you find such a thing?"

Grandma is so mad her cheeks are bulging out and she's red as a beet.

"There are several widows who are renting out their upstairs. And that's what they're calling it. An apartment. I've looked at a couple of them and they're nice. They have two bedrooms, a kitchen and a living room."

"Where do you propose to eat?

"In the kitchen. We eat in the kitchen when there's no company here."

"Well, don't expect me to eat in somebody's upstairs bedroom they're calling a kitchen. I don't intend to set my foot up there if you choose to do such a thing."

"Well, that is perfectly fine with me," Elizabeth tells her, and walks out the door.

For quite a while after that Grandma completely stops talking about Vivian. It's Elizabeth and her job as secretary at Batten's Plumbing Shop she talks about. Plus what a crazy thing it is to rent an apartment to live in when she has a perfectly good place to stay at the Grays'.

But Grandma does love little Tommy. All of us do. He won't even be a year old until January and he can already say words. The funny thing is that Vivian doesn't like little Tommy a bit. She treats him just about like Grandma Motley treats her. She never speaks to him when he's visiting, and every time, just after he leaves, she accuses him of messing up something in her bedroom. But I don't know how she could even tell. She's the messiest person I've ever seen. Even Sallie says so.

But there's something that keeps me from saying anything bad about her. Even to Courtney. It's because I still blame myself for Johnny joining the navy. It's true that by now he'd have been drafted into the army, but then he wouldn't have been a sailor in a USO canteen in Los Angeles and met Vivian.

One Saturday morning, Mama sends me upstairs to Grandma's room with some clean laundry to put away. Grandma is sitting in her rocking chair with her eyes closed, holding her Bible on her knees. I put her underwear in the drawer and am tiptoeing out in hopes she is so deep in prayer she'll never know I'm there. I keep my eyes on her face as I walk backward toward the door. And just as I get there, she opens her eyes.

"I've been meaning to talk to you, Margaret Ann," she says. "Close the door."

I close the door, but otherwise I don't move a muscle.

"Step closer," she says.

"Yes, ma'am?"

"There's something wrong with you and I want to know what it is. You won't say boo to a duck these days. Are you sick?"

"No, ma'am. I'm not sick."

"What is it, then? You've changed completely. Walking around here just as lifeless."

"I'm trying to help Mama. I'm trying to be what all of you always wanted me to be."

"Well, don't. I don't like it."

"I don't think you like anything, Grandma Motley. I don't think anyone in the world could act to suit you."

"Now," she says, smiling, "that's the old Margaret Ann."

I'm not at all sure I want to be the old Margaret Ann. The old Margaret Ann wasn't nearly as happy as the new me. If there really is a new me. But right this minute I don't feel like explaining it. So I just say thank you and start for the door. Just as I have my hand on the doorknob and am twisting it, Grandma says one more thing and it stuns me.

"You know," she says, "you always were my favorite."

In the middle of September, one of Bobby Holland's married brothers is drafted into the army. In the beginning of the war, married men weren't drafted. But now everybody says there's no choice. More and more gold stars are hanging in the windows of people's living rooms. And that means a serviceman, just like Tommy Gray, has been killed. It means a lot of mothers and wives are crying all over the country.

Another thing it means is that Bobby Holland has to help his own daddy part of the time.

"If I could have Bobby Holland every day, I could make it," Daddy says. "But we have got some acres to harvest. I don't see any way Junius and I can do it all by ourselves."

During this time when Daddy is trying to decide how in the world he can get the crops harvested, there's an article in the *Smithfield Times* that says farmers can get two British sailors to live with them for two weeks and help with harvesting. It's the same two weeks the schools are let out. The thing is, if we get them, which bedroom can we possibly put them in?

Grandma absolutely refuses to have any of us sleeping with her. So that means more pallets. Vivian insists that Courtney and I sleep in her room, and Aunt Mary Lee says she'd just love to have the twins. Which shows how good Aunt Mary Lee really is. Anybody who would love to have the twins sleeping in the same room with them is a living saint.

So we sign up to get some sailors, and Daddy drives to town on a Sunday afternoon to pick them up from the county agent's office. Courtney and I are sitting on the front porch, waiting, when they get back.

"Girls," Daddy calls to us, "this is Jim Derbyshire and Dick Gregory. Come say hello."

I mumble something about how glad I am to meet them and keep on rocking, but Courtney walks quickly down the steps and shakes their hands, one after the other.

"It's wonderful to see someone from home," she says.

"Home? You're from England?" the one named Jim asks.

"Yes, I am. I've mostly lived in London, but Grandmother and Grandfather live in York. Where are you from?"

"I live on the prettiest farmland in Derbyshire. Just like my name. And don't I miss it. I can hardly wait to get my hands in real dirt again."

"We've got plenty of it," Daddy says. "What about you, Dick? You live on a farm at your home?"

"No, sir. I'm straight out of the coal mines. I was never clean a day in my life till I joined the navy. But I don't mind a little bit of dirt from the colonies."

We all laugh at that. A little too much, I think, because we're all a bit uneasy. Except for Courtney. She keeps right on asking them questions until Daddy breaks in and asks if the boys would like some refreshments.

"I never turn down an offer of food," Jim says.

When the four of them get to the porch steps, I get up and I shake the sailors' hands just like Courtney. But for some reason I feel foolish. Like it isn't really me standing there. Like there's something terribly wrong. And when I look at Courtney, I figure it out. And I get a bad feeling in the pit of my stomach. It's almost like she's home in England while she's hearing them talk. And I don't want her to feel that way.

· · ·

After that first day, I get used to having Jim and Dick in the house. Daddy says they're good workers too, which is important, because everything needs digging or picking right then. Daddy and Bobby Holland—what little time he's here—and Sallie's husband, Junie, have been working as hard as they can, but they're behind on everything.

Monday things go fine. The men work from daylight till long after dark. But by the time Daddy gets in the field on Tuesday morning, we have to ring the dinner bell to call him home, because Vivian thinks maybe she needs to go to the hospital.

"I just don't know," she says. "I think it hurts, but, then, I can't really be sure. My gosh, I never had a baby before."

"Well, that's good news," Grandma Motley says. Right out where Vivian can hear her.

"If a woman can't tell when her baby's coming, I'd scratch her right off my list."

Of course, poor Vivian has never been on Grandma's list. But I think Daddy's list is shortening too.

"Look here," Daddy says. You can tell he's really mad. "Don't call me to the house until she's ready to step in the car with her suitcase. I need to be in the field. Bobby Holland's just as good as any man in running a farm. But it's not fair to ask him to teach those British boys how to harvest like we do, and keep the machinery running, and make all these decisions just because Vivian doesn't know if she's having the baby or not."

Courtney looks at me and we grin.

"As good as any man," she whispers.

I nod my head.

"Exactly."

By this time everybody likes Jim and Dick. Not just Courtney. Of course, we females don't get to see them much. Mostly they're working in the field or else sleeping. At mealtime all the men eat at a table on the porch, because they don't have time to change clothes or anything. And harvesting is dirty work. Even their eyelashes are fringed with dust. I think it makes Bobby Holland's eyes even prettier.

Courtney and I help Sallie serve the food. She's standing over the cookstove frying chicken or ham slices or pork chops, while we're carting out platter after platter. But once during every meal, Jim calls her out to the porch to compliment the food and she beams and smiles.

"Sallie," Jim says. "You could cook for the finest eatery in London. Not that I ever ate a bite of food in London. But them that has says it's good eating. What do you say, Courtney? You ever eat in a fine place like that in London?"

"Not often," she says. "Mostly I was left at home with one of the maids."

"Pretty posh, huh?"

"Yeah, Jim," Aunt Mary Lee calls out from the kitchen. "Pretty posh. But don't hold it against us. We like Sallie's food much better. Right, Courtney?"

Courtney smiles and nods.

Vivian spends most of the time in her bedroom trying to decide whether the baby is coming or not. I think the real reason she doesn't want to see Jim and Dick is because she's so bulgy. I know I wouldn't want to be seen if I looked like that. But she doesn't eat hot buttered toast and tea like Grandma Motley. She's as hungry as the men in the fields. Courtney and I are running up and down the stairs all day with trays of bread and preserves and canned peaches with whipped cream. She even eats a piece of old fruitcake Sallie finds in the pantry.

Jim keeps asking about her.

"I sure wish that baby would hurry and get here," he says. Several times a day. "I'd sure like to see the little thing before we go."

And then he tells us about his two children back in England.

"They're growing up," he says. "And all I have is a picture or two. They won't even know me when this bloody war is finally over."

"Yes, they will," Courtney says. "I'm sure of it."

. . .

The baby is finally born early on Friday morning of the second week the boys are here. About eleven o'clock that Thursday night, everybody in the house knows it's on its way. Vivian is screaming at the top of her lungs. Of course, Courtney and I are right there in the room with her. And as it happens, Vivian hasn't packed her suitcase ahead of time like she's supposed to. So Courtney and I have to do it while Mama gets a decent gown and bathrobe on her. We're wide awake by the time Daddy has hauled her down the stairs and into the car.

"Want to get in Vivian's bed?" I ask Courtney.

"Yes," she says. "Even if it's only for one night. A real bed. How long has it been since we slept in a real bed?"

"I don't even remember."

Vivian's sheets smell just like her perfume. And somehow it keeps me awake. Or maybe all that screaming gets me to thinking about having babies and how hard it might be. But people have to do it. There have to be more people. And then I get to thinking about how much mothers love their children . . . and about all the boys who are dying in the war . . . and how sad their mothers must be. And then I get to thinking about how much longer this war is going to last. And how if it lasts a few more years, Bobby Holland will have to go into the army or the navy. Or the marines, which is even more dangerous. And then I get to thinking how it will be if I join the WACs or the WAVES. I can see myself in one of those uniforms. I wonder what Bobby Holland will say about my being a WAC or a WAVE. After that there's no way I'm going to get back to sleep.

Daddy drives in around daybreak. Mama is staying at the hospital to help look after Vivian.

"It's a girl," he says. "And Vivian named her Joanna Vivienne Motley. That's the way she wants it spelled. And we have to pronounce it funny like that too. Vivienne. And do you know why? Because there is no doubt in her mind, she says, that the baby will grow up to be a movie star."

"Well," I say, "that sounds pretty good for the next generation of Motleys, don't you think? A movie star and the president of the United States."

Daddy starts laughing so hard he can't even say, "Aye, Lord."

Vivian stays in the hospital for a week, so Jim and Dick never get to see the baby. They have to go back to their ship late on Saturday afternoon. We're all sad to tell them good-bye.

"Now, Bobby Holland," Jim says as they're getting in the car with Daddy. "I want you and Margaret there to come to England when you're grown and see how we farm in Derbyshire. When the war's over, that is. And Courtney, maybe I'll come up to London with my wife and take you to one of those posh eateries. And we'll let Dick come too if he promises to wash his hands."

Dick nods and holds out his hand and we shake.

"We'll see you again," he says. "And be sure to bring Sallie, too."

Bobby and Courtney and I stand there waving as long as we can see the car through the cedars.

"I doubt we'll ever see them again," Bobby Holland says. "And I expect there's plenty more we won't see besides."

"Don't talk like that," I say. "I don't like to even think about it."

"I don't like to think about it either. But I can't help myself. It just comes to my mind."

Of course he's thinking about his brother Charlie. And I get to thinking about Johnny. What if he never sees his new baby?

"Well," Courtney says, "that's that. Let's get our minds on something else. It doesn't help anyone to think about what might happen."

"You're right," I say. "Come on. Let's see if there's a crumb or two left of that jam cake Sallie made."

The twins move back to their room that afternoon, but Courtney and I sleep in Vivian's bed until the day she comes home. Then we move our pallets back to Aunt

Mary Lee's room, so we're all settled in when Mama and Daddy get home with Vivian and the baby.

Grandma is standing on the front porch between Courtney and me, watching with her hawk eyes, when they drive up to the front door. Mama is holding the baby and Daddy is helping Vivian.

"Who does she look like?" Grandma says right out loud. "Here, let me look at her."

Mama pulls the blanket down from her face and holds her so we can see.

"She favors Johnny," Grandma says. "That's a relief."

When Bobby Holland gets out of the field, he comes to the house to see the baby.

"How can you get word to Johnny?" he asks.

"Aunt Mary Lee says the Red Cross can help with things like that."

"Reckon he'll mind that it's not a boy?"

"Bobby Holland, what a terrible thing to say. As if that could make any difference," I say.

I look down at the baby sleeping in the bassinet. She doesn't have much hair, but what's there is dark brown. And her eyes are dark too. Like Johnny's.

"She doesn't look much like you, Miss Vivian," Bobby says. "Your hair is about as yellow as I ever saw."

By this time all of us in the house are well acquainted

with the peroxide bottle. But I never told Bobby Holland.

"Well," says Vivian, who is lying in her bed like she's too weak to move a muscle, "I still think she looks just like me. And I know Johnny would like that."

"Yeah," Bobby Holland says, "but he'd like a boy better."

If Johnny wants a boy, he sure doesn't say so. The next time Vivian gets a letter from him, she reads every word of it to Courtney and me. He writes for a whole paragraph about how much he's hoping the baby has blond hair like Vivian. So Johnny doesn't know about Vivian's hair either. Maybe only girls know things like that. And maybe there's a lot more Johnny doesn't know about Vivian. What's going to happen when this terrible war is over, and he finds out?

Part Three

With Aunt Mary Lee

Christmas this year isn't all bad. At least not for me. When Bobby Holland comes to see me Christmas Eve afternoon, I know right away what he's holding in his hand. Mistletoe. I don't turn my face away either. First he gives me a silver necklace to match my identification bracelet, and then he kisses me. Standing in the front hall, as close to the door as we can get so nobody will see us. He doesn't touch me with his hands. He touches my lips with his, like he's trying out a new flavor of candy or something. Like he isn't sure he's going to like it. But I sure like it. I decide I want him to kiss me every day, three times a day maybe, as long as I live.

Grandma Motley catches us, though.

"What is this?" she says. "Kissing downstairs in the front hall? I've never heard of such a thing. In my day a couple never kissed at all until the engagement was announced. Let's have no more of this."

"Yes, ma'am," Bobby says.

So then he turns back to me and I know he meant to say, "See you later." But what he says is, "Kiss you later, Margaret Ann."

Grandma Motley laughs right out loud. And she tells Aunt Mary Lee, and Mama and Daddy, and Elizabeth, and Sallie. Everybody in the house she's speaking to. It keeps her laughing straight through till she goes to bed. By Christmas morning she's forgotten it, of course.

Vivienne, as Vivian insists on pronouncing it, gets a few things in her stocking, but I have to say, Vivian isn't nearly as excited about her daughter's presents as she is about a ruby ring that comes in the mail from Johnny. We have no idea how he's able to send it to her, but it comes. And she looks at her hand all day. And talks about how Johnny has promised her she's never going to have to ruin her hands with washing dishes.

Daddy doesn't much enjoy his Christmas dinner, but at least he doesn't leave the table till he's done.

New Year's of 1944 comes in without any of us watching for it. And the year seems to slip by without us watching it either. In the spring, for the first time, I don't need to let my dress hems down. I haven't grown an inch. Grandma says I never will grow any taller. "But if you don't watch how you eat, you may grow broader," she says.

It's strange to think that when I choose a new dress or coat, I better really know I like it, because I'll have to wear it a long time. Especially if the war keeps going. But I don't think I have to worry about growing broader. I still eat like a horse, and just the other day Bobby Holland gets his hands to meet around my waist. Of course he has to squeeze like crazy. I'm still not as tiny as Mama and Elizabeth.

I'm growing up, and our country is growing up too. All the fighting and dying is changing how we feel about everything. Men are used to driving old cars and not having enough gas to go where they want. They roll their own cigarettes too, the ones who smoke. Women are used to having runs in their hose. You can't buy new ones, so it's okay. Other things are more important.

And it seems like America is going to have to look after the rest of the world from now on. I wonder if it will be like Mama, not saying much, but really doing everything people need. Or will it be like Grandma Motley? Talking . . . talking . . . saying what she will do, what she has done, but not doing a blessed thing.

As for myself, I can't decide how fast I want to grow up. I want to be free to do whatever I like. On the other hand, I don't want all the responsibilities. But it seems like I don't have a choice. My birthdays are clicking by. In June I'm going to be fifteen. Mama says I can have dates if anybody asks me.

"After all, Margaret Ann, you're little Tommy and Vivienne's aunt."

Think of it. Two little people who weren't even alive when the war started. And think of all the people we know nowadays. People we'd never have met except for the war.

Grandma Motley is changing too. She's gotten shorter and skinnier as Courtney and I've gotten taller. And her face is wrinkly as a turkey gobbler. Aunt Mary Lee finally convinced her to see a doctor. He tells Grandma she's fine, but he tells Aunt Mary Lee and Mama these spells she's been having are really small strokes. "At her age," he says, "you can expect a big one anytime. There's nothing to be done about it, so I think it best to say nothing to her." So we don't say a word. We let her go on just like she always has, talking by the hour. But every time she stares, or blinks, or says her hands feel numb, I expect the worst.

Another thing that's changed is Paige and Polly and the way I see them. I guess it starts in the summer of 1944. Mama doesn't have enough matching feed bags to make dresses for them. And it's almost impossible to buy enough dress goods. So Polly has a green flowered dress and Paige has a yellow one. And I find I can tell them apart, just like Courtney does.

Then it occurs to me to ask the question, why couldn't I

tell them apart before? Courtney could almost from the second she met them. I decide it's because I didn't really look at them. They were a nuisance to me. I never wanted them around. But now I see them as two separate girls. Each has a way of speaking, of expressing herself. Paige turns her head slightly to the left every time she says my name. And Polly sticks her tongue out between sentences.

Besides this, they're no longer interested in exactly the same things. Polly loves reading. She borrows all my books and laughs and cries over them, just like I used to. Paige is learning to play the piano. She asks Aunt Mary Lee to teach her. And Paige can sing really pretty, whereas Polly can barely carry a tune. It's a miracle.

There are a lot of miracles actually. Some of them are sad, but they help me to understand more about life than happier things would. Take Joanne Cox's brother, for example.

Just like Johnny, he's stationed on a destroyer, only he's an officer. Joanne brags about it all the time. "My brother is an ensign, you know," she says at least once a day. Well, one day his ship is blown up and sunk by a kamikaze pilot. When I hear it, it's like Tommy Gray gets killed all over again. I can hear Tommy's voice, the way he used to tease me about Bobby Holland. I'd never said a word to Joanne's brother in my life. I have no idea how his voice sounded, but I remember how he looked. Blond, curly hair and blue eyes. I can see him just as plain.

At first I can't look at Joanne. But then I remember what Courtney said when Uncle Walter was missing in action. And so I make myself do it. I go to Joanne after English class one day and I say, "Joanne, I'm sorry about your brother."

She looks at me like she's shocked. I think I've made her angry, so I start to walk away. But then she reaches out and touches my arm.

"Thank you, Margaret Ann. It means a lot to know somebody remembers him."

We talk all the way to algebra class about things I remember. And while we are never close friends after this, Joanne and I understand each other. Joanne is changed and I'm changed by all that happens in the war. In fact, she invites Courtney and me to a Christmas party later that year. And we go. The funny thing is that her mother serves ham biscuits—not big floppy ones, like Sallie makes, but tiny, delicate ones that taste delicious. So Paige and Polly knew what the elegant thing was all along.

Everybody says the spring of 1945 has a different feeling to it. And what we don't say, because we're almost afraid to believe it, is that things are winding down. In the Pacific, all during 1944, American troops have been capturing one set of islands right after the other. Islands with names like Saipan and Guam and Peleliu. Old Mr. Gray, Tommy Gray's grandfather, just shakes his head whenever anybody at church mentions the wonderful victories. Sometimes he whispers, "The boys . . . the boys . . ." And we know he's talking about all the American marines and soldiers and sailors that are dying for each one of these victories.

Of course, it's exciting when General MacArthur returns to the Philippines, just like he said he would. And then there's an island called Iwo Jima. And that is too horrible to even imagine. In less than a month's fighting, almost seven thousand of our boys are killed, and close to twenty thousand are wounded.

In April, U.S. marines and soldiers land on an island called Okinawa, and that's even worse than Iwo Jima. Besides all the troops who die fighting on the island, five thousand sailors, boys just like Johnny, are killed by the kamikazes. The planes keep coming in wave after wave. That's how the newspapers say it. I think about waves and how I looked at the pictures in my geography book the day the Japanese attacked Pearl Harbor. And I think about the waves at Virginia Beach. The year I was ten, Daddy took our whole family to Virginia Beach, and we stayed the night and went swimming in the ocean.

The first day when we get there, the waves are crashing in along the beach. I can hardly stand up. Mama has to hold my hand. But the next morning they're no more than a ripple. Johnny and I walk way out and swim back to where Mama and Daddy are waiting for us with the twins.

I've never forgotten those waves, the way they kept coming and coming. One day tall as houses and the next a ripple. The war is like that. It keeps coming and coming. Sometimes crashing on the beach and sometimes only a ripple. Until, in the midst of all this fighting in the Pacific, there really is an ending. On April 12, Franklin D. Roosevelt dies.

We get home from school to find Mama and Aunt Mary Lee in the living room listening to the radio.

"What's going to happen?" I ask. "How can the war get won without him?"

"I surely hope Mr. Truman can carry on," says Aunt Mary Lee.

And he does. Daddy even says Truman is doing a good job. Soon the waves of kamikaze attacks end. Our troops take Okinawa. And then we don't hear much that's new. But we listen. And we wait.

On the twenty-ninth of April, a part of the waiting is over for Aunt Mary Lee and Courtney. Allied soldiers liberate the prison camp at Moosburg. There are 100,000 men there and Uncle Walter is one of them. They fly him back to England right away, and I think it's harder than ever for Aunt Mary Lee to be here in Virginia with us.

On May 7, the Germans surrender to the Allies. The day we hear it, Aunt Mary Lee kind of loses her senses for a while. We're all in the kitchen when Daddy comes back from town and tells us the news. Aunt Mary Lee sticks her head in the kitchen sink and gets her hair all wet.

"For the Lord's sake, Mary Lee, what are you doing?" Daddy asks her.

"I don't know, John. I really don't know. I think I was planning to swim the Atlantic."

Everybody is laughing, but I just can't. I sneak out the back door and go down to the dog pens. I have to get my thoughts together. I know I'm glad for Uncle Walter to be liberated from the prison camp. But I also know this means that Aunt Mary Lee and Courtney will be getting on a ship someday soon to go back to England. I don't like to even think of it. Courtney will want to go, but all I can think of is how much I want her to stay.

Aunt Mary Lee decides to stay in Virginia until Courtney gets out of school, which will be the end of the first week in June. I try not to think about it. Just enjoy what you have, I tell myself. But it's hard. Aunt Mary Lee is constantly telling us about her plans. Worrying about whether she's going to find a ship leaving out of New York or whether she'll find one leaving Hampton Roads. She and Uncle Walter send telegrams back and forth across the ocean.

One day while all this is going on, Vivian gets a letter from someone other than Johnny. From the first I can tell she wants to talk about it. And sure enough, the very next morning she calls Courtney and me into her bedroom, closes the door, and whispers the whole thing.

"I don't know what to do," she says. "I thought maybe you girls would help me decide about whether I should answer this letter."

She extends it in our general direction, but I won't take it, so Courtney has to. I can see that it's addressed to Mrs. Johnny Motley.

"Read it, Courtney," she says. "I love the way your voice sounds with that English accent. You ought to be in the movies."

"No, thank you," Courtney says. "But I'll read it if you want me to."

"If you please," Vivian answers.

"Dear Sara—"

"Who's Sara?" I blurt out.

"That's me. I mean, it's my real name. I only use Vivian because I think it sounds like a movie star. You know Vivien Leigh, don't you?"

"But, Vivian, does that mean you're not really married to Johnny? I would think if you use a phony name, it'll be a phony marriage."

"Oh my God. Do you suppose I'm not married? And here I've got a baby and everything."

"I have no idea," I say. "But it's something to think about.

Anyway, go on and read, Courtney. I won't say another word."

"Dear Sara,

"How joyful we were to receive your letter telling us your whereabouts. When you first left home, we searched the county and then the state of Kansas. We were sure you were lying dead somewhere. We could not believe that you would run off and leave us.

"But all is forgiven, Sara. If only you and your baby will come home to us, we will ask no questions and you will have all of our love. Just as you had three years ago when we last saw you.

"We are enclosing a bus ticket from the town of Smithfield, Virginia, to Elmo, Kansas. Please come soon. There have been many changes, most of them for the better.

"We love you,

"Mother"

All the time Courtney is reading, I'm watching Vivian's face. The way her eyes brighten when she hears her name. And how her lips form the words as Courtney pronounces them. But when Courtney finishes, when the mystery of Vivian's family is finally solved, I look away. I'm seeing more than I want to know. I mean, think of it. Three years she has been away from her family. What was she doing all alone in Los Angeles before she met Johnny? Where had she been living? How did she get money to buy food? I know she's just stupid enough to tell me if I ask her, but now, more than ever, I don't want to know.

"So, girls, what do you think?"

I look over at little Vivienne sitting on the floor chewing on a rattle. She smiles up at me and makes little bubbles that drool off down her dress front. She's so beautiful.

"I mean, do you think I should go home? After all, they did send a bus ticket. And I would be that much closer to California when Johnny gets back in port."

"Families shouldn't be separated if it can be prevented," Courtney says.

"That's true," I say. "Except it's too late to think of that. If you take the baby from Mama, then that's separating a family."

"Oh, I hadn't thought of that. Aunt Emily will be devastated if you take the baby away."

"But what about my mother? She's sad. You can tell from the letter that she misses me."

"It's a bit late to think of that," I say.

And then I can see Courtney tense up a little bit. I know her so well now that I can almost read her mind. She never wants to hurt anybody's feelings. Sometimes I think she's more like Mama and I'm more like Aunt Mary Lee. So I backtrack.

"What I mean to say is that it's a bit late in the afternoon to think about going anywhere."

"But you won't hate me if I go, will you?"

"Of course not," Courtney says.

I let it stand at that. I'm thinking about Mama. I walk over to where Vivienne is sitting, and right away she holds her little china-doll arms out to me.

"May I hold her, Vivian?" I ask.

"Sure. You hold her all you want. Because I guess I'll be leaving tomorrow or the day after."

"That soon? Then you'd already decided before you asked our opinion."

"I guess I had. But don't say anything to your mothers. I'll find the best way to tell them. Now, if you girls can look after the baby, I'll start my packing. But I think I'll need another suitcase for the baby things."

The next morning at breakfast Vivian announces that she's going to leave on the two o'clock bus that afternoon. Mama just sits there at the kitchen table, staring at her.

"You can't mean it," she says.

"Yes, I do. I should have told you before, Mrs. Motley, but I was actually dreading it. I have a lot to confess to you. I have a mother and a father in Elmo, Kansas, and they want me to come home to them right away."

"Does Johnny know this?"

"No, Mrs. Motley, he doesn't. But I plan to write him all about it as soon as I get home to Kansas. I think he'll be glad. After all, I'll be a lot closer to California, if he gets back in port sometime."

"I don't know what to say."

"There's nothing to say, Mama. I don't think we can change Vivian's mind. So . . . why don't you spend the morning playing with the baby?"

"But there's so much to do. . . ."

"We'll do it, Emily Ruth," Aunt Mary Lee says. "You just go upstairs and get her."

"She's asleep," Vivian says.

"Then wake her. Go, Emily Ruth. I'll take care of everything. Vivian, you can have my small suitcase. I'll need to buy another one before we leave for England. And Courtney and Margaret Ann can help with the packing. And the twins can help by picking some vegetables for Sallie to cook."

When Daddy comes home for dinner, he is so shocked he just turns around and walks back out the door. Then I think he gets mad. He doesn't even tell Vivian and the baby goodbye. I don't think he can. So Aunt Mary Lee drives Vivian and the baby, and Courtney and me, to Turner and Griffin Service Station to meet the bus. When it comes, we manage to get them in a seat, and then we go back to stand on the sidewalk. All I can see and all I can think of are Vivienne's little china-doll arms. She's stretching them out toward the window like she's asking me to hold her. And it isn't only that. It's that I feel like Johnny is on that bus with them. And Vivian is taking him away too.

Aunt Mary Lee finally manages to get passage on a ship leaving at the end of the second week in June. That means two days after the box supper at church, they'll be getting on the train in Suffolk to go to New York City. The day after that they'll leave on a ship for England.

Bobby Holland tells me that James Whitley has been dying to ask Courtney for a date for a long time. Finally he gets the nerve to ask her. They're double-dating with Bobby Holland and me, since Bobby can drive. I know Courtney isn't particularly interested in James. He isn't handsome like Bobby, but he's as funny as any comedian on the radio. I feel like I can use some jokes.

Sallie fixes a box supper for me and one for Courtney. Nobody is supposed to know whose box is whose, but Sallie ties my box with a blue ribbon and Courtney's with yellow.

"I don't want those boys wasting their money buying some other girls' food," she says.

She tells Bobby Holland about it, so he and James can bid on the right box and get to eat with us. That's how box suppers work. The highest bidder gets to eat with the girl who fixes the box.

Bobby Holland doesn't have any trouble with mine. He

gets it for exactly fifty-nine cents. But lots of boys want to eat with Courtney, and somehow the word about the yellow ribbon gets around.

"I had exactly fifteen cents left in my pocket when the bidding was over," James says. "All I can say is I hope it's worth two dollars and twenty-two cents to eat with you, Courtney Liveley."

"Sallie's fried chicken is worth every penny," Courtney says.

Bobby Holland and I and Courtney and James take our boxes of fried chicken and ham sandwiches and potato salad and caramel cake down to some wooden benches by the cemetery gate. But I can't keep my mind off what I'm going to do when Courtney is gone.

"Hey, Margaret Ann, why aren't you laughing at my jokes?" James asks me.

"What jokes?"

"Shall I tell it again?" he asks.

"It wouldn't do any good," Bobby Holland says. "Margaret Ann's got her mind on something else. She hasn't heard a word I've said in two weeks."

"That's not true," I tell him.

"It's true," he says. "But I'll just wait it out. I've waited out plenty before."

Bobby grabs my hand and smiles.

"Hey," he says. "You want to drive us home tonight?"

"I do if Mama and Daddy aren't looking."

"Wait a minute here," James says. "I want to live to get home."

"Don't worry. Margaret Ann can drive. I teach her every chance I get."

"Not with me in the car you don't," James tells him.

So I don't drive home, but having Bobby offer lets me know he understands how I feel about Courtney.

Courtney and I are back in Johnny's bedroom, so we have a place to talk when we get home that night.

"And," I say, "what do you think of James Whitley?"

"He's nice. But he isn't Bobby Holland."

"What do you mean by that?"

"I mean you're a very lucky girl, Margaret Ann. I only hope that I'll find someone as gentle and handsome and hard working when I get back to London."

Back to London. It won't be much longer.

The last day Aunt Mary Lee and Courtney are with us is terrible. Every time I start to say something, I stop, because I know I'll cry. Finally I write it all down and hand it to Courtney to read.

"Dear Courtney,
    There is so much I want to tell you and I can't get the

words out. For one thing, I know it's really wrong of me to be glad there was a war so I could meet you. And I don't really mean that. I wish there had been another way that we could have known each other. But the war happened, and it gave us the chance. For that I will be grateful as long as I live. You have changed my life. You have taught me so many things. I could almost say that you have opened my eyes to the world. I might never go to all those places, but I am aware of them. I have an idea of what is out there to see.

And because of you, I have come to know myself better. I can make decisions about what is really important to me. I know that I matter to people and so I must control my words and my actions. I think a lot of people hurt others simply because they don't know they can do it.

I will never forget you. You will always be my favorite cousin and my best friend.

Sincerely,

Margaret"

Courtney reads the letter and then she smiles.

"Oh, Margaret, I would be so sad to leave you that I don't know how I could manage, if it were not for seeing Father. And knowing how happy Mother will be when we're home at last. But you'll always be my favorite cousin and my best friend too."

She folds the letter and puts it in her dress pocket. And then she pats the pocket and smiles.

"When you and Bobby Holland get married in a few years, I expect to be a bridesmaid."

"Get married?" I whisper.

"You know, Margaret, that you are sure to marry him."

"Do you think so?"

"Of course. He'll never let you go."

"Or it might be the other way around."

We both laugh and hug and cry a little. Then Courtney takes my hand and starts pulling me toward the door.

"Come on," she says. "There's something that has to be done right this minute. I planned to do it tomorrow morning, but there might not be time."

I follow her down the stairs and out the front door without a question. But then she starts wandering around the yard like she's lost her mind or something.

"Courtney, what are you doing?"

"Never mind. Just follow me until I tell you to stop."

We come around the corner of the house and there stands Gladwin, stretching himself and licking his chops. He seems to be getting up from one of his numerous afternoon naps.

"Here," she says. "Stop right here beside Gladwin. Okay, give me your hand."

I look down at Gladwin. He's looking at me now and yawning.

"Stand still, both of you. It won't take long."

"What is this?"

"Just listen. I wrote the whole thing out, but then I lost it, so I'll just have to ad-lib."

"Ad-lib what?"

"Quiet. This is a solemn occasion. Margaret, do you take Gladwin to be your faithful dog, to feed him and take care of him, to train him to fetch sticks, and to keep him from jumping on Grandma till death do you part?"

"I do," I say solemnly. "But—"

"I'm not finished. Gladwin, do you take Margaret to be your new mistress, to love her and obey her, to stay out of the flower beds, and to look after Paige and Polly till death do you part?"

Gladwin yawns again, then wanders off across the yard.

"You tried, Courtney. And I will take care of him. Don't worry about that."

"I know," Courtney says. "It's just that I'm going to miss this farm, and all the family, and Gladwin. But most of all I'm going to miss you, Margaret Ann Motley."

"Me too," I say. "Miss you, I mean."

Our sorrow is lost on Gladwin. He comes wandering back and starts licking my fingers like he's eating a lollipop.

The only reason I'm able to say good-bye without crying is Grandma Motley. It's a good thing her tear ducts are dried up, else she'd never have made it through like a Motley.

"Oh, Mary Lee," she says, over and over. "Oh, my dear, dear girl."

And then she turns to Courtney.

"You must promise me to come back. Will you?"

She hugs them and holds their hands in hers. Grandma doesn't usually hug anybody. Not even if they are her favorites.

A few days after Courtney and Aunt Mary Lee leave, I'm so sad I can't seem to do anything right. I'm helping Sallie cook dinner, and I burn the ham slices. Then I drop the pitcher of iced tea on the back porch and break it. The tea runs all over the floor, under the table, under the chairs. So I have to get out the scrub mop and clean it up.

But then something happens that takes my mind off everything except Grandma. It's that stroke. The big one. We're all sitting on the front porch, shelling butter beans to cook for supper. She gets this funny look like she does, but then one side of her face goes rigid. And then she slumps back in the chair and the pan of beans slips off her lap and rolls across the floor.

"Margaret Ann," Mama says. "Go get your daddy. Take the car."

"You mean drive it? You mean me?"

"Of course, you. I know Bobby's been teaching you. Now go get your daddy."

I have to go inside to get the car keys, so I stop by the kitchen door to call Sallie.

"It's Grandma," I say. "Like the doctor told us. You know. The stroke."

"Lord Jesus," Sallie says.

She gets up quickly from the kitchen table and starts toward me, but I turn and am out the front door before she gets halfway down the hall. Paige and Polly are standing beside Mama, fanning Grandma as hard as their arms will go.

"Hurry, Margaret Ann," Mama says.

I open the screen door and jump way past the steps and the tree roots. I'm at the garage and in the car before Mama can say another word.

When I drive up to the field at the Crumpler place, Bobby Holland is just finishing up plowing a row, so he gets off the tractor and comes running.

"Are you crazy, Margaret Ann? Driving up here for your daddy to see? He's going to ask me if I've been letting you drive, and I can't lie to him. He's going to be so mad. Oh, God."

"Bobby, Mama told me to do it. It's Grandma. She's had a bad stroke. We've got to tell Daddy. Where is he?"

Bobby points off in the distance. In a few minutes I see the tractor. And then Daddy sees us. It doesn't take many minutes for him to get there.

"It's Grandma," I holler. "She's had that stroke the doctor was talking about. Mama needs you."

"I better go," he tells Bobby. "You see how much of this field you can finish before dark."

"Yes, sir."

We're halfway home when Daddy turns his head and looks at me.

"Were you driving this car, Margaret Ann?"

"Yes, sir."

"Ever done it before?"

"Not this car," I say.

"But you drive the Hollands' car. Right?"

"Yes, sir."

"It's a damn good thing."

That's all he says. Not another word passes between us before we get home.

Grandma is in the hospital for two weeks. At first the doctor tells us she's going to die. Day after day she just lies there, staring into space. Mama stays over in Newport News at the hospital all that time. Then one afternoon she calls and says Grandma is improving.

"She spoke a word. It was hard to understand because she can't move one side of her face, but she said 'home.' I just know it."

A week later they let Grandma leave the hospital. Daddy

carries her upstairs to her bedroom in his arms. When he starts toward the bed, she gets real nervous. With her good hand she points toward the chair, so Daddy sets her there. She looks around the room for the longest time. And she smiles. That is, half of her face smiles.

She motions to me and I'm pretty sure she calls me Mary Lee. I look at Daddy.

"What did she say?"

"She thinks you're your aunt Mary Lee," he says.

"But—"

"It would sure help her to think that."

"But then it would be like there's nobody named Margaret Ann."

"That's true. But maybe we can overlook certain things around here, such as you driving the Hollands' car."

We stare at each other a long time.

"Okay, Daddy. It's a deal."

After supper that night, Mama takes my hand and leads me up the back stairs.

"Now, let's talk things over. First I want to thank you for all you did to look after the twins and to help Sallie while I was gone."

"That's okay, Mama. I didn't really do so much."

"Yes, you did. Sallie says you were wonderful."

"Really?"

"Yes, really. So I was thinking about this. You can take your choice. You can stay where you are, in Johnny's room, or you can have Elizabeth's room. What do you think?"

We walk back and forth from room to room, holding hands, looking out of windows, poking at the beds to see which is more comfortable.

"I'll take Elizabeth's," I say. "Johnny's is larger, but I always dreamed of having this one. I always thought it was the best room in the house."

"Then it's yours, Margaret Ann. I promise I won't let anyone take this room away from you again."

Mama hugs me and goes back downstairs. I stand there in the quiet and think about Grandma. I haven't even asked if anyone has called Aunt Mary Lee. She and Courtney will be so upset.

It's terrible to be so far away from people you love.

I walk over to sit down on the bed, but I find I can't do it. Not with Grandma down the hall, smiling her half smile. And Courtney so far away. She says she'll take some pictures and send me. Maybe I'll send her some too. But before I do, I'll get this room fixed up. Just like it looked when Elizabeth was here. Maybe Elizabeth will teach me to sew. It isn't likely that I'll ever learn, but I really ought to try.

The summer days go by so slowly, I have the feeling someone has put more than twenty-four hours in them. We sit on the front porch in the afternoon. It's too hot to do anything else. And I read every book I own at least twelve times. Paige plays and sings the same songs over and over. And Bobby Holland is too tired to go on a date except for Saturday and Sunday night.

Then, on the sixth of August, a B-29 bomber called the *Enola Gay* drops an atomic bomb on Hiroshima in Japan. At first we have no idea what it means. Daddy says it's the most powerful explosion the world has ever seen. And the radio says thousands and thousands of people are killed. Three days later we drop another one on Nagasaki. Thousands more people are killed. When I think of it, I feel like I can't breathe.

"How could we do such a thing?" I ask Daddy.

"Sugar," he says, "I know it sounds terrible, but if it can save American boys—boys good as Tommy Gray was— then I say do it. Drop whatever bomb we have. We didn't start this war, but it looks like it's up to us to end it."

"I know, but—"

"Sugar, do you want your brother to die?"

"No. Of course not."

"Well, nobody else wants their brother to die either."

On the fourteenth, Japan surrenders. And by the time they sign the agreement on September 2, we're back in school. And happy as we all are that the war is over, it's a hard thing to go back to school without Courtney. And hard to be a senior. To know that in another year I have to make a decision about things more important than what room I'll sleep in. I think I want to go to college. Grandma's going to be happy if we can make her understand. But Bobby Holland isn't sure if he wants to go.

"I just want to farm," he tells me, "and I already know how to do that."

"Yes, but I want to know everything. I want to read every book in the world."

"Well, you can't do that, Margaret Ann. But if you want to go to college, it's okay with me. I'll be right here whenever you learn all you want to know."

"That will never happen, Bobby. I will always want to read another book."

"That's okay. Just say you won't go off like Johnny did and find somebody else."

"I promise you that. There will never be anyone to take your place."

"Okay, then."

But Elizabeth does find someone to take Tommy Gray's place and we're all glad of it. He's from Smithfield and gets to come back early to the U.S. because he flew fifty bombing raids over Europe. His girlfriend married someone else while he was gone, and Elizabeth says he's lonely. He works at the same place she does for a while, but then decides to go to college on the GI Bill. So Elizabeth is going to be Mrs. Sam Lawrence and move to Blacksburg so he can attend Virginia Polytechnic Institute. And Elizabeth says Sam really loves little Tommy.

"How could you help it?" I ask. "He's the sweetest child I ever saw. I don't think I can ever love a child the way I love him."

"You will," Elizabeth says. "Just you wait."

· December 1945 ·
Always,
Elizabeth's Room

J ohnny and Vivian, whose name is now Sara, come
home for Christmas in 1945, and they are now calling
the baby Joanna. I want to ask if they had to get married again using Vivian's real name, but before they get here,
Mama makes me promise I won't. Everything is so strange
after they arrive. Johnny isn't Johnny. I can just as easily call
him Charlie, or Percy, or any other name. He's losing his
hair and his eyes look different. But worst of all, he doesn't
play with the dogs. Or check on the cows. Or look at the
pictures of the new tractor we're getting.

Elizabeth and Sam and Tommy stay with his parents in
Smithfield, so we have plenty of room. And we have plenty
of sugar to make a fruitcake. And there's enough gasoline for
Bobby Holland to take me to the movie in Smithfield. And
to a party Joanne Cox is having on Christmas Eve. After
that, while we're sitting in his car underneath the maple

trees, Bobby gives me the prettiest ring I've ever seen. It has my birthstone in it. And it fits my finger just perfect.

"How did you know what size to get?" I ask him.

"I know everything about you," he says, then laughs. "About your hands, anyway."

This time he doesn't need a piece of mistletoe and his lips don't bounce off my cheek. We've been practicing kissing a lot.

"Margaret Ann," he says. He holds my hand and looks at the ring on my finger. "I want to tell you something."

"Okay. Tell me."

"Okay."

He looks right into my eyes then and he isn't smiling.

"I sure do love you. I think I have loved you since I was five years old."

"Okay."

"Well, is that all you're going to say?"

"I guess it is for right now. But later, after I've been to college and come home, I will probably tell you that I've loved you too. Since I was five years old."

"Margaret Ann . . . what am I ever going to do with you?"

On Christmas Day the Liveleys call from London, and after Daddy and Mama talk to Aunt Mary Lee and Uncle Walter, I get to talk to Courtney for ten whole minutes. Elizabeth says it costs a lot.

"Uncle Walter must be rich," I say.

And then I tell her everything Courtney told me. All about the university she's going to next year. And how hard she's working to catch up with her classes. But I don't say a word about her boyfriend, because she told me not to. He sounds great. Someone a couple of years older than she is, but she's always known him. He's a viscount or something like that. I need to look it up to know exactly what she means. But she definitely promises she'll come to Virginia in the summer. Uncle Walter wants to come too, so they'll all come over in July or August.

Paige and Polly are disappointed they don't get to talk.

"I love Courtney too," Paige says. "And I wanted to tell Aunt Mary Lee we found a new piano teacher. Mrs. Whitley says Aunt Mary Lee was her very first student."

"Yes," Polly says. "And she looks so old you might be her last."

"That's mean," Paige says.

I notice the twins don't always get along these days. Each has her own friend.

"I tell you what," I say. "Why don't we all go in the living room and sing Christmas carols? You can play the piano, Paige. And you can choose what order to sing them in, Polly."

Of course that doesn't work out very well. Vivian—that is, Sara—wants to sing a solo . . . and she doesn't look after

Joanna . . . and Joanna breaks three ornaments on the Christmas tree . . . and then she hits little Tommy on the head with a truck he got for Christmas. It's a mess.

The only good thing about it is that it makes it less noticeable that Daddy and Johnny can't seem to talk. Johnny doesn't want to talk about farming, and Daddy never talks about anything else. Daddy and Bobby Holland sit around all afternoon talking about which fields to plant peanuts in and which to plant corn. And about hunting. And hunting dogs. Johnny doesn't seem to care about any of it anymore. He just looks at Sara all the time.

I sure hope he's happy.

The day Johnny and Sara and Joanna leave for California, and Elizabeth and Sam leave for Blacksburg, the weather turns warm. The thermometer shows 71 degrees that afternoon. Paige and Polly are spending the afternoon with their new best friends. Grandma is asleep. She sleeps most of the time now. People at church cluck their tongues and tell us how sad it is about Grandma, but it isn't really. She's happy all the time. She only knows what she sees right in front of her. She has no memory of how things used to be or how she wants them to be. When I take her hot buttered toast and tea to her bedroom, she always says, "What a feast. Thank you, Mary Lee." So I'm Aunt Mary Lee, but that's okay too. As long as Grandma's happy.

. . .

I tell Mama she ought to take a nap too.

"I can't," she says. "There are too many things for me to see after."

"Just tell me what it is, and I'll see it gets done."

"Are you sure?"

"Very sure, Mama."

"Okay, then. The table has to be cleared. And there's a load or two of laundry to do. Sheets to be changed. And you can tell Sallie to go on home as soon as it's done. Tell her we'll eat leftovers tonight. She has worked so hard."

"You have too, Mama."

"And what about you, Margaret Ann? What would I ever do without you?"

After I tell Sallie good bye and check on Grandma, I go to my own bedroom. Elizabeth's room. I walk to the window and push aside the blue flowered curtains. They're faded now from so many washings. But I still love them.

I lean down and look between the two large maples and along the row of cedars. So many people have driven down that long lane who will never come back. Tommy Gray. Joyce Darden's cousin who was killed on Iwo Jima. Jim Derbyshire and Dick Gregory. And I'm afraid Johnny won't be coming back much either.

"We live in a world of change," Edward R. Murrow says.

And Elizabeth says it, and my teachers at school say it, because now married women can teach.

I pull up a chair and lean my forehead against the windowsill. I'm thinking all kinds of deep and mostly sad thoughts when I turn my head slightly to the left and glimpse Bobby Holland's truck. Not his, of course, but an old one his daddy lets him drive. The truck moves slowly past cedar tree after cedar tree, then brakes under one of the big maples.

Bobby Holland gets out of the truck and starts toward the door. I knock on the window to make him look up at me. He smiles and motions for me to come down. So I open the window and whisper as loud as I can and have it still be a whisper. "Grandma's asleep." I know he doesn't hear me, but he gets the idea, because he points to the truck, and then he points up at me, and then he puts his hands in front of him like he's driving. And finally he shrugs his shoulders. I'm pretty sure I know what he means, but I put out my hands, palms up, and try to look like I have no idea. So he does the whole thing again.

This time I decide to put him out of his misery. I pull the window down, grab a sweater and run downstairs.

"You should have climbed out of the window," he says.

"Are you crazy? If I'm going to drive this thing, I prefer not to be a cripple."

We walk over to the truck. Bobby opens the door on

the driver's side and I get in. He walks slowly around to the passenger's side, like he's pretending to be too scared to get in. Finally he makes it and closes his door too.

"So, where are we going?" I ask.

"What do you think? We're going to feed up."

"Why are you feeding up today?"

"Because your daddy said so."

"What do you mean? Did he call you this afternoon?"

"No. He's at my house right now talking to my daddy about hiring me full-time."

"No kidding?"

"That's what he said. And Daddy says he doesn't really have that much work for me now that my brothers are both home."

"So that means you'll be here every day, huh?"

"Looks like it." Bobby leans over and kisses me on my nose. "That okay with you?"

"Yeah. As long as you let me drive your truck every day."

"Deal. So go ahead. See if you can do it without choking out the motor."

"I can do it without choking the motor."

"Then do it," Bobby says. He hands me the key.

I roll the window down an inch or so to get some air.

"Okay," I say. "Here goes."

I put my foot on the brake pedal and release the emergency brake. Push the clutch in, and turn the key. Move my hand to the ball of the shift stick, and feel Bobby's hand close over mine. That's what he did when he was first teaching me to shift gears.

"I can do it, " I say.

"Pretty sure of yourself, aren't you?"

I'm not, but I shake my head yes. I push the shift stick left then forward into reverse while I let up on the clutch and push down on the accelerator. We move backward as smooth as water.

"Okay," Bobby says. "That's far enough."

"I know it."

"Then stop."

I push in the brake and the clutch. The truck stops. Then I move the stick to low gear, push on the accelerator and let out the clutch all at the same time. The truck moves forward, and I turn the wheel toward the path that leads to the barn.

"Now, can you get it into second?"

My hand glides back to neutral, and then forward to the right.

"Made it to second," he said. "How about high?"

"You just watch me."

I let up on the accelerator slightly, then pull back out of second, push in the clutch and slide the gear back into high. Not a wobble or a waver.

"Good going, Margaret Ann," he says as he kisses my cheek.

Life is surely going to be fun with Bobby Holland.

Journey back in time with Simon & Schuster!

CHAINS

FEVER 1793

THE WALLS OF
CARTAGENA

STELLA STANDS
ALONE

THE YEAR OF
THE BOMB

ESCAPING INTO
THE NIGHT

If you loved this book · · · try these great reads!

Anything But Typical
by Nora Raleigh Baskin

My So-Called Family
by Courtney Sheinmel

The Homework Machine
by Dan Gutman

Magic in the Outfield
by Loren Long and
Phil Bildner

H.I.V.E.
by Mark Walden